For Jams

ONE

It was quarter to nine when Sheila arrived home. The first thing she did, as always, was turn on the radio as loudly as she could bear. She needed noise. If it ever got too quiet, she worried she'd hear him again.

When he was alive he'd filled every corner of the house with his presence. Every wall, mirror and surface had seemed to scrutinise, criticise and chastise her.

"You'll never be good enough."

She'd see the words on the television screen as she rubbed at the children's handprints so they didn't interfere with the news; she'd smell them in the bleach as she scrubbed the toilet, and taste them in the meals she cooked him every night.

Tonight though, the house felt different, lighter somehow, as though it had sensed her brighter mood.

She placed her car keys and handbag carefully on the kitchen counter then went back out into the hallway where she hung her scarf on the bottom of the banisters. She peeled off her thin leather gloves and was about to take off her coat when she remembered. It was Tuesday tomorrow. Bin day. She hadn't put them out yet.

As she turned back towards the kitchen, the phone on the hall table rang, its shrill tone making her jump. She glanced back at the caller display and hesitated. There was only one reason for her employer's son ringing her at this time of the evening. She was tempted to leave it, but what was the point?

He'd only keep trying until she answered and, if she didn't, then he'd call her mobile.

Taking a deep breath, she steeled herself and picked up.

"I can't get hold of Lauren." It was the unmistakable voice of Mark Hampton. Soft, deep and melodious. "I know it's your day off but have you heard from her?"

"Why aren't you on stage? I thought it was your play tonight."

"I'm not on for another ten minutes," he said. "Listen, I can't find my wallet. I've rung Lauren to ask if she's seen it, but she's not answering."

"Oh," said Sheila. She knew what was coming next.

"Can you nip up and see if she's OK?"

She wondered why he bothered phrasing it as a question. They both knew she'd say yes.

"I'll leave now," she said. "I'll ring you when I get there."

She grabbed at her handbag and keys; didn't bother turning off the radio. As she pulled open the back door, the local headlines came on. Another woman had been raped on Saturday night. She was the third one in as many months.

***

Tonight, more than ever, Elmtree Manor seemed to sneer at Sheila as she completed the winding approach of gravelled driveway. It was a greedy house, she thought. Over the years, along with its owner, she'd felt the place consume her, until she was nothing but an empty carcass.

Lauren Hampton's silver Mercedes was parked in its usual spot. Sheila climbed out of her Polo and crunched her way towards the front entrance. The security lights snapped on, illuminating the gravel path in front of her and plunging everything else into a thick, velvety darkness. She couldn't see the Tor, but she felt its presence looming behind her, its ruined tower dark and imposing.

Reaching the panelled front door, she knocked loudly and waited, imagining the clipped tones of her employer, "For God's sake, I'm coming." But there was nothing. She knocked again and waited. Still nothing. She'd try the old servants' entrance, she decided. It was normally left unlocked, as though personality alone could keep intruders at bay.

She turned away from the front door and took the path leading to the right of the house. Another light flashed into life allowing her to follow the damp stone path until she reached a small, wooden door. It was unlocked, just as she'd thought.

"Hello?" she called as she edged it open. "Mrs Hampton? It's me. Sheila."

Nothing, just an ominous silence. She let herself into the narrow corridor, pushed the door shut behind her and turned into the vast kitchen, feeling a waft of hot air against her face.

"Mrs Hampton?" She glanced across at the kitchen worktop. It was a jumble of cereal packets, dirty plates, bowls, cups and glasses. *Lazy bitch*. It had only been a day. She shuddered to think what state Elmtree would fall into if she were allowed to take more time off.

She crossed the room and stepped out into the brightly lit hallway, calling out as she moved. "It's me. Sheila." She stood for a moment, listening intently. The familiar sounds of the house seemed amplified; the rumble of the old boiler like distant thunder, the ticking of the Grandfather clock like a loud mocking clap. She crossed the hallway slowly and hesitated before entering the drawing room through the open door.

The sudden drop in temperature after the stifling warmth of the kitchen and hallway made her shiver. The vast room was faintly lit by a small, tasselled lamp in the far corner of the room and it took her a moment to adjust to the half-light. Her attention was caught by a sudden movement to her left. Heart thudding, she turned quickly only to see the floor-length white curtain wafting up; the patio doors that led out onto the terrace had been left wide open. *No wonder it feels so cold in here*, she thought.

She started to cross the room towards the doors to close them. And it was then that she saw Lauren Hampton. She was lying in a heap beside the leather armchair, its back to the open doors and stretch of invisible lawn beyond. On the floor, next to her head, lay a crumpled white and blue carrier bag. Sheila tried to focus on it, but a perverse curiosity insisted on dragging her eyes back to the face instead. It looked twisted, bluish-grey and ugly, as though Lauren's true essence had seeped out through her skin and was now visible to the world.

She was dead. There was no doubting it. Sheila had seen a corpse before, but that didn't make it any easier. Now, in contrast to the inanimate body before her she was aware, more than ever, of how vital her own was. Her skin tingled, the hairs on her arms and neck rose up, her heart pounded uncomfortably and a rush of noise, a sort of gurgled roar, filled her head.

She tried to move. The phrase 'frozen to the spot' came to mind and along with it a memory of her daughter and grandson, when he was a year old. They were out shopping. Heather had given him a plastic bag to play with in the pushchair. He liked the noise it made when he scrunched it up.

"You can't give him that," she'd said. "It's dangerous."

"Oh mum," her daughter had replied. "I'm watching him the whole time. I'll stop him if he starts to put it over his head. And anyway, how many people do you know who've been suffocated with a plastic bag?"

At least one, she'd now be able to say.

She felt herself stagger backwards. *The police*, she thought, trying to pull herself together. *I need to ring the police.*

Her legs were trembling but somehow she managed to stagger out into the hallway.

"I need to ring the police," she said, as though saying it aloud would confirm her intention. She could hear and feel the shake and judder in her voice.

The phone was on the sideboard, cradled in its black holder, a small green light flashing to show that Lauren had messages. *Messages she would never hear*. Sheila grabbed at it but her fingers felt as though they didn't belong to her. She managed to grasp the phone and as she did she noticed a white envelope, lying face down next to the dead woman's handbag. Instinctively she turned it over. It was addressed in Lauren's handwriting. The name on the envelope was familiar. Michael Fenn.

How did Sheila know that name? For a moment she couldn't think straight, her heart was beating too fast. She felt sick, dizzy, as though she might faint at any moment. She clutched the side, staring at the name. Reading it over and over again.

Michael Fenn. Michael Fenn. Michael Fenn.

Then it came to her. Of course. She'd seen his name so many times before; it was only because it was out of context she hadn't placed him straight away. She picked up the envelope and slipped it into her handbag.

It was only then she punched in the three numbers.

TWO

Detective Sergeant Kate Linton fidgeted on the velvet-covered seat in a futile attempt to stop her backside from turning numb and decided that in future she'd be more outspoken.

If only she'd said, "No thanks. I'd rather watch paint dry," she could've spent the evening lying on her sofa enjoying repeats of *CSI*. Instead, here she was watching her best friend's husband in the amateur production of *Beauty and the Beast*, while Gemma clutched her arm with excitement every time he appeared on stage.

The second half had only just started and Linton was already losing interest. Her mind drifted momentarily before coming to rest on the subject she'd been dwelling on for the last couple of weeks. The wedding reception she was invited to on Saturday night. Detective Inspector Rob Brown had offered to be her plus one, claiming it was to stop her incessant moaning about having to go alone. *But was that the real reason?*

She thought back to that moment on Wearyall Hill a couple of months ago when they were chasing the serial killer the media dubbed the Ley Line Strangler. She'd tripped and fallen on top of Brown, his physical attraction embarrassingly obvious.

And then there was the drunken message he'd left on her answerphone a couple of nights later. He'd been out with Turley that night, a pretty policewoman drafted in from Dorset to help with the investigation. He'd phoned Linton from the pub but she'd been in bed with tonsillitis, too ill to pick up. At the time she'd felt certain if she had, he'd have admitted his true feelings for her. But the next time she'd seen him nothing was said. And now she wondered if she'd completely misread the situation.

"Oww!" she squealed, as a sharp elbow from Gemma brought her musings to a painfully abrupt end.

"Nick's on again," Gemma hissed.

Linton forced herself to watch, an inane grin plastered on her face as she wondered what possessed an otherwise sensible man to prance about dressed as a grandfather clock.

The moment Gemma's husband flounced off stage Linton surreptitiously picked up the programme she'd bought from the familiar-looking Welsh man who'd shown them to their seats. Reading it would at least pass some of the time.

She turned the pages quietly, hoping Gemma wouldn't notice, skimming the local ads for carpet fitters and opticians until she found the photos and blurb about the performers. She looked up at the man on stage dressed as the beast, then back down at his picture in the programme. His portrait had a practised look, head on to the camera. It was a cliché, but the word she would've used to describe his expression was smouldering.

She glanced at his name then nudged Gemma who turned to her with a frown.

"Is that Lauren Hampton's son?" she whispered. Gemma nodded impatiently and turned back, apparently hypnotised by the love scene taking place between a giant candelabrum and a teapot.

Mark Hampton. He was the sort of bloke Linton hated on sight. She'd seen him marching through Glastonbury High Street, a smooth, sleek look of public school about him, which wasn't about money or even class, but something inbred. He had that glossy, polished appearance that made everything around him appear shabby and had obviously inherited his looks from his mother – the former fashion model turned author turned semi-recluse. Linton had recently read she was trying to get her latest novel published, but no one was interested.

At that moment her phone vibrated against her leg. A text. She pulled it out of her trouser pocket and glanced at the sender's name. Brown. At least he'd remembered she was going to the theatre and had had the decency not to ring. Perhaps there was hope for him yet. She opened the message and changed her mind. It simply said, "Fuck the panto. DB. Ring me. Now."

"I've got to make a call," she whispered to Gemma, nodding her head towards the exit. "Work."

"I thought it was your night off," she hissed back.

"Which means it's important." She didn't show her the text. Even Gemma could've worked out what the code stood for. Dead body.

She nudged her way to the end of row Q, apologising to the tops of people's heads, feeling guilty for disturbing them and even guiltier at her relief that someone had died so she didn't have to watch any more of this torturous crap.

She rang Brown as soon as she reached the foyer. "Where are you?"

"Just around the corner from you," he said. "Elmtree Manor. See you in couple of minutes."

Elmtree, she thought. What a coincidence. Wasn't that where Lauren Hampton lived?

"Who's dead?" she said quickly, sensing Brown was about to ring off.

But he'd gone before she'd finished asking the question.

***

An hour later and Linton was beginning to wish she were still at the theatre. At least it had been warm.

When she first arrived she'd thought how attractive Elmtree Manor looked but the house was rapidly losing its appeal. She didn't know or care much about architecture, but at a push she'd have said that the white, ivy-covered building with its panelled door and sash windows was Georgian. She couldn't risk asking Brown. He'd only launch into a history tutorial riddled with facts and dates she'd never remember.

Across the lawn she could see the Scene of Crime Officers moving slowly in and out of the open patio doors, their white boiler suits and boots painfully bright in the glare of the floodlights they'd set up. She stamped her feet in a useless attempt to bring some feeling back into them. The latex boots she'd changed into when she first arrived might ensure the crime scene wasn't contaminated but they offered little in the way of warmth.

Brown sighed and banged his blue-gloved hands together. "Another long night for that lot," he said, exhaling a cloud of warm air. "What with the rape last night."

Linton nodded. "Have you heard any more about it?"

"Hooper filled me in," he replied, the curl of his top lip demonstrating how he felt about the trainee detective. "Said it was the same as before except she'd been to Sainsbury's this time. Apparently she was taking a detour home along the moors around five o'clock when the bloke jumped out in front of her car. Told her his wife had gone into labour and asked her to help."

"It doesn't make sense," Linton said. "Not after what happened to the other two women. Why would she drive that way unless she had to?"

"It was a different part of the moors," he said, mimicking Hooper's slightly nasal tone. "Down near Godney. As if that makes a difference. Tosser." He shook his head. "You know what he reckons? That these women are meeting this nut job on purpose. That he finds his victims online. Through a dating agency."

"But they're all married, aren't they?"

"So?" he said impatiently. "Anyway, that's not the point I'm making. Would you *really* agree to meet a bloke in the middle of nowhere when this sick fucker's on the loose, raping women at knifepoint?"

She turned to face him, flinching at the familiar jolt in her stomach as she took in the rugged face, the tousled blond hair, the intense blue eyes. She quickly looked away, feeling the predictable rush of heat rise up from her chest and crawl its way onto her neck and face.

"I..." she began, but was interrupted by the crackling of Brown's walkie-talkie followed by Hooper's voice breaking through the static.

"There's some bloke in fancy dress at the bottom of the driveway." The excitement in the disembodied voice was evident. "Says he's Lauren Hampton's son."

"Two secs and we'll be there," Brown grunted. "That'll be your beast," he said to Linton, marching off in the direction of the entrance.

She followed, slightly off balance thanks to the numbness in her feet, desperately trying to keep her gaze off Brown's improbably pert backside but failing.

***

They found Hooper at the bottom of the long, tree-lined driveway hopping impatiently from foot to foot in front of the yellow and black fluorescent police tape.

"He's just there," he said, pointing eagerly into the gloom beyond. "He keeps asking if he can come in."

Brown ignored Hooper and shone his torch past his spindly frame causing a shorter, more well-built man standing just behind the tape to squint into the intense, white light.

"Fuck me," mumbled Brown, under his breath, as they moved towards him. "It's the dandy highwayman. I thought you said he was playing the beast."

"At the end he turns into the prince."

"Of what?" he hissed. "Camp?"

Linton did her best to suppress a smile. Mark Hampton was wearing a ruffled white shirt under a bright blue silk suit trimmed with gold. His tight trousers were pushed into black knee-high leather boots, the heels as high as the ones Linton was planning to wear to the reception on Saturday night. A large enamelled brooch was pinned to his chest. As they reached the tape and stopped she could see his face was the colour of a pumpkin, his lips and eyebrows painted on. He looked like a drag queen.

"I'm Lauren's son," he said breathlessly, his eyes darting around nervously. "I got here as soon as I could."

Brown pushed down the police tape and was about to step over it when his mobile rang. "Two secs," he said, snatching it from the pocket of his white paper suit. "The Toad," he mouthed at Linton, pressing the torch into her hand before moving back into the shadows to take the call from their DCI.

Linton stepped forward and held out her hand to take Hampton's outstretched one. It was strong and reassuring and she could feel its warmth through her thin, rubber gloves.

"DS Kate Linton," she said. "Has anyone told you what's happened?"

"Our housekeeper left a message on my phone," he said, breathlessly. "I got it at the end of the show. She said Lauren's dead. What happened?"

"Until the Scene of Crime Officers have finished..."

"Is it true? That she was murdered?" he interrupted. "That's what Sheila said."

"As I said, until SOCO have completed their investigations, we won't really know."

For a moment neither of them spoke. Hampton was staring at the ground, his eyes unfocused, chewing anxiously on his bottom lip. Linton watched as he traced a semi-circle in the gravel with the tip of his right boot. He swallowed hard and when he eventually spoke, his voice was thick with emotion.

"How did she die?" he asked quietly, still not looking up.

It was obvious the housekeeper hadn't gone into detail. And Linton wasn't about to either. He didn't need to know that some sick bastard had pulled a plastic bag over his mother's head, held it there until she'd stopped breathing and collapsed onto the floor.

"We're not certain," she answered gently.

"Did she..." he said, then stopped, expelling a long, shuddering breath. He cleared his throat then tried again. "Do you think she suffered?"

"She would've died quickly," Linton replied, although of course that depended on the definition of quick. Lauren Hampton's last few seconds had probably felt like hours.

"What do I do now?" he said, looking around him distractedly and Linton got the impression he didn't just mean at that particular moment. She noticed his hands had started to shake.

"We'll need to question you, but you're obviously in shock. We can wait until the morning. Have you got any friends you can stay with?"

"Friends?" he said, frowning in confusion.

"I'm afraid you won't be able to stay here tonight."

"Why? I don't live in the main house. I live on my own. In the cottage."

"It's still in the grounds of Elmtree," she said apologetically. "So we need to keep it clear for the investigators."

"Can I at least collect some overnight things?"

She shook her head. "I'll get someone to pick up some supplies for you and drop them off. Toothbrush, toothpaste." She paused. "Maybe some clothes."

He laughed but stopped abruptly, obviously embarrassed that he'd found some humour in the situation. Turning slightly he nodded towards the road beyond. "My clothes are in the car. I didn't get changed. I was in too much of a rush. Nearly knocked some poor bloke off his bike on the way over."

"You're shaking. I really think you should sit down."

"You know, I always thought she'd live forever," he said, as though Linton hadn't spoken. "I'm sure everyone thinks that about their parents, but with Lauren it was more than that. I thought she'd manage to outwit death. She was seventy-five last month although you'd never have known it. Sorry," he said stopping suddenly, "I'm babbling."

"I think it might be an idea for you to see a doctor," said Linton. "You don't look well."

"I'm fine. Please. I don't want any fuss. If you could just book me into a hotel, I'd be very grateful."

"OK," she said reluctantly, pulling out her phone. "I'll see if the Pendragon have got any rooms."

"Thank you. I'm very grateful."

"I was at the theatre tonight," she said, as she scrolled through her numbers. "I thought you were very good."

"It was our first night," he said, sounding genuinely pleased. "But I won't be able to go on again, not after… I don't think I could…" He stopped again then said, "You know I can't help thinking this is my fault."

Linton looked up from her phone and placed her hand on his arm, feeling the slippery material of his suit through her gloves. "It's a common feeling," she said gently. "Feeling guilty because you weren't there to protect her."

"It's not that," he said, shaking his head. "She's been distracted for a while. Worried. Something was bothering her."

Linton was instantly curious. "Did she say what?"

"I asked but she got cross. I should've pushed her for an answer."

"How long had she been acting like that?"

He shrugged. "For the last couple of weeks. Maybe a little longer."

"Did you get the impression she was worried about her safety?"

"Possibly. But she's not normally the anxious type." He paused then said, "There was one thing I noticed that was out of character."

"What was that?"

"She started putting on the security lights on at night. I had them installed years ago, but she refused to use them. Said it was a waste of money."

"She seems to have left the side door and patio unlocked though."

He rolled his eyes. "That doesn't surprise me. Lauren was a mass of contradictions. She may have given into security lights, but she'd never have locked the doors. It was something she liked to boast about. How you can keep them unlocked in the countryside. If she'd locked them, it would've been admitting that she was wrong."

"Is there anyone you can think of who might have wanted to harm your mother?"

Hampton looked at her as though he was about answer, then without warning his eyes rolled backwards into his head. Linton stepped forward quickly and grabbed at his arm, but there was little she could do as he staggered forwards with a grunt before collapsing onto the ground in front of her.

"Linton?" shouted Brown, emerging out of the darkness. "What the fuck have you done to him?"

She shone her torch along the motionless body. "Shit! I think he's fainted."

"That's gotta be a first, Linton," said Brown laughing. "Having a bloke fall at your feet like that."

Before she could form an answer, Hooper appeared suddenly from behind Brown.

"What's happened?" he asked excitedly.

"I think you better radio for an ambulance," said Brown with a satisfied smirk. "It turns out Mark Hampton's more of a fairy than a beast."

THREE

Linton returned to Elmtree Manor at seven the next morning. She'd eventually left the house along with Brown just after midnight when it was obvious that SOCO weren't going to finish examining the crime scene for another few hours.

As she approached it along the secluded road, she realised how isolated Elmtree was. A high stone wall surrounded the property and only the tops of the chimneys were visible from the bottom of the long gravel drive.

The house looked sinister in the eerie half-light of the January morning, much more so than it had the previous night. Perhaps it was the Tor behind, its silhouette barely distinguishable through the ethereal mist. Or maybe it was the dark blanket of ivy covering its walls. Linton could imagine the stonework beneath fighting to breathe, suffocated by the leafy parasite crawling over it. She thought of Lauren's distorted face, the crumpled carrier bag lying on the floor nearby and shuddered.

Brown was getting out of his own car as she pulled up.

"I wonder how Prince Charming is this morning," he said. "Do you think he made it through the night without keeling over again?"

"He'd just found out his mum was dead," she replied, as she clambered out of her Mini, clenching in response to the frosty air. "And not everyone's as tough as you are, Brown."

He grinned. "Too right they're not. Which reminds me. You haven't sponsored me yet."

"What are you doing?" she asked, slamming her door and following him up the stone path towards to the entrance to the house. "A shagathon? How many different women you can work your way through in a month?"

"Hardly a challenge for someone like me," he said, turning to her and waggling his eyebrows.

"What then?"

"The Bath half marathon. In March. I'm aiming to run it in one hour forty."

"Is that fast?"

"Seven-minute miles? I should think so."

"I could do that." *Couldn't I?* She had no idea. The last time she'd run more than a few metres was in 1996 for Sport Aid. She still had the same trainers.

"I didn't know you were a runner," he said grinning.

"There's a lot you don't know about me." *Such as the fact that, despite thinking you're a womanising prick, I spend half my time fantasising about you.*

"There's an app you can download on your phone," he said. "Next time you go for a run you can record how long it takes."

"Right. I'll do that. And I bet I'm as fast as you are."

The Scene of Crime officer who greeted them heartily at the door was as busty as she was enthusiastic. Even the baggy suit couldn't hide the fact that, if she hadn't fancied criminology as a career, she could easily have enjoyed one as glamour model.

"As I said last night, nothing was forced open," she said, ushering them in, her eyes lingering on Brown for longer than Linton felt was necessary. "The patio doors were unlocked. So was the side door near the kitchen. Our carrier bag killer could've got in through either of them."

"What about footprints?" Brown asked and Linton

wondered how much self-control it was taking him not to glance down at the SOCO's breasts.

"It was dry last night. Nothing visible on any of the carpets, but he could've slipped his shoes off outside either of the doors."

"How long had she been dead when the housekeeper found her?"

The SOCO shrugged, twisting a clump of her long, blonde hair round her finger. "The police surgeon said less than an hour, but of course we won't know for certain until later."

"So was it a robbery?" asked Linton.

"It's hard to tell because we don't know if anything's missing. The bedroom's in a bit of state, but mine's no better. Half the time I wouldn't know if I'd been robbed."

Brown laughed obligingly and Linton wondered why it was that people bragged about their untidiness, as though it made them more interesting. Knowing that if she boasted about her tidiness, they'd think she was an uptight freak.

"At the moment there's nothing to suggest that anything's been taken," the SOCO continued. "She's got a number of jewellery boxes in her room. None of them were open; they were still in the drawers of her dressing table. As far as we can tell, nothing electrical is missing. And her handbag was still on the side in the hall with a purse full of cash, credit cards and an expensive mobile. Basically none of the hallmarks of a robbery."

"Better get Hooper to check for mobile messages," said Brown, turning to Linton. "And the landline as well."

"Perhaps Lauren came home and found the burglar before he'd had time to look through anything," Linton ventured. "He might've panicked and killed her by mistake."

"I'll show you where she was killed," said the SOCO leading them down the oak-floored hallway and into what

Lauren Hampton had probably referred to as the drawing room.

It was the sort of room that Linton had only ever seen in a National Trust house. Occasional tables were scattered artfully around, their surfaces covered with an array of ornaments, silver picture frames and candelabra. The thick, white carpet gave the room a muffled quality, the only sound a ticking from an ornate carriage clock on the long mantelpiece above the fireplace. There was a sweet smell, like sherbet, which Linton guessed was coming from the large vase of lilies on a table near the door.

"She was found there," said the SOCO, pointing to an area on the floor in front of an antique-looking armchair. "That plastic marker represents her head. The other two are her feet. Here," she said, handing Brown the digital camera she'd been holding. "You can see for yourself."

Brown held the camera down and flicked slowly through the photos, whilst Linton looked over his shoulder, breathing in his crisp aftershave. Every now and then he stopped at a picture and zoomed in, studying the enlarged details.

"I don't buy the disturbed robbery," he said after a few minutes.

"Why not?" asked Linton.

"Look at the way she's collapsed on the floor. She obviously fell forward off the chair."

"Meaning?"

"The chair's got its back to the patio doors which means she must've been sitting down with her back to the killer when he came in. That indicates he surprised *her* rather than the other way around. Add to that the fact her car was here and a light was on. It's obvious she was at home. And that says to me it was premeditated."

The next few photos were of a crumpled Tesco carrier bag, taken from different angles. "I'm assuming that's the weapon," he said, flicking through them. The SOCO nodded. "So much for the holes on the bottom to stop people from suffocating," he said as he handed the camera back to her.

"They were hardly going to make any difference. Anyway," she said looking at Brown and stifling a yawn, "I'll leave you to get on with it. I'm off home. To bed."

If that wasn't obvious flirtation, thought Linton, then she didn't know what was. She watched with disdain as the SOCO sauntered back across the room. It was obvious that the exaggerated movement of her hips was for the DI's benefit. The performance was wasted though. He wasn't even watching.

"You're losing your touch, Brown," she said, as she heard the front door slam shut. "No date lined up with her. Not even her phone number?"

He turned and winked at her. "I'm saving myself."

"What for?" she asked, feeling the familiar rush of warmth curling up her neck.

"I'm concentrating on my training. I don't want any distractions."

"Let's check out the rest of the house," said Linton, anxious to leave the room before he'd noticed she was blushing.

"Do you think the fact that the killer used a Tesco bag is significant?" she asked as they went back out into the hallway.

"Why? Do you think if he'd used a Waitrose one we'd be looking for a different sort of person? A more middle-class murderer? I bet she'd have preferred something posher. Like Fortnum and Mason. Mind you," he laughed, "at least it wasn't Lidl."

"You're horrible."

For the next ten minutes they worked their way through the downstairs rooms before mounting the wide staircase. As they reached the top and turned on the landing Linton came to an abrupt halt in front of a large oil painting of the Tor; the silhouette of the tower in stark contrast to the blazing sunset of red, yellow and gold.

"One of your mum's?" said Brown. Linton nodded, glancing automatically at the signature in the right-hand corner. "It's good, isn't it?"

"She would've spent a lot of time making sure she got it just right." *A lot more time than she did with her own kids. Her paintings were her real babies, the ones she loved and nurtured and agonised over.*

Each of the five bedrooms they entered looked untouched, impressively clean to the point of sterility. That was until they reached the one at the end of the landing.

"Christ," said Linton, as they stepped into the large square room. "Tell me again why you don't think it's a robbery."

"I assume this is Lauren's," said Brown.

The floor and unmade bed were strewn with clothes: underwear, dresses and shoes. A couple of drawers were pulled open and Linton spotted a black, lacy bra hanging out of one and what looked like a pair of stockings from the other. Beauty products were scattered across the dressing table: moisturisers, foundation, perfume and hair products.

"That's the thing with getting older," said Linton, as Brown began taking photographs of the clutter with his phone. "It takes twice as much stuff to look half as good."

"She was gorgeous once though," said Brown, nodding at one of the many photographs and portraits of Lauren that papered the walls. There were framed magazine covers, an enormous poster in which she was advertising a perfume. A large black and white print of her, staring into the camera, her chin in her hands.

"She's got a bit of Elizabeth Taylor about her," he said, with genuine admiration. "I wouldn't have chucked her out of bed."

"That's not saying much."

"What's that proverb?" he said grinning. "Women are like melons. You have to try a few before you find a good one."

"That's not a proverb. That's a Brownism."

"I like that! Maybe I could write a book. Rob Brown's book of Brownisms."

Linton rolled her eyes in response. "What's in here?" she asked, moving towards an open door to the left. She'd expected to walk into an en suite bathroom and was surprised to find a small study. On the desk was a laptop and printer.

"A silver surfer," said Brown, as he followed her in. "I'll get SOCO to take the computer in. You never know. We might find something useful."

Above the desk was a long wooden bookshelf with dozens of hardback books, all with identical spines. Brown walked towards the shelf and picked one up.

"Talking of writing books," he said. "Look what we've got here. *How to Get a Man and Keep Him* by Lauren Hampton. There we go, Linton," he said holding it out to her, with a smirk. "I wonder if there's a chapter about how to keep your boyfriend away from your mum's lesbian lover."

Linton let out an exaggerated sigh. "Do you think the day will ever come when one of the most humiliating episodes of my life will cease being funny?"

"Nope," he said, turning the book over to study the back cover. "Listen to this," he said. "'This book is your secret weapon for success. In ten easy-to-read chapters, it will show you how to get the man of your dreams and keep him. Say hello to a new confident you and say goodbye to the endless worry of ending up unloved and alone…'"

"Talking of worrying," she interrupted, "do you think there's anything in what Hampton said to me last night?"

"About what?" said Brown, replacing the book on the shelf before walking back into the bedroom.

"About how Lauren had seemed anxious for the last couple of weeks," she said following him. "I wonder if she thought she was in some sort of danger."

He shrugged. "If she was, she obviously didn't want anyone to know about it. You said she wouldn't tell Hampton what was bothering her. Anyway," he said, "odds are, whoever killed her knew her. And that she'd be on her own last night. I'd put money on the housekeeper. Or the son."

"But Hampton couldn't have done. He was at the theatre. I saw him myself. And as for Sheila. Well, you saw her when we got here. She was genuinely shocked."

"Not upset though," he said. "And besides, if she did kill her, you'd expect her to be shaken up. She probably hadn't counted on being called back here to find the body."

Linton wasn't convinced. "What about her motive?" she asked.

"One of the usual. Anger. Jealously. Revenge. But more than likely money. She might've been left something in the will. Same for Hampton. Although that depends on whether there *is* any. Half these places are mortgaged up to the hilt and propped up with massive loans. Whoever stands to inherit, and I'm assuming it's the son, could find themselves lumbered with a fat load of debt."

"But we know it wasn't him," she said impatiently. "He was on stage. I saw him myself."

"What? For the whole time? There's an interval, isn't there?"

"It was twenty minutes long."

Brown pulled a face. "Long enough to get up here and kill her." He picked up a gold tube of lipstick and rolled it around in his gloved fingers absentmindedly before placing it back on the dresser. "I've been thinking," he said, "I reckon that whoever killed her hated her."

"What makes you say that?"

"The carrier bag was on the floor and not still over her head."

Linton raised her eyebrows.

"I'd say the killer pulled it off so he or she could see her face," he explained.

"Maybe it was to check she was dead."

"Or to get pleasure from it."

Linton jumped as the vintage-looking clock on the bedroom mantelpiece chimed.

"We need to get back to the station," said Brown, heading for the bedroom door. "I've arranged for Sheila Martock to come in this morning. I've got a feeling she knows a lot more than she was letting on last night."

***

The woman pushed her shopping trolley back across Morrison's car park and wished that something would happen. Something to distract her from the day-to-day monotony of cooking, cleaning and childcare. Something dramatic and exciting.

Anything.

She went over her purchases in her head, wondering if she'd bought enough to last the week. She'd got chicken, pork chops, some rump steak and a leg of lamb to roast. *Or she could always stick her head in the oven instead.*

Come on, she thought, *pull yourself together. Things weren't that bad.* Actually things weren't really anything. That was the problem. It was just all so bloody boring.

She slammed the trolley into the waiting backside of its replica, pushed the plastic clip into the slot and took out her pound. She would put the coin into the glove compartment of her Renault Espace so it would be there the next time she came here to shop.

How very fucking sensible.

She turned and walked briskly towards her car, zipping up her coat as she moved. She'd parked it in the far corner of the car park as part of her New Year's resolution. *Another one she wouldn't keep.*

"If you go to work by bus," her book advised, "why not get off a couple of stops before you need to and walk the rest of the way?"

But she didn't do anything as exciting as taking buses or going to work, so parking as far as possible from the shop's entrance was the best she could manage.

As she half-jogged across the tarmac, her head bent against the cold, she passed a man in a suit, hurrying in the other direction.

There was no one else around.

In about half an hour the car park would be packed, full of mums on their way home from the school run. It was why she'd come early. So she could be in and out and back in time to have the kids before her husband started his shift at nine.

She reached her car, opened the door, climbed in and pulled it shut. She put on her seatbelt, *clunk click for every trip,* started the engine and pulled out of the parking space.

It was the beginning of her journey into hell.

FOUR

DCI Hargreaves was barking into his mobile, his claret face clashing with his mismatched attire of brown suit, blue shirt and purple tie, when Linton and Brown entered the incident room fifteen minutes later. He scowled at them and jerked his head at their desks, his way of telling them to get on with it, causing his multitude of chins to wobble with the movement.

Linton raised her eyebrows at Brown. "What's up with The Toad?" she asked, as they passed Hooper's desk.

"Haven't you heard?" he whispered. "The doctor's put him on a new diet. That's why he's in such a foul mood."

"Let's have your paper then," said Brown, swiping it from Hooper's desk before he could protest. "I want to see what they're saying about the murder."

He turned it over, studying the back page as he crossed the room, before flinging it onto his own desk. The newspaper landed on top one of the many heaps of paperwork that covered its surface, fighting for space between the clusters of mugs and pens and the yellow sticky notes that were so old and ignored they were curling at the edges.

"You're going to have to let the cleaners near your desk one day," Linton said.

"I've told you," he replied, pushing a couple of the mugs aside and sitting down to switch on his computer. "I don't like my stuff being moved around."

"It's unhygienic."

"You need a few germs to build up your tolerance. It's why I'm never ill."

Linton sat down at her own desk feeling instantly calmed. It was clean and uncluttered with a single stack of paper neatly piled, a notepad and a pen tidy.

No doubt her friend Gemma, obsessed with self-help books and pop psychology, could tell her what their desks said about them. Probably that Brown was a spontaneous, multi-tasker, able to dip in and out of things easily. That she was conscientious; preferring to focus on one thing at a time. And she'd probably say it reflected the way they approached their relationships too.

"That's interesting," Brown said, interrupting her thoughts. "There's a message here from Wells. Apparently Hampton's got a gun licence for three firearms. Uses them for hunting."

"Where's the gun cabinet? It wasn't in the main house."

"Somewhere in the cottage apparently. Wells checked and everything's kosher. Hampton's licence was reviewed at the end of last year."

"So presumably he's considered mentally stable then. They wouldn't have renewed it if he wasn't."

Hampton shrugged. "It doesn't mean he *is* mentally stable. Or that he didn't suffocate his mother."

Linton nodded at the paper. "If you're not reading that, I'll have it."

"I am now," he said smugly picking it up and turning it over to the sports page again.

"Fine," she said, "I'll go online." She had to restrain herself from clicking on the page she had saved in her favourites, a shortcut to the showbiz page of a newspaper she wouldn't ever dream of buying but had recently become addicted to. Instead she clicked on the BBC news home page and skimmed the headlines before clicking on a link to Lauren Hampton's obituary.

LAUREN HAMPTON, 75, A 'SUPERMODEL' DIES

Lauren Hampton, widely regarded as the nation's first supermodel, died last night at her home in Glastonbury. She is considered to be one of the early modelling icons of the British fashion industry. Police are treating her death as suspicious.

Described as possessing a 'mesmerising beauty', she once featured five times on the cover of *Vogue* in a single year. During her modelling career, she appeared on more than 60 magazine covers. When she retired she went on to write two best-selling books: *Lauren Hampton's Beauty Secrets* and *How to Get a Man and Keep Him*.

She was born Laura Matthews in Wandsworth, the youngest daughter of a baker. Discovered at the age of seventeen whilst working in her father's shop, she was the first model to command the sort of money that's now considered par for the course by modern-day supermodels.

She suffered great tragedy in her personal life. She married Joseph Hampton in 1954, a foreign diplomat with family money. He died of a heart attack when he was just 42. Unknown to him, Lauren was pregnant with his child. Two weeks later, she was devastated when her daughter, Sophia, committed suicide. Lauren went on to have her son Mark a few months later. She never married again. In her last interview with *The Sunday Times* she talked about publishing a novel.

"Did you know about Laurens's daughter?" she asked, when she came to the end of the article.

"She topped herself, didn't she?" he said distractedly, not looking up from the paper. "Sorry," he said, wincing, a couple of seconds later as the reality of what he'd said obviously hit home. Linton's brother had tried to kill himself a couple of months before. He was still undergoing treatment for depression at a clinic near Bristol.

"It's fine," she said. "You don't have to apologise every time you mention someone who's killed themselves."

"I can't remember how or why she did it," he said, still looking awkward. "It was before my time. But I remember my mum and dad discussing it."

Not for the first time Linton wondered what it must've been like to grow up in a household with a family that had ordinary conversations. Where people talked about the news; the weather; local events. Her parents had existed in their own selfish worlds, oblivious to the real one that went on around them. Her mum was an artist and her dad a university lecturer; their conversations had revolved around reviews of artists and books and world films, around what their amazingly interesting and creative friends had done and said. Their intellectual debates had bored Linton senseless and her friend Gemma was convinced they were responsible for her love of popular fiction and lowbrow telly. "It's your subconscious way of rebelling," she'd once said.

Brown glanced at his watch and said, "We'll ask Sheila in a minute. She'll know how she died."

"I'm not looking forward to seeing her again," Linton replied. "She's not exactly the warm and friendly type."

"Don't worry," he replied, with a loud yawn. "I'll have her eating out of my hand by the time I've finished."

***

A harassed-looking policeman had plonked Sheila in an interview room with the promise that one of the detectives working on the case would be along shortly. He'd returned a minute later with mug of tea and now the lukewarm cup of beige liquid sat uninvitingly on the Formica table in front of her.

Her head was pounding and she felt nauseous. She pushed the mug away and pulled her handbag onto the table. She was sure she had some headache tablets in there somewhere. Groping around, she touched the smooth surface of her leather purse, the bulk of her phone and then something unexpected. An envelope.

She pulled it out perplexed, staring at it blankly for a moment before turning it over and reading the name. Michael Fenn.

She'd forgotten all about it after the endless questions, the enforced journey home in a police car, the cup of tea the policewoman had insisted on making before leaving her to crawl into bed long after midnight.

She ran her trembling finger along the edge of the seal. The envelope popped open easily, too easily, as if it had been opened once before.

She knew it was wrong, reading someone else's letter, even in the circumstances. But curiosity – or was it survival? – got the better of her and she yanked out its innards.

There were two pieces of paper, neatly folded. She opened the top one. It was a letter. Lauren's looping handwriting covered three quarters of the page, her oversized signature the rest. She speed-read it, feeling her throat tighten and her stomach constrict.

Dear Michael Fenn,

Please find enclosed the information as promised. I thought you might like to have a bit of background reading before we meet next week to discuss what really happened. I promise you. It's quite a story!

Since we spoke, it's as though the floodgates of my memory have opened and I'm recalling all sorts of fascinating things from my life. Things I've never told anyone but I feel that the public have a right to know.

Hands shaking, she picked up the other piece of paper, dreading what she would find, but as she started to unfold it, she heard footsteps and muffled voices. A man and a woman's. Hands poised in midair, she watched the handle on the door pull downward. She grabbed at the letter and envelope, shoved them back into bag and looked up to see the detectives she'd spoken to the night before.

***

Brown's boast that he'd have the housekeeper eating out of his hand had yet to be realised. For the last couple of minutes, he'd done his best with some one-sided small talk, but Linton could see that his charm offensive was having little effect on the rigid woman with the cast-iron face. She was dressed entirely in grey, sitting stiffly opposite them.

"So how long have you worked for Lauren Hampton?" he now asked, leaning forward and smiling.

"Forty years," she said abruptly. "I started just after Henry did."

"Henry?"

She sniffed. "My husband. He was their gardener. He got me the job after Mrs Hartry retired."

"Does he still work at Elmtree?"

"Hardly," she sniffed again. "He's been dead for years."

"I'm sorry," said Linton, only now glancing at the women's left hand and noticing the absence of a ring. "You must miss him."

"He was my husband," Sheila replied, her tone oddly neutral.

"What are you duties at Elmtree?" asked Brown.

"My *duties*?" she said, emphasising the word with a sneer. "I clean the main house and Mr Hampton's cottage. Do all the cooking, washing and ironing."

"I could do with someone like you," said Brown, winking. "You might find it a bit of a challenge though."

She sniffed again. "I find there are far more challenging things in life than a bit of housework, don't you?"

"When did you last see your employer alive?" he asked. Linton could hear the lightness had left his voice.

"Sunday evening. About five. I have Mondays off."

"How did she seem?"

"I don't know what you mean."

"What sort of mood was she in?"

Sheila shrugged again. "The same as always."

"Which was?" She didn't answer. "Mrs Martock," he said, with exaggerated patience. "How would you generally describe Lauren Hampton?"

"I'd describe her as my employer," she said, her lips thinning to a hairline crack. "I was paid to clean, not have opinions about her."

"What was she like to work for?"

Sheila looked up, a note of defiance in her intelligent, blue eyes. "Fine."

"Can you tell us what happened yesterday evening?"

Brown took her slowly through her discovery of the body, asking questions as he went. *What time did she get the call from Mr Hampton? Had she seen anyone whilst she was driving to Elmtree? What exactly happened when she arrived there?*

Linton watched her carefully as she answered Brown's questions, noting that she seemed on edge, but not upset.

"What about earlier?" Linton asked when Brown reached the end of his questioning. "Tell us how you spent your day off."

"I caught up on my own cleaning."

"And in the evening? Before you got the call."

She paused then said stiffly, "I had tea. Watched a bit of telly. Then Mark Hampton rang me."

"What did you watch?"

"I can't remember," she said warily. "Whatever was on BBC One. That's what I tend to have on. I wasn't paying much attention. I was doing my crossword."

"Can anyone vouch that you were home all evening?"

"I was in when Mark rang," she said, her eyes narrowing. "He phoned my landline at quarter to nine."

"What about before that? Would your neighbours have seen you?"

"You'll have to ask them."

"The crime scene photos aren't back yet," said Brown picking his mobile from the table. "But I took some of Lauren's bedroom this morning. I'd like you to have a look."

"Why?"

"I thought you'd be able to spot if anything's out of the ordinary."

He passed her the phone. "See the button to the left?" he said. "You click…"

"I know how to use a camera phone," she interrupted. "I'm not stupid."

Linton watched her carefully as she flicked through the photos. The woman's face was devoid of emotion.

"Nothing," she said finally, handing the phone back to Brown. "It always looks like this when I've had a day off."

"We noticed she had a laptop in her study," said Linton. "Did she use it much?"

"She was always on it. Writing her novel. And when she wasn't writing, she was on Twitter."

Sheila must've noted the surprise on Linton's face because she said caustically, "Just because she was old didn't mean she couldn't keep up."

"What about you? Are you online?" asked Brown.

"I've got a laptop. I'm not on Twitter. But I know how it works. You put up your profile and people can follow you. That was right up Lauren's street."

"What do you mean?" asked Linton.

"She was used to having fans. People wanting to know all about her. She had a lot of Twitter followers. At least that's what she told me."

"Was she on Facebook as well?"

"That's about having friends, isn't it?"

"Meaning?"

"Let's just say I can't imagine Facebook would be her cup of tea."

"I read her obituary in the paper," said Linton. "It mentioned her daughter, Sophia. How did she die?"

"Suicide," she said coldly. "She threw herself off Hornsey Lane Bridge."

"Where's that?" asked Linton.

"London," said Brown, before Sheila could answer. "One of the capital's favourite suicide spots. Did you know it's the only significant suicide bridge in the world which passes over land rather than water?"

Fascinating, thought Linton sarcastically, wondering what it was about blokes and their inherent need to show off their general knowledge. "Why London?" she asked. "Had she moved there from Elmtree?"

Sheila shook her head. "She'd only gone up there for the operation."

"What was wrong with her?"

"Nothing. Apart from being seventeen and pregnant. She went to London to have an abortion. Lauren wanted to keep it covered up, but it all came out after Sophia died. Reckoned she regretted getting rid of the baby and that's why she did it. And on top of that, her dad had died a couple of months before."

"So who got Sophia up the duff?"

Sheila's eyes narrowed suspiciously. "What's this got to do with Lauren's death?"

"Do you know who got her pregnant or not?"

Sheila shook her head. "There were rumours. That he was married and that's why they kept it quiet."

Linton smiled in what she hoped was a conspiratorial manner. "But you would've have seen all the comings and goings in the house. You must have had your own suspicions."

"I told you," she said sharply. "I don't know who he was."

"Come on, Sheila," said Brown. "It's obvious you're hiding something. I can tell."

"She was a tart," she blurted out hurriedly. "She was always disappearing into the arboretum with different men. It could've been any one of them."

"Which men?" Brown asked, leaning forward in his seat. "Did you know any of them?"

"The ones who used to come down from London to all the parties. Lauren's friends. I was never introduced to them. And before you ask, I'm bad with faces. I couldn't describe them. Not after all these years."

"I think you know who it was, don't you, Sheila?" said Brown. "Are you worried you might get into trouble if you tell?"

"I said I don't know! Why would I lie?"

"There's no need to shout, Shelia."

"What about Lauren?" asked Linton, taking over the questioning as Brown sat back in his chair defeated. "Did she know who slept with Sophia?"

Sheila pursed her lips and shook her head. "I don't know."

"There's a big age gap, isn't there? Between Sophia and Mark? Seventeen years."

"Lauren found out she was pregnant just after Joseph died. Sophia was dead before Mark was even born."

"How did Mark get on with his mother?" asked Linton.

"Fine."

"Did they ever argue?"

"You'll have to ask him."

"What about other people? Had she fallen out with anyone?"

"I was her housekeeper. Why would she tell me if she had?"

"What about you?"

"I got on with her fine."

"Have you seen anyone hanging around Elmtree Manor recently?"

"Like who?"

"Someone you didn't know?" Linton asked, feeling increasingly impatient. "Someone who made you suspicious?"

Sheila shook her head, keeping her steely gaze fixed on Linton.

"What about the day before?" said Brown, taking over the questioning again. "Did anyone come to the house?"

"Only the postman."

"What about other employees? Does anyone else work for Lauren?"

"There isn't anyone else," she answered tightly. "Only me."

"Just one more thing before we finish," said Linton. "Did Lauren seem worried about anything? Anxious?"

Sheila laughed abruptly. "I've never seen Lauren Hampton anxious in my whole life."

"But her son said she'd seemed worried about something. That something had been bothering her for the last couple of weeks."

Linton watched with interest as a flush of colour curled up the woman's neck.

"Mrs Martock," she pressed, "did something happen a couple of weeks ago?"

Sheila shook her head vehemently. "I don't know what Mark's on about."

***

Linton and Brown left Sheila in the interview room with the promise that someone would be along to take her fingerprints, explaining they were needed for purposes of elimination.

They were silent, as they walked along, each lost in their own thoughts. The stuffy corridor smelt of disinfectant and Linton could hear the swishing of a mop and the clink of a bucket somewhere behind them.

"She got very defensive when we mentioned Lauren being anxious," she said eventually.

"She was defensive full stop," said Brown. "She's got a right chip on her shoulder."

"Do you think she was lying? About being home before Hampton rang her."

"Definitely." He shuddered. "She's a cold-hearted bitch. You could feel the chill coming off her. I could easily imagine her killing Lauren, then slapping her hands together and getting on with her cleaning. In fact suffocation would be perfect for her. No blood to clean up afterwards."

"We need to speak to the neighbours," said Linton.

Brown nodded his agreement. "And once we know what's in the will we'll know if she's got any financial motive. I'd like to take a look at Lauren's Twitter account as well. Look at her recent activity. See what she's been saying. Who's been following her."

As they reached the double doors of the staircase they saw Keen coming towards them from the direction of the canteen.

"Clothes pegs at the ready," said Brown under his breath, "here comes Trench mouth."

"Have you heard?" he said, as they came to halt in front of them. "There was another attack. First thing this morning."

For a moment, Linton thought it must've been too cold for Keen to have produced his legendary body odour. But a second later the meaty odour of stewing beef reached her nostrils.

"This morning," said Brown. "That's a first. He's always attacked in the evenings. Where did it happen?"

"Out near the garden centre on the Sharpen road." Linton could smell Keen's breath now. It was fusty, mildewy; like a pile of damp clothes left in the washing machine for too long. As she looked closer, she noticed a tiny piece of egg white, attached to the bristly blond hairs above his lip. She gagged involuntarily.

"The same as before," Keen continued oblivious to the effect he was having on her. "Except she needed a lot more stitches than the last woman. She sustained a lot of damage to her face. It's covered in cuts and bruises. He had her face pushed into the ground whilst he raped her."

"But he did that to the others."

"This time he literally ground her face into the dirt. He held onto her hair so tightly she lost a massive chunk of it from the back of her head."

"Had she been shopping first?" asked Brown, lightly brushing his own top lip with his finger, presumably in the hope that Keen would copy the gesture and remove the egg.

"Morrison's this time," Keen replied, not taking Brown's hint. Linton watched with fascinated disgust as the blob of albumen wobbled up and down, clinging resolutely to the bristly hairs. "And she lives in Street, so she had no reason to be anywhere near there. Her story about him jumping out in the road and waving her down is bollocks."

"What do you think happened?"

"My guess is he's getting into their cars at the supermarket and forcing them to drive out to the moors. He knows the area's too big for us to patrol properly. Even if we sent out every car at Glastonbury, we couldn't cover it all." He stopped for a second to wipe the back of hand across his sweaty forehead, revealing a damp patch beneath his arms. "What I can't understand," he said thoughtfully, "is how he's doing it without anyone seeing him. You'd think someone would've spotted a bloke threatening a woman with a knife or whatever method he's using to force himself into their cars."

"Nothing on CCTV?"

"The cameras tend to cover the entrance to the supermarket

and not much else. We've been through hours of CCTV but there's nothing."

"It's obviously not about the sex," said Brown thoughtfully. "He wants to hurt them. Punish them. I'll bet you they're a stand-in for a woman he hates from his past. An ex-girlfriend who humiliated him. A teacher that picked on him at school."

"Listen to you," said Linton laughing. "The amateur psychologist."

Brown grinned. "There's nothing amateurish about *anything* I do." He turned back to Keen. "Did she give a description of him?"

He shrugged. "She's claiming the same as the previous victims. That she hit her head and got amnesia, although there's no evidence she suffered any sort of concussion. She can remember exactly what happened to her, but not what he looked like. Just like the other women."

"Amnesia doesn't work like that," said Brown, "it's not that selective. If it was a bump to the head or even if it was caused by psychological trauma, she'd forget the whole event, not just his appearance. I reckon the rapist must've threatened them. Said if they gave the police any details he'd come after them."

"So why bother reporting it at all?" said Linton.

"Their husbands made them," replied Keen. "They've all been in a too much of a state to hide what had happened when they got home."

FIVE

Elmtree Manor was still off limits, so Hampton agreed to meet Linton and Brown in the bar of The Pendragon hotel. He'd spent the previous night there, insisting he was fit enough to drive his own car after coming round from his fainting fit.

It was a good excuse to get out of the incident room, something the detectives seized at every opportunity. And with the mood that The Toad was in due to lack of food, getting away from the station seemed like an even better idea.

As they entered the bar Linton immediately spotted Hampton at a table tucked away in a corner. He looked up and raised his hand in acknowledgment. As they got closer, Linton could see he was back to his everyday self, all signs of make-up gone from his tanned, clean-shaven face. His hair looked artfully ruffled and he was wearing a striped blue shirt under a soft, corduroy jacket. He looked like a model from a Boden catalogue.

"How are you?" she asked smiling as they reached the table.

"Terribly embarrassed about fainting," he said with a grimace. "That's never happened before."

"It was the shock, I expect," said Linton, pulling back a chair to sit down. "And you'd been on stage all evening."

"We've got a few questions we need to ask you," said Brown, taking the seat next to Linton. "I hope it won't be too much for you."

"Of course," he replied. There was no hint in his tone that

he'd noticed the sarcasm, but Linton was aware of a flash of emotion in his eyes. Embarrassment? Or was it something else? "I'm assuming I'm not a suspect," he said, looking at her for confirmation. "I was at the theatre all night."

"It's so we can eliminate you from our enquiries," she smiled reassuringly, "and start moving forward with the investigation."

He nodded. "I understand."

"So," said Brown, opening his notebook. "When did you last see your mother?"

"Yesterday morning," Hampton answered promptly. "Just before I went to the skydiving centre in Taunton."

"You skydive?" said Linton, impressed. "I've always wanted to have a go at that."

She watched his face light up. "I'd be happy to take you some time. I'm a trained tandem instructor."

"Really? Is that your job?"

He laughed. "Nothing quite so exciting, I'm afraid. I work from home, managing the family money, our investment portfolio, that sort of thing." He paused, his expression changing to a more serious one. "My marriage broke up last year, so I moved back to be near Lauren." He stopped to take a sip from his water and then looked suddenly stricken. "I'm so sorry. I'm not myself at all today. Could I get either of you a drink?"

"We're fine," said Brown curtly before Linton had a chance to answer. "Did your mother say how she was planning to spend her day yesterday?"

"I asked, but she was unusually vague. All I know is she was going to her book club at six thirty. She always did on a Monday."

"Do you get the impression she was deliberately vague?"

"What do you mean?"

"Perhaps she was going somewhere she didn't want you to know about. Meeting someone perhaps?"

"Possibly," said Hampton, thoughtfully. "But then it's easy to read things into situations in retrospect."

"Last night you told me she'd seemed anxious," said Linton. "Do you think she was worried about something in particular?"

"I've been thinking about that. I'm probably just making a mountain out of a mole hill. If it's a robbery gone wrong, then what does it matter the sort of mood Lauren was in?"

"What makes you say it was a robbery?" asked Brown leaning back in his chair, his hands clasped behind his head. With his chest strained against his shirt, the thin white material was transparent. Linton could see the outline of his nipples and the dark surface of hair spreading from his neck down to his stomach. She swallowed and looked back at Hampton.

"Because it makes the most sense," he answered. "She's well known in Glastonbury. To be honest, that's probably why she moved here all those years ago. I expect she liked the idea of being a big fish in a small pond. Everyone knows she's got plenty of money. And that she doesn't take security seriously. Anyone who'd ever spent any time around the place would know that."

"We're not sure if anything was taken. There were no signs of a break in or anyone searching through her things."

"Perhaps she disturbed the burglar. And that's why…" He stopped, cleared his throat awkwardly. "Besides, how can you know nothing was taken? My mother owns a lot of expensive jewellery."

"Which, as I'm sure you know, she catalogued for insurance purposes, so we're working our way through the list." Brown paused. "There is one thing we need to check with you though."

"Please do."

Brown nodded at Linton and she passed him the manila folder. He opened it, yanked out a pile of paper and began riffling through it. He finally grabbed at a sheet, shoving the others untidily into the folder.

"The Scene of Crime Officers have made a list of what your mother was wearing when she died," said Brown, glancing down at the piece of paper in his hand. "It's possible the killer took something from her body. Something valuable." He looked up at Hampton. "Perhaps you could tell us what jewellery she had on last night."

Hampton nodded. "That's easy," he said. "She always wore earrings, her watch, her eternity bracelet, her engagement ring and her wedding ring." He tapped the fingers of his left hand as he listed each item, stopping at his little finger. Linton noticed he was wearing a thin, gold band on it. As he spoke he began fiddling with it, twisting it one way and then the other. "Lauren doesn't, or rather didn't, often wear much of her other jewellery," he said. "Unless it was a special occasion. Most of it's rather large and showy. She wouldn't admit it, but I think as she got older, it weighed her down."

Brown handed the list back to Linton with a nod and said, "What time did you leave the skydiving centre?"

Hampton hesitated. "I'm not sure exactly, but I got home just after five. I knew Lauren was in because her car was on the driveway. I didn't see her though."

"And after that?"

"I showered and changed and left for the theatre at quarter to six. In time to get ready for the performance."

"Was Lauren's car still there?"

He nodded. "Her meeting didn't start until six thirty and it was only down the road."

"What time did you get to Avalon Theatre?"

"A couple of minutes later. I drove."

"And you were there the whole evening?" said Brown.

He nodded. "I had to be. I've got one of the main parts. I'm the beast."

"Which means you're on stage for most of it."

"Mainly in the second half," he said, looking at Linton again for confirmation. "But don't worry. I've got someone to vouch for me for the first half. And the whole of the interval."

"Who?"

"Our family solicitor. Jonathan. Jonathan Baines. He's one of the patrons so he helps out doing front of house, showing people to their seats and selling programmes. He spent the entire first half in my dressing room and stayed until the end of the interval. We had a couple of drinks and a chat." He paused. "No doubt you'll be speaking to him anyway. He's the executor of the will."

"Why did he come backstage?" Linton asked.

"He'd watched the rehearsals a couple of times and, to be honest, I don't think he could face seeing it again. I told him to come to my dressing room and we'd have a drink. Put the world to rights." He paused. "He's a good chap, is Jonathan. Salt of the earth."

"I understand you rang Sheila Martock during the interval," said Brown, "because you were concerned about your mother."

Hampton took a sip from his water and nodded. "That's right. I realised I didn't have my wallet with me. I rang Lauren because I wanted to know if it was in the cottage. I was worried I might have dropped it somewhere. Turned out I'd left it in the car. Anyway, I tried her mobile and her landline.

Three or four times, but she didn't answer. Sorry," he said pausing for breath. "I'm rambling on again."

"What time was this?" asked Linton.

"Between eight thirty and nine."

"Were you worried?"

"A bit, to be honest, so I rang Sally Hughes."

"Who's that?" asked Brown, scrawling the name in his notebook.

"One of the ladies from Lauren's book club. She hosted last night's meeting. Apparently it finished slightly early. Lauren left at eight twenty-five and, as far as Sally knew, she was going straight home."

"How far is her house away from yours?"

"Just down the road. Frogmore Cottage. It's probably less than a minute by car." He frowned. "Lauren was driving. She should've arrived home by half eight. I couldn't think why she wasn't answering. She wouldn't have gone back out again and she never left the phone to ring. She considered it to be the height of rudeness."

"Do you know who the beneficiaries of Lauren's estate are?" asked Brown.

He nodded. "As far as I know, the only people in her will are Sheila and myself."

"Do you know what she's left Sheila?"

He nodded again. "A painting."

"Does Sheila know that?"

He shrugged. "Possibly. Lauren might've wanted it to be a surprise although I don't think it's particularly valuable."

"So you've never told her."

"No. It's not something you really discuss, is it?"

"And presumably you know how much Lauren's estate is worth."

Hampton started fiddling with the gold band on his little finger again. "An awful lot. There's the manor house itself of course. The land alone is worth a chunk of money, although I'd never dream of selling it. Then there's all her stocks and shares, her antiques and jewellery and I imagine she's got a fair amount in the bank."

"It sounds as though you stand to become a rich man."

He frowned. "I suppose I do as I inherit the house."

"And everything else presumably," said Brown, looking up from his notes.

"Oh no," said Hampton. "Only Elmtree Manor. She's left everything else to charity."

None of them spoke for a few seconds. "Charity?" said Linton eventually, trying to hide her surprise. "That's very generous of her."

"Isn't it?" She could hear the sarcasm in his tone. "Still, I suppose it looks good, which is what Lauren wanted. Sorry. I must sound bitter."

"Was that her reason? Because she wanted to look good?"

There was a slight pause before he said. "Lauren was very concerned about how she was perceived by others."

"So she wasn't in any financial difficulty?" Brown interrupted.

Hampton knitted his eyebrows together. "Why? What makes you ask?"

"I thought she might be keen to get her latest book published because she needed the money."

Hampton made a noise, somewhere between a laugh and a grunt. "That wasn't about money. It was about recognition. Fame. She liked people worshipping her from afar."

Linton thought of what Sheila had said about Twitter, how Lauren had liked the idea of people following her. She was rapidly creating a picture of Lauren in her mind and it wasn't a pleasant one.

"Is there anybody else who might've expected to gain from her death?" asked Brown. "Any other family?"

"Lauren was an only child. Her parents died years ago. She had another child, my sister, Sophia, but she died before I was born."

"She committed suicide, didn't she? After a termination," said Brown.

Hampton nodded.

"Just out of interest, did Lauren ever tell you the identity of the man who got Sophia pregnant?"

"Obviously it happened before I was born, but it's something I've always wondered about. Who he was. Whether he's still alive."

"Did *Lauren* know who he was?"

"I asked her once and she said no. I didn't believe her."

"Why not?"

"Because I can't imagine my sister could've kept a secret from her."

"Have you got any ideas yourself?"

"I did wonder if…" he stopped, as if he'd said too much.

"What?" Brown asked, leaning forward slightly in his chair.

"Apparently there were rumours at the time. About him being someone well known – a married man. Someone much older. I think we might've found out if Lauren hadn't died."

"What makes you say that?" asked Linton.

"Lauren's been talking a lot about the past recently. She was in contact with Michael Fenn. I don't know if you've heard of him."

"The investigative journalist? He works for *The Times*," said Brown. Linton waited for the Wikipedia entry, which invariably came with any imparting of information from Brown. Birth date, place of birth, school, A level grades. But curiously he had overcome his temptation to show-off and simply added, "Go on."

"Fenn was planning to run something in the paper. I think it was Lauren's way of getting back into the public eye; trying to get publishers interested in her novel. For years, people have wondered about the truth surrounding Sophia's death. A revelation like that would've sold papers."

"What was her novel about?" asked Linton curiously. "Have you read any of it?"

Hampton grimaced. "It was a romance."

"Is it purely fiction?"

"You mean is it based on her life? Were there any revelations in it that might have got her murdered?" He shook his head. "It's basically *Pride and Prejudice* set in modern times. But with none of Jane Austen's wit. I hate to say it, but it's bloody awful. I can't see anyone wanting to publish it."

"What about Lauren's friends? Old employees? Would any of them think they might have gained financially from her death?"

He shook his head again. "I'm afraid she didn't really have friends as such. She didn't keep in touch with the people she knew when she was modelling. She'd cut them out of her life. I think she was ashamed of growing old."

"What about locally? She must've known people round here."

He shrugged. "She had her book group of course, but I wouldn't say that any of the members were her friends."

"Why not?" Linton asked.

He paused and then said, "Lauren wanted everyone to admire her so she spent time with people she thought looked up to her."

Neither Brown nor Linton said anything, waiting to see what else he might say.

"I'm sorry," he said eventually, rubbing his eyes. "I know I shouldn't speak ill of her. I loved her. I mean she was my mother for God's sake. But she wasn't always…" He paused, as if searching for the right word.

"She wasn't always what?" Linton pressed.

He sighed. "She could be difficult sometimes. Critical."

"Of what?"

"Anything and everything."

"Can you think of anyone in particular she might've upset?"

He sighed again. "She upset everyone eventually. She had a habit of drawing people in and then throwing them out, once they served their purpose. The only people who stuck by her were Sheila and myself. If it wasn't for Sheila staying, I don't know what Lauren would've done. No other employee would've lasted more than a few weeks." He stopped. "Look, please don't think she was all bad. She couldn't help it. It was the way she was."

"What about your ex-wife?" asked Brown.

He looked puzzled. "Elizabeth?"

"Were she and your mother close?"

He shook his head sadly. "I'm afraid not. She hated Lauren. That was one of the things, amongst many others, that led to us splitting up. Elizabeth couldn't understand why I wanted to spend so much time with her. She thought my mother was a bitch. But I felt sorry for Lauren. Underneath, she was a sad and lonely old woman. Elizabeth couldn't see that, she was jealous of my relationship with her." He paused. "Actually, she was jealous full stop."

"Of what?"

"I'm involved in a lot of charity work and she even resented that. She couldn't understand why I'd want to give up my time for anyone else other than her. I'm sure that's why she didn't want children. I don't think she liked the idea of having to compete for my attention."

"Elizabeth Hampton," Brown said, noting the name down in his book, next to Michael Fenn's. "Do you have an address for her?"

"I'm afraid I don't. After I left her, I didn't want to keep in touch. She did something so..." he stopped. "Sorry. Listen to me babbling on again. You're far too polite to tell me to shut up. This isn't relevant, is it?"

"It could be. What exactly did she do?" Linton asked. She was genuinely curious.

He chewed his bottom lip as though debating whether to say anything. "I'd rather not go into it, to be honest. It's personal. And I can assure you it's got nothing to do with your investigation."

Linton waited to see if Brown would push for an answer, but he didn't. Instead he asked, "Do you keep in touch with her at all?"

He shook his head. "We lived in Bournemouth, but I've heard from mutual friends she'd moved away. No one is sure where."

"Surely one of them would know?"

"To be honest, after what... after we split up, our friends tended to take my side on account of... I shouldn't think any of them would have kept in touch with her."

"You said you both lived in Bournemouth," Linton said. "Did she have a job?"

He nodded. "She worked in advertising. For a company called CDA."

"Perhaps we can trace her through them. They might have a forwarding address."

Hampton nodded.

"Did Lauren keep in touch with her?"

He shook his head. "She'd asked Elizabeth to leave her alone."

"Why?"

"A month or so ago she went to Lauren asking for money. Told her she'd fallen into debt since we split up."

"Did your mother give her any?"

"Lauren said she didn't."

"Did you believe her?"

"I'm not sure. She was a very convincing liar."

"Did Lauren mention your ex-wife recently?" Hampton was silent for a moment. "What is it?" Linton asked.

He shook his head, as though throwing off a thought. "Nothing. No. She didn't."

"You looked as though you were going to say something else."

He was twisting the ring more vigorously. He swallowed. "Sorry. It's just that talking about my ex-wife gets me agitated. As I said, we didn't part on very good terms."

"Let's go back to your housekeeper for a moment," said Brown. "Sheila said she tried ringing you from your mother's house, after she'd contacted us."

"I switched my mobile off as soon as I rang her because I knew I had to go on stage. I didn't get her message until the end of the show. I rushed back straight away. Nearly knocked that poor bloke off his bike."

"Going back to the people she's upset," said Brown. "Have you got any idea who could've hated her enough to do something like this?"

"Lauren was definitely better at making enemies than she was friends. The number of people she upset over the years is endless, but I don't know anyone who would do something like that." He paused. "Killing a defenceless woman. Well, it's pure evil."

"Could you write down a list of people she might have wronged and why?"

He shook his head. "It would be easier to write a list of people she hasn't upset. In fact, I don't know if there would be anyone on it."

"What about Sheila?" Linton asked. He looked confused. "You said she stuck by your mother. Didn't Lauren she ever upset her?"

"She's old school, Sheila. Not the sort to ever give in. And underneath it all, I think she was genuinely fond of Lauren, warts and all."

***

Really? You're a sky diver?" Brown said, mimicking Linton's earlier words, as they stepped out of the hotel and onto Glastonbury High Street.

"Piss off," she said, wincing at the cold air after the warmth of the bar. "I was being polite. Trying to put him at ease."

"What a smarmy git. With his poncy jacket and his sparkling water."

"I liked him," said Linton pulling her scarf tighter round her neck. "He's a gentleman."

Brown grunted as they sidestepped a sallow man sat cross-legged on the pavement in front of the cash point. He was wearing a grubby white turban and playing a piccolo.

"His hands must be freezing," said Linton as they passed him.

"Which might explain why he's playing it so bloody badly."

They walked up the gentle hill heading towards St John's church, where Brown had left his car. Linton couldn't help smiling at the window display of broomsticks and carved wands as they passed the Witch and Wand shop.

"The bloke who knocked Sophia up," said Brown, "What if he got wind that Lauren was going to name him? He could've killed her to shut her up."

"After all these years?" she replied. "That sounds a bit far-fetched."

He shrugged. "It depends on who the bloke is. Maybe he thought he'd got away with it. Even after years, it could still ruin a reputation, break a family apart." He paused. "You know what they say about the past."

"What?"

"Eventually it'll catch you up and bite you in the arse."

"Ooooh. Another Brownism. That's two you've got for your book."

He laughed, then said more seriously, "We need to get hold of Michael Fenn. Find out what Lauren told him."

They walked in a silence for a bit, stepping round a group of tourists spilling out of Café Continental, then ducking the stream of bubbles being pumped from a machine just inside the door of Gothic Image.

"What about Hampton's ex-wife?" said Linton, as they passed The Helping Hand, her friend's favourite bookshop, thanks to its proclamation of being the largest purveyor of self-help books in the south-west. "Perhaps she asked her for money and Lauren refused so she killed her out of anger."

"And then there's Sheila," said Brown. "If she thought the painting was worth something. You know what though? If I had to go on gut feeling, I'd plump for Hampton."

"Why have you got it in for him? I was there! I saw him on the stage. And when he wasn't, he was with his solicitor."

"Or so he says."

"But he knows we're going to talk to Baines so why lie?"

"Baines," said Brown thoughtfully. "I know that name. It's familiar, but I can't think why." He paused and then said, "Going back to Hampton, I'm just saying he's got the most to gain. And he wasn't exactly flattering about Lauren. It sounds like he hated her."

"Haven't you ever felt like that about your own parents?"

"They got on my tits sometimes, but I never hated them."

"Not even when you argued with them?"

"They aren't like that."

Linton had met Brown's parents a few times over the years. They were always so thrilled to see him, acted like they hadn't seen him for weeks, even though they only lived round the corner. No wonder Brown was so confident, so self-assured. He'd been brought up by his two biggest fans.

"Did you notice how he referred to her as 'Lauren'?" Brown continued. "Never as 'mother' or 'mum'. It's like he's trying to distance himself from her."

"It's the criminal psychologist again."

"You've got to admit it's odd."

"But look at the way he reacted last night. He fainted with shock."

Brown grunted again. "Was he any good in the play?"

"All right, I suppose," said Linton confused. "But what's that got to do with anything?"

"If he's any good at acting, he could've faked the faint. He'd make a lot of money from the house if he sold it. Not to mention the plot."

A freckled woman with her hair pulled back in a ponytail

walked towards them pushing a pushchair. She smiled bashfully at Brown as she passed him. Linton looked sideways at Brown, watched him look over at his shoulder at the retreating woman.

"What?" he said, as he looked back and caught Linton's expression of scorn. "I was looking at the pushchair. It was one of those Land Rover thingies. My sister's thinking of getting one for the next one."

They walked in silence for a while, snaking in and out of the steady flow of people streaming down the High Street; shoppers, more mums with pushchairs, a man wearing a tunic made from a potato sack. As they passed the open doorway of Alchemy, panpipe music drifted out along with the sickly, sweet smell of patchouli oil. Linton shuddered. The smell would always remind her of the Ley Line Strangler.

"Do you know what really intrigues me?" she said eventually.

"Whether Mark Hampton's single?"

She rolled her eyes in disdain. "What his ex-wife did to him that was so terrible."

***

The first thing Sheila did when she got home, after switching on the radio, was to take the envelope out of her handbag and lay it on the kitchen table.

She'd thought about reading the rest of its contents in the police station car park, but the fear that one of the officers might see had stopped her.

Heart thumping uncomfortably against her rib cage, she pulled out the two bits of paper. She pushed the letter to Michael Fenn to one side and unfolded the other piece. It was a cutting from the *Central Somerset Gazette* dated July 19th

1985. The headline alone made her feel sick, but she forced herself to read it.

INQUEST CONFIRMS ACCIDENTAL DEATH

The coroner at the inquest of a gardener who died of a gunshot wounds has recorded a verdict of accidental death.

The Taunton inquest was told how Henry Martock, age 40, was found by the teenage son of his former employer Lauren Hampton in the grounds of Elmtree Manor, her home in Glastonbury. He had tripped over a raised tree root and had accidently shot himself in the chest.

The coroner was told how Mr Martock, a father of two, had become obsessed with the upkeep of Mrs Hampton's arboretum, despite being sacked from his job as the groundsman at Elmtree Manor.

He told his wife he'd seen rabbits that were causing damage to some of the newer trees he'd originally planted, and that he was going to shoot them. He was reported to have been drinking heavily before the incident.

Drinking heavily before the incident... Reading the words immediately brought that fateful evening back. Sheila could see Henry now, staring blankly at the flickering television screen, picking up his beer glass so often it was like he was lifting weights.

At seven o'clock the phone had rung, making her jump.

She'd pulled herself up from the crossword she was pretending to complete and wondered if she risked getting up to answer it. But Henry was already there, shoving his way into the hallway, slamming the sitting room door behind him. She heard a thump and a mumbled curse. The ringing stopped, followed by a gruff 'what?' She edged her way towards the door, scared he might see her outline through the frosted glass, and tried to decipher what he was saying. But he spoke too quietly. Her stomach clenched as she wondered if this was it.

He stumbled back into the room a minute later, his face distorted. She'd already run back to her chair and picked up her crossword. As he moved toward her, she could feel her heart in her throat, threatening to block her airways. She stiffened, waiting for him to yank her out of the armchair but he simply scooped up his keys from the table.

"I'm going out," he slurred. A couple of seconds later their front door had slammed shut.

Back in the present, her hands shaking, Sheila laid the photocopy down on the kitchen table. So after all these years, had Lauren been about to expose the truth?

Thank God the bitch was dead.

SIX

Michael Fenn was at work. According to the woman who answered, Linton was in luck because he wasn't often at his desk.

She was prepared for someone well spoken and authoritative so his voice, when she finally got through, was something of a shock. He sounded like an old woman with a heavy cold. High pitched and nasal and with a strong Bristolian accent.

"After speaking to her on the phone, I can't say I warmed to her much," he said matter of factly, when she explained why she was ringing. "She thought she was being terribly charming, but she came across as a bit of a cow. Still it's a terrible tragedy. For me. If nothing else. That's my piece down the proverbial pan."

"Actually, that's what I wanted to talk to you about. I understand from her son that you were planning to write an article about her life."

"I was hoping to run it in a couple of weeks' time."

"Why now?"

"I'm sorry?"

"She's been out of the public eye for a long time. I'm curious why you'd want to write about her."

"Do you read our paper?" he asked.

She hesitated. "Sometimes. Well, only the magazine," she admitted. "Does that count?"

He laughed and cleared his throat. "She got in touch with us recently and asked us if we'd be interested in featuring her in the *Best of Times, Worst of Times*. You're probably familiar with it if you read the magazine."

Linton was. Every week a well-known person was asked to talk about the high and low points in their life.

"It's obvious why," he continued. "She's been trying to get her new novel published but no one's interested. She's desperate to get back in the public eye."

"What made her think you'd want to print anything about her?"

"According to Lauren, she had some information she thought the public had a right to know. Secrets from her past that would have had our paper flying off the shelves. That's when I got involved."

"Did she tell you what these secrets were?"

"She hinted at them."

Linton looked up to see Hooper in front of her desk, waving a mug and mouthing 'tea'. She nodded and stuck her thumb up. "What exactly did she say?"

"She told me her gardener died in the grounds of her garden. Twenty-eight years ago. At the time the police thought he'd tripped and his gun had gone off, but according to Lauren there was more to it than that."

"Did she say what?"

"She said she'd send me some background info about him, which incidentally hasn't arrived, but she wanted to tell me what happened in person."

"What sort of background information?"

"She didn't say. I googled the gardener anyway. She'd told me his name. Henry Martock." *Sheila's husband*, Linton thought. "According to your lot, he was trespassing in the

Hampton arboretum when he fell over a tree root and his gun went off. He'd been drinking heavily."

"Were there any witnesses?"

"Apparently not. But Mark, Lauren's teenage son, heard the shot and got there a few seconds later."

"Do you think it's odd Lauren wouldn't tell you over the phone?"

He laughed his high-pitched squeal. "She was stringing it out. I think she liked the drama of it all. I don't know if she meant he'd killed himself or if there was something more to it."

"Did she mention any other secrets?"

"You mean did Lauren tell me who got Sophia pregnant before she killed herself?"

"Exactly."

"Funnily enough, I asked her the same thing. It's always intrigued me. I remember the tragedy well."

Linton waited.

"She said she didn't want to talk about it over the phone. She said we could discuss it when we met in person."

"Did you get the impression she knew?"

"Definitely. And it's a great story. A lot of our readers would've remembered it. People love an unsolved mystery. Even if it's from years ago."

***

Linton recounted her conversation with Fenn to Brown.

"If Sheila's husband was murdered," she said, "maybe his killer found out Lauren was about to expose him and suffocated her to shut her up."

"It could've been Mark," Brown said. "He was first at the scene. And he's got a gun licence. He knows how to use a weapon."

Linton shook her head. "I worked it out. He would've been about fifteen."

"So?"

"Why would he want to shoot their ex-gardener? Plus, would Lauren really want to implicate her own son?"

"I wouldn't put it past her. She sounds like a right bitch."

"Anyway. Mark Hampton's got an alibi."

"Which we haven't confirmed yet. And besides, even if it does check out, there's every chance he's still responsible for her death."

"How?"

"He could've paid someone else to do her in. Then made certain his solicitor was with him all evening so he had the perfect alibi."

"And the motive?"

"Elmtree Manor! All right, so she's left everything else to charity, but if he sold the house, with planning permission he'd make a packet."

He had a point. "I'll speak to Hooper, shall I? Get him to look into Hampton's bank accounts and see if there are any unusual withdrawals."

"Which reminds me, did he check with Sheila's neighbour?"

"He couldn't get hold of the one who lives on her right, but he's left a message. The others couldn't be certain whether she was home or not."

Brown sighed. "I feel like we're getting nowhere. Which reminds me. Whilst you were on the phone to Fenn, I rang CDA."

Linton frowned, trying to link the initials to something.

"The advertising agency in Bournemouth that Elizabeth Hampton worked for."

"And?"

"She left abruptly, about four months ago. Around the time she and Hampton split up. They haven't got a forwarding address for her."

"Did she tell them why she was leaving?"

"No. But it didn't surprise them."

"Why not?"

"They said she was a very private person, often seemed preoccupied. Kept herself to herself. Never went out with any of them after work. Took a lot of time off as well with various illnesses. They couldn't prove it, but they thought she was skiving. The odd thing is, they tried to pay her last month's salary into her account, but it bounced back. When they rang the bank to find out what happened, they told her she'd closed the account. They thought she might get in contact with her new details, but she never did." He paused. "It's like she didn't want to be tracked down."

"Perhaps it was to do with what she did to Mark?"

"Possibly."

"She can't have just vanished," she said. "What about her family? Surely someone must know where she is?"

"I've still got Hooper trying to track them down, but Boy Wonder hasn't had much luck yet."

"What about her landlord?"

He shook his head. "She told him she'd contact him with a forwarding address so he could return her deposit but she never did."

"I expect she's moved onto the next unsuspecting bloke."

"By the way," said Brown. "I've got to give my sister a lift to the hospital tomorrow morning. She's got her scan. You go and see Baines, then we'll speak to Sheila again. See if she can shed any light on what Lauren was inferring about her husband's death."

"I can't wait," said Linton. "Hopefully she'll be as warm and accommodating as she was this morning."

**

It was after seven by the time Linton got home. She thought about going for a run; got as far as downloading the app for her mobile when it rang. It was Gemma.

"Do you remember I said I was going to see that psychic?" her friend said breathlessly. "Well, before you interrupt with your cynical comments, she was amazing. You'll never guess which initials she came up with."

"C.R.A.P? As in 'what a load of'?"

Gemma tutted loudly. "No! K.L."

"As in Kuala Lumpur? Karl Lagerfeld?"

"God, you're a cow sometimes. It was obvious she was talking about you."

"Why?"

"Because she said KL was an important person in my life. Which you are. And that I needed to give you a message."

"Go on then. What is it?"

Gemma paused, obviously feeling the announcement warranted a build up, then said dramatically, "She said to tell you that you needed more colour in your life. That you should actively embrace it."

"That's it?" said Linton. "That's the message?"

"Don't you see? More. Colour. In. Your. Life."

They both waited for a few seconds, Linton unsure of what to say. "Well, I'm wearing red shoes to the wedding reception on Saturday, if that helps?"

"Christ, Kate. Do I have to spell it out?"

"Sorry, Gemma," she said laughing. "I'm not psychic."

"Don't you see what she meant? Colour. *Brown*. It's obvious. It's a sign. That you should be together."

***

JULY 26TH

So much for a happy birthday. She did everything she could to ruin it for me. All I wanted was a party with my friends, but of course that wasn't to be. I know why. It's because she wouldn't have had complete control and we can't have that, can we? How many other mothers insist on holding a dinner party at home for their daughter's 17th birthday and decide who should be invited? Not a single person my age was there. Only the great and the good, the people she thinks are worthy of her company along with a couple who aren't, because they make her feel superior.

As always, she dominated the conversation regaling everyone with her stories, which she thinks are so dazzling and witty and brilliant. When she wasn't talking about herself, she was parading me around, telling them all what a genius I am. It was embarrassing.

"Sophia darling, play them something on the piano. You know her teacher begged me to let her audition for the Royal Academy of Music when she was younger, but I didn't think it was fair, pushing her into the limelight like that."

Firstly, that isn't true, I'm mediocre at best and secondly I can't understand how she can show me off in public like that and yet constantly belittle me in private. It happened again while we were getting ready this evening. I'd put on the dress I wore to the end of term ball, hoping that by making an effort I'd be showing her how grateful I was for the trouble she'd gone to arranging the evening (even though Sheila had done everything). She was still in her robe, sat at her dressing table, carefully applying her make-up. I asked her how I looked. She didn't even attempt to turn round; she simply studied my reflection in her mirror. The sneer she produced was theatrical – as though someone was pulling on her top lip with piece of string.

"Ridiculous," she answered. "It's a dinner party, not a dance. For God's sake, put on a blouse and a skirt. Something less revealing. You look like a slut."

When she finally made her grand entrance, she was wearing the very dress she'd told me to take off. Once she'd lapped up the compliments she wandered over to me and said under her breath, "Darling. You could have made an effort. You look so dowdy."

I think though, the most infuriating part of it was the birthday cake, or rather the lack of it. I know Sheila had bought one because I'd seen it on the side in the kitchen. I thought Mother must have forgotten, so after Sheila had served coffee to the guests I quietly reminded her. She looked at me as though I was insane and said loudly, "Darling. Fancy getting cross because I didn't buy you a cake? You know you're allergic to egg. It wouldn't be fair to have got you one and then you not be able to eat any of it, would it?"

There were a couple of "ahhs" from the guests as they considered what a thoughtful mother I had. It was at this point I thought I was going mad. I'm not allergic to eggs. I never have been.

And then I realised what it was. She couldn't bear the thought of everyone singing 'Happy Birthday' to me, of letting me be the centre of attention for once. Instead, she told everyone this story about how, at her own seventeenth birthday party, Jerome Du Galle, the famous milliner, had presented her with a cake in the shape of the hat he'd specially designed for her to mark the occasion. I looked over at Father at this point. He had a bewildered expression on his face and no wonder. At seventeen, she was probably still living with her parents in their semi-detached house in Wandsworth.

As the guests were leaving, the only consolation was that mother seemed to have had a good time. This would mean Father and I would be off the hook. Hopefully we'd be able go to bed without her having one of her tantrums. I was wrong. Apparently I'd made too big a fuss over the present Angela Deacon had given me. She'd bought me some beautiful silver earrings and I must admit I gave a little squeal of excitement when I saw them. *Did I like them more than the present she had got me?* she demanded. *No, of course not,* I replied. *Then why had I acted like it?* She cannot stand it if I am ever happy or pleased about anything that doesn't include her. The truth is I did like Angela's present more. Mother bought me some clothes in a size smaller than I am as an incentive for me to lose some weight. Ironically, we are the same size although she would never admit it. After I'd persuaded her I loved the clothes she'd bought me and that she was very thoughtful to worry about my figure and that the earrings Angela had bought me were cheap and nasty, she launched into a tirade against Mrs Harper, the Mayor's wife. Apparently when she'd remarked to her that no one could believe she was old enough to have a seventeen-year-old daughter, she hadn't replied. Of course Mrs Harper hasn't had the years of training I've had and didn't realise that she was supposed to say, "*My goodness, you don't look old enough to have children at all, and how do you manage to have beautifully smooth skin? You are the most beautiful woman I've ever seen, I wish I looked like you.*" Poor Mrs Harper. Being Lauren Hampton's enemy is no fun at all as no doubt she'll soon discover.

SEVEN

"This is a lovely office," said Linton, as Jonathan Baines ushered her in. The room was light and spacious with a large, solid oak desk and a set of antique-looking leather armchairs.

"Could I offer you some tea?" he asked, waving her into one of the chairs. "Traditional English, Earl Grey, Lapsang Souchong?"

"Traditional English," she replied, thinking that if it weren't for his gentle Welsh accent, it would be exactly how she'd describe the man sitting opposite her. There was something instantly reassuring about him, with his meticulously neat hair, dark suit and sober tie.

She'd immediately recognised him from the theatre; he was the man who'd shown her and Gemma to their seats. But he seemed familiar for another reason that she couldn't yet place.

He picked up his phone and said tightly, "Gillian, a pot of tea when you're ready please."

Linton cleared her throat. "I understand from Mark Hampton that Lauren's estate has three beneficiaries. Himself, Sheila Martock and a charity. Is that correct?"

Baines nodded, swallowing hard. "Mark inherits the house and land. Lauren left the housekeeper a painting. And the rest goes to Rape Crisis."

Linton looked up from her notebook. "That's not one of your run of the mill charities."

"I, um, I suppose not."

"How long has her will been like that?"

"For the last month. Originally, everything apart from the picture was to be left to Mark. Lauren came in a month ago and asked to change her will."

"I hadn't realised it was so recent. Did she say why?"

"Why the charity or why the change of will?"

"Both."

He took a few seconds to think.

"I don't know why she chose Rape Crisis," he said, picking up a fountain pen absent-mindedly from his desk. "As for changing the will, she simply said she'd changed her mind. She didn't elaborate and I didn't ask. Lauren wasn't the sort of person you questioned. I just did was I was paid to do."

"Mr Hampton mentioned the land is worth a lot to potential developers."

He nodded, rolling the pen between his thumb and forefingers. "If planning permission were ever granted, we're talking a couple of million. However, Mark's always maintained he wants to preserve the grounds of Elmtree Manor. I've spoken to him about it a number of times and he's very much against this idea of digging up gardens and filling them with blocks of flats."

"Do you believe him?"

"Absolutely." He nodded vigorously. "He's the most honest person I know."

Linton looked at her notes and continued, "Were you surprised that Lauren wanted to leave so much of her estate to a charity?"

"Not particularly," he said. "I'm used to requests like that. Some of my clients are quite prone to changing their mind on a whim." He paused then said, "Anyway, she rang last week and told me she wanted to make an appointment for next week so she could change it yet again."

Before Linton could ask how, there was a gentle tap on the door.

The solemn receptionist Linton met earlier treaded softly in. She was balancing a tray with a white china tea service and a plate of assorted biscuits. Gently pushing aside a framed photograph of Baines embracing a large fish, she positioned the tray neatly on the desk and tiptoed back out again.

"You said Mrs Hampton spoke to you about changing her will," she continued while Baines poured tea into one of the cups, his face furrowed in concentration and his hand shaking slightly from the weight of the teapot. "In what way?"

He settled the pot back onto the tray and looked up. "She wanted to revert back to her original will and leave everything to Mark again."

"Did he know that?"

"Look," he said rubbing his large hands together awkwardly, "I know this is unprofessional, but I told him. Not because he wanted the money. He'd have probably ended up donating it to charity in any case, but he was hurt by the whole episode." He stopped suddenly, as though he'd said too much.

"What episode?" she said sharply. "You said Lauren didn't tell you why she was changing it."

"That's the truth." He licked his lips nervously. "She didn't tell me. But Mark did. In confidence."

"What happened?"

"They had an argument."

"About what?"

"They got into a debate about charity and Mark told her that she ought to give more. She didn't like that, so she changed her will out of spite."

He passed Linton the teacup. It rattled slightly, spilling tea over the side of the saucer.

"Did Mark know why she chose that particular charity? Is it significant?"

"He didn't mention it. You'd have to ask him."

She waited while he poured tea into the second cup, noticing for the first time how tired he looked. The skin was grey and baggy beneath his eyes.

"The night Lauren was killed," she said. "Mr Hampton says you spent the first half of the play and the interval in his dressing room. Is that correct?"

Baines nodded. "I went in there just after seven."

"Apart from when he went on stage, did he leave the dressing room at all?"

"No," he said, shaking his head adamantly. "Definitely not."

"Did he share the dressing room with anyone else?"

"It was too small. It was more of a cupboard if I'm honest. Like a bloody sauna in there with the heating on full blast. If we hadn't had the fire escape open, we'd have boiled alive."

"Hampton says he thought he'd lost his wallet."

"That's right. He rang Lauren just after eight thirty to ask if she'd seen it. She didn't answer. He rang a few times. He was very worried. He thought something must've happened. When she didn't answer, he phoned Sheila and asked her to check up on her."

"And you're quite sure you were with him the entire time."

"Quite sure," he replied tightly.

When Linton eventually got up to leave, she handed him her card. Perhaps it was the angle of his head but as he leant forward to take it she instantly remembered where she'd seen him. It was in the local paper, a few months ago. He'd been campaigning to get a dating agency to stop advertising on late night local radio. They were called *No Strings* or something similar and encouraged people to have extra-marital affairs.

"How did your campaign go?" she asked. "To stop that dating site from advertising."

He looked up; obviously taken aback that she'd mentioned it. "Apparently there's nothing rude or offensive, so the ASA won't act on it."

"I agree with you by the way. It's wrong to encourage people to be unfaithful."

He nodded then said awkwardly, "Extra-marital affairs can get people into all kinds of messes. Messes which can take years to untangle."

***

It was inevitable, thought Sheila, that reading about Henry's death would unearth painful memories. Memories she'd buried long ago; in a shallower grave than she'd realised.

She was doing her best to distract herself and was part-way through *The Times* quick crossword – *twelve across, five letters, 'snarl'* – when her phone rang.

The caller display told her it was Heather. Wednesday was her daughter's day off and she was at home with Toby. She was tempted to leave it. She was probably only ringing to tell her about Toby's potty training. Did her daughter really think she wanted to hear every detail of it? She'd been there, done that, thank you very much.

"God, mum," she said breathlessly when Sheila eventually picked up. "I'd have rung earlier, but I've only just heard."

"It's all over the news." Sheila tutted.

"Toby's had CBeebies on most of the day."

Sheila sniffed, hoping to indicate her distaste at children being plonked in front of the television.

"Are you all right, mum? You sound like you're crying."

She felt herself stiffen. "I'm fine," she replied tightly.

"They said you found the body," Heather persisted. "Why didn't you ring last night? I could've come over."

"Why? To gloat? I know how much you hated Lauren."

"God, mum," she snapped. "I don't know why I bother sometimes. I rang to see if you were OK. It must've been a shock."

She sniffed. "I think I'm used to them by now."

"What's that supposed to mean? If you're talking about Toby again…"

"I wasn't actually…" said Sheila.

Heather ignored her and continued, her tone icy, "It's bad enough his father wouldn't have anything to do with him. Now, you're turned against him as well."

"Not this again," Sheila sighed. "You know I love Toby. He can't help it if…"

"What? If his mum's a slag. I know that's what you think."

"It's not his mother that's the problem."

"Save me the lecture." She paused and waited. "I'm presuming there's something for you in the will," she said nastily, when Sheila didn't answer. "I can't see why else you'd have stuck around."

"I don't know and I don't care."

"So will you be staying on there?"

"What else am I supposed to do?"

"You're unbelievable," said Heather. "After everything that's happened."

"Entangle," she said suddenly, marvelling at the mind's ability to make connections.

"What?" said her daughter, her voice thick with spite.

"Nothing," she replied. "I was doing the crossword when you rang."

"Well, don't let me hold you up," said Heather and slammed the phone down.

EIGHT

When Linton returned to the station, Brown was already back from the hospital, sitting at his desk.

"My sister's scan," he said grinning proudly, passing a grainy black and white photograph across the desk. "They took a few so she let me keep one. You can see all its fingers and toes. It's amazing."

Linton looked at the blob and smiled, more at his enthusiasm than anything else.

"So what did Baines have to say?" he asked, as she handed it back.

"Lauren only changed her will a month ago. Up until then, everything, apart from Sheila's picture, was left to her son."

"So that's another couple of motives in Hampton's favour. Anger and revenge."

"Except that Baines said he was with him the whole time. He went backstage just after seven thirty and was with him until the second half, which Hampton spent most of on stage."

The disappointment was evident on Brown's face. "It makes me uneasy though," he said. "His only alibi happens to be his solicitor."

"But why would Baines lie? What's he got to gain?"

Brown shrugged. "Hampton could've put him up to being his alibi. Said he'd split the inheritance."

"But wouldn't questions be asked, further down the line? When suddenly Baines is given all that money. And besides,

Hampton would've been better waiting if he was going to kill her for the money."

"Why?"

"Baines said Lauren was about to change her will again in Hampton's favour. She was about to leave everything to him again."

Brown looked suspicious. "Or so Baines says. He might be lying."

Linton shook her head. "Honestly, Brown. He's the sort who wouldn't park on a yellow line because he's terrified of breaking the law. He was nervous just having me there. He's the one who was campaigning to get that extra-marital dating site closed down."

"Him! Mr Knickers-in-a-twist-about-nothing. I knew that name was familiar!" He laughed. "Maybe he found out Lauren had joined the agency. This might be part of his campaign to rid the world of marriage breakers."

Linton rolled her eyes. "You're hilarious."

"Anyway," Brown continued, "you're wrong about him. Hooper checked him out this morning. He's broken the law."

"Really?" said Linton, taken aback, unable to imagine the gently spoken man doing anything illegal. "What's he done?"

"Drink driving. He lost his licence. It's a bit ironic, isn't it? After taking the moral high ground."

She remembered the shaking hand as he handed her the teacup. The dark circles underneath his eyes. *The trademarks of an alcoholic?*

"Just because he was done for drink driving," she said, "doesn't mean he's lying about Monday night."

"Did he say why Lauren wanted to give most of her inheritance away?"

"Apparently Hampton accused her of not donating enough

to charity, so she changed it to spite him. But the charity she chose is interesting. Rape Crisis. It made me wonder if she'd been a victim."

"Or perhaps her daughter was raped," said Brown thoughtfully. "That might explain the termination. If Lauren was going to expose something to the paper that would certainly shake things up. Even if it couldn't be proved, it could still destroy someone's reputation."

"Which leads us away from Hampton again," said Linton.

"*Are you a skydiver?*" he said, in a singsong voice.

"What?"

"You really don't want it to be him, do you?"

"I couldn't care less one way or the other."

"*I look after the family money,*" he continued. "*And when I'm not doing that, I like poncing about on stage dressed in high heels and a silky jumpsuit.* Tosser."

"Which is the whole point. It's not that I don't want it to be him. I just don't see how it can be him. Like you said. He was at the theatre, poncing about on stage."

Brown pulled a face. "I've already got Hooper interviewing the other actors. And everyone working backstage. We'll soon see if they can pick any holes in Hampton's and his solicitor's story."

"Right! You lot!"

Linton jumped and they both looked up to see The Toad advancing towards them, his eyes bulging.

"I've had Chief Inspector Milne on the phone," he barked. "Wanting an update on the Hampton case. So let's hear what you've got. Come on. Gather round. Chop-chop."

They followed Hargreaves to the front of the room, pushing their wheelie chairs and stopping in front of the desk he'd plonked himself on, his stumpy legs dangling awkwardly down.

"Detective Inspector?" he said, turning to fix his rheumy glare on Brown.

"As you know, Sir," Brown said, sitting down, "there's an outside possibility that it was a robbery. We're still checking to see if anything's missing from the house."

"You don't sound convinced."

"On the face of it, it doesn't look like the house was robbed. And there were better times to commit the burglary. When she was at her book club meeting for example."

"So if you don't think it's a robbery," said The Toad impatiently, "what have you got?"

"A number of leads, Sir."

"Such as?"

"For a start Sheila Martock. The housekeeper who found the body. She maintains she was home all evening until she got a call from Lauren's son, but I'm not certain she's telling the truth."

"Have you checked with her neighbours?"

Hooper's long spindly arm shot up. "I have, Sir. None of them can remember but I'm still waiting to hear back from one."

"Her motive?" said Hargreaves, ignoring Hooper and directing his question at Brown.

"She's been left a painting in the will although the solicitor's not sure if she knows."

"Is it valuable?"

Brown shook his head. "Not according to Mark Hampton. But again, Sheila might not know that."

"And if it's not the housekeeper?"

"We've also found out that Lauren Hampton was in contact with an investigative journalist before she died."

"And?"

"Sheila's husband used to be Lauren's gardener. He died a few years ago; apparently tripped and shot himself. But according to Lauren, his death wasn't an accident. If he was murdered and Lauren was going to expose the killer, maybe he strangled her to shut her up."

"She had a daughter who killed herself, didn't she?" said The Toad. "Some families are just sodding drama magnets."

Brown nodded. "That's the other thing. The journalist we spoke to thinks she may have been about to name the man who got Sophia pregnant."

"Anyone else?" said The Toad caustically. "Or do you think perhaps that's enough to be getting on with?"

"There's also Hampton's ex-wife," said Linton. "She's asked Lauren for money in the past. There's a possibility she asked again and killed her when she didn't get what she wanted."

"Well, you need to get her in then," said The Toad. "Find out where she was on Monday night."

"She's proving difficult to track down, Sir."

"Hard cheddar! And all the more reason to get her in," he snapped. "She's hardly going to make herself visible if she's got something to hide!"

"There may be another reason for her disappearing," said Brown.

"What d'you mean?"

"I get the impression there was domestic violence. On her part, towards Hampton. She could be afraid that he's reported her."

The Toad grunted. "What about Hampton himself?"

"I was coming on to that, Sir. It makes sense for it to be him. He's got the most to gain financially although apparently Lauren was about to change her will so it would've worked even more in his favour if he'd waited. He's also got an alibi.

His solicitor was with him at the theatre. But Hooper's about to interview the rest of the actors. See if they can find any holes in his story."

Hooper opened his mouth about to say something but The Toad put up a podgy hand before he could speak. "Have you checked to see if Hampton's car was gone from the theatre car park? They must have CCTV."

"Not yet, Sir," said Brown. "But we'll certainly do that next."

"The whole thing sounds like a bloody mess to me."

"There's certainly a lot to think about, Sir."

"Well, you better get up with it then," he said clapping his hands together. "Chop-chop."

***

An hour later, Linton found herself perched next to Brown on the edge of Sheila Martock's beige sofa. She glanced around the room feeling oddly unnerved. As much as she advocated clutter-free living, Sheila had taken it to the extreme. There was a total absence of what she was certain the older woman would've referred to as *knick-knacks*. No pictures, no ornaments, no vases of flowers. There was only one photograph and a professional had obviously taken it in a studio. It was of a chubby-faced toddler, her grandson perhaps, and it was propped up against the magnolia wall on the otherwise empty mantelpiece. It was still in its cream and gold cardboard frame.

The only other thing suggesting this was a home, and not just a display of furniture, was the shelf of books near the door. It was neatly lined with classics: Austen, Dickens and Tolstoy.

This time Brown didn't bother with small talk, just launched straight into questioning Sheila.

"So tell me, Sheila. How did your husband Henry die?"

Linton watched the colour drain from the woman's face. "What's he got to do with any of this?"

"You sound anxious," said Brown.

"I get upset talking about him, that's all. He was my husband."

"You still haven't answered the question."

"You're the police," she said harshly, "I'm sure you already know how he died."

"It was a long time ago, Sheila. Way before I joined the Force."

"He died in a hunting accident. He tripped and shot himself."

"Was there ever any suspicion that your husband's death wasn't an accident?"

Sheila's eyes narrowed. "What do you mean?"

"Not long before Lauren Hampton died, she told an investigative journalist that there was more to your husband's death than everyone initially thought."

Linton watched Sheila stiffen. "I still don't know what you mean."

"Lauren didn't say exactly how," continued Brown smoothly, "but we're assuming she meant either suicide or murder."

Shelia laughed – an unpleasant, brusque sound. "It was an accident. The coroner said so."

"Do you know anyone who might have wanted to harm him?"

"I told you," said Sheila adamantly. "There was nothing suspicious about his death. He was drunk and he tripped. The gun went off."

"Did Mrs Hampton ever say she suspected anything to you?"

"Why would she confide in me? I just cleaned her house."

"Surely you were more to her than a cleaner," said Linton. "You've been with her for years."

Sheila frowned. "So?"

Linton took a deep breath. "It's possible that if your husband was killed, whoever did it might have wanted to shut Lauren up."

"I've never heard such a load of rubbish in my life," said Sheila hurriedly. "There was no suspicion at the time. No one wanted him dead. Lauren Hampton was an attention-seeking liar."

"Well, at least we know how you really felt about your employer," said Brown.

Sheila's face flooded with colour.

"You said no one else was employed," said Linton remembering something from before. "Who looks after the garden now?"

Sheila hesitated for a moment. "Mr Hampton."

"It must be a lot of work."

"He enjoys it," she said stiffly.

"Why didn't they get another gardener after your husband died?"

"They did," she said quickly. "But he retired." She pulled herself up from the sofa suddenly. "I suppose I should've offered you a cup of tea. Isn't that the usual custom?"

"Sit down," said Brown sharply. "One more question and we're done. Do you have any idea where we might find Elizabeth Hampton?"

"Why would I know that?" she said, sounding relieved by the change of subject. "I've only met her once."

"What did you think of her?"

Sheila sniffed. "I don't have any opinion of her."

"Why doesn't that surprise me?" said Brown getting up from the sofa. "We'll be in touch."

"What will you do now Lauren's dead?" asked Linton as Sheila ushered them out the front door.

"I'm sorry?"

"About your job?"

She laughed. The same abrupt sound. "Mr Hampton's still there, isn't he? I'll carry on of course."

***

"Frosty old bitch," said Brown, as they made their way back down Sheila's front path.

"Do you know what amazes me most?" Linton replied.

"Apart from her not succumbing to my charms?"

She rolled her eyes. "Apart from that, of course. Sheila found her employer murdered in the place where she works. Why on earth would she want to carry on working there?" She stopped suddenly and pointed at the recycling box at the bottom of the driveway. It was full of tins, cans and plastic milk bottles. "What day do the bin men come on?"

"Tuesdays."

"So why didn't she put that lot out before she went up to Elmtree Manor?"

"Because she wasn't at home," said Brown, catching on immediately. "Let's see if her neighbour's in."

They repeatedly rang the doorbell of the house next door but nobody answered.

***

Sheila didn't know what to do with herself after they'd gone. She felt restless, stirred up by an irritating energy she couldn't calm. She picked up a cup from one place and put it down in another, then shuffled mechanically through her post before shoving it into the kitchen drawer. She sorted through a pile of clothes, but couldn't decide what to iron first. Perhaps some gardening might help, but there was only a bit of weeding out at the front. She needed something more physical.

She'd go for a walk, she decided. A proper one in the countryside, where there were trees and plants and birds. Where there was life that had nothing to do with hers.

She drove to Street Hill, parking in the lay-by opposite the Hood monument, remembering the last time she'd come up here with Henry and the kids.

He'd started to give them a lecture, about how the monument was built in honour of Lord Nelson.

No, she'd corrected him without thinking; *it was erected to commemorate his fellow officer, Admiral Hood. Hence its name.* His look had filled her with an icy fear. War had been unintentionally declared.

For the rest of the day, she and the children had remained under fire. Hostages of time, held in a Sunday from which there was no escape as they struggled to take cover from the insults he hurled at them. She and five-year-old Heather were 'ignorant bitches', and 'thick as shit'. Nine-year-old Mike, who cried when he fell off a rope swing and twisted his arm, was nothing but a 'bloody poof'. Sheila had cringed under the shield of words she'd held up, hoping to deflect his attack.

"Of course you're right, Henry. I don't think you're stupid. I would never think that."

He'd chucked his dinner at her head; smashed two plates. She'd spent the evening scraping roast potato off the kitchen walls.

"Strip," he'd said, when she eventually crept up to their bedroom, praying he'd fallen asleep. He was lying on their bed fully clothed and holding open one of his magazines. She did as she was told.

"Stand there. Against the wall."

She'd stood trembling as his eyes made the mortifying journey down her body, as he pointed to each part with a look of contempt on his face, explaining in detail why she was deformed, comparing her to the glossy perfection he was holding in his hands.

"You make me sick," he'd said, taking his magazine into the bathroom.

Now as she walked around the back of the monument the steady rhythm of movement began to settle her. She thought about the website she'd discovered a few weeks ago. San.co.uk it was called. She'd heard about it on the radio. Was it a coincidence, she'd wondered at the time, that the initials of the website were the first syllable of sanity? She'd certainly questioned her own over the last few years.

SAN stood for Surviving a Narcissist. It was what Henry was, although she hadn't known it until she'd heard the item about personality disorders on *Woman's Hour*. She'd thought he was unique, not believing there were other monsters like him out there. But he'd had every single trait they'd mentioned: no conscience, cruel, critical, grandiose, competitive, craving admiration, always needing to be right, a liar, an exaggerator, manipulative.

There were lots of people's stories on the website. Many of them were still living the hell she'd endured. But she was one of the lucky ones, wasn't she? Her husband's death had meant she'd escaped; at least that's what she'd thought until she read something which made her question whether her freedom was simply an illusion: *"The narcissist is there in spirit long after he's physically gone. The real danger for victims of the narcissist is that they'll become like him – bitter and self-centred. This is the last bow of the narcissist, his final curtain call."*

She knew she couldn't claw back the wasted years of her life, but at least she could change what was left of it. That was advice that the others gave; buying the books she'd always wanted to read was the first small step.

And now that Lauren was dead, there was only one other person standing in the way of her happiness.

NINE

A further appeal for information concerning Lauren's death had gone out on the local lunchtime news. As afternoon turned to early evening, Hargreaves came marching over, his chins wobbling in every direction.

He stopped at Linton's desk and folded his stubby arms across his chest. His fleshy jowls continued to quiver for a couple of seconds, like an optical echo.

"Where's Brown?" he said, his eyes unblinking in their hooded lids.

"Over with the computer lot," said Linton. "He's still looking through Lauren's Hotmail and Twitter accounts."

"You'll have to do then. There's a call that needs following up. A local man; went for a run past Elmtree Manor the night Hampton was killed. Reckons he saw someone on a pushbike."

A pushbike. Hadn't Hampton said he'd almost knocked a cyclist over on his way from the theatre to Elmtree? But that would've been over an hour after Lauren was murdered.

"That's his number," said Hargreaves, pushing a piece of paper towards her. "Get him in and get a statement from him."

Half an hour later, Linton was sitting in an interview room opposite a man she guessed was in his late forties. He had small dark eyes and saggy skin that made her think of a bulldog. Before sitting down, he'd apologised for being so dusty, brushing at the seat of his trousers with his grimy hands.

"So tell me about this man you saw."

"I'm probably wasting your time. I mentioned it to the wife

and she said I ought to ring you. It might be important."
Linton nodded encouragingly. "He was on a pushbike.
Coming along the road from Elmtree, heading back towards
town. My missus said for all I know, he could've been the killer.
On his way back from Mrs Hampton's."

"What time did you see him?"

"I normally leave my house around eight, so I reckon it
would've been between eight forty and eight fifty. Give or take
a few minutes."

"And you were running?"

He nodded. "I go out a couple of times a week."

"Tell me about the man you saw."

"It was dark so it was hard to see. And he shot past me
pretty quickly."

"Can you remember anything about him? His build? The
colour of his hair? What he was wearing?"

The man paused, then frowned. "He was dressed in fishing
gear. A khaki jacket. Long trousers. The sort you wear when
you're fly-fishing."

"Did you see his face?"

"Only a glimpse. There wasn't much to see. He was wearing
a helmet."

"Do you know what colour?"

He shook his head. "Like I said, it was dark. Colours look
distorted, don't they?"

"Did he seem in a hurry?"

"It's hard to tell because he was going down the hill."

"Did you happen to notice the make of the bike?"

He shook his head again. "Sorry."

"Colour?"

"Silver," he said doubtfully. "Or maybe blue."

"Did you recognise him?"

He shook his head. "No," he said slowly.

"You don't sound very sure."

"It's just that for a minute I thought it was Mark Hampton."

Linton kept her expression blank and did her best to sound casual. "What makes you say that?"

"Only because he was near the manor. And he was the same build. Broad across the shoulders. I said that to my wife and she told me not to be so bloody stupid. '*He's in the pantomime, isn't he?*' she said. She went to see it Monday night. Anyway, why would he be out on a pushbike in January dressed in fishing gear?"

"Do you know Mark Hampton well?"

"Only from around. He seems like a decent bloke. Not like his mother." He stopped, as he realised what he'd said. "Sorry, speaking ill of the dead and all that."

"So you knew her too?"

"I did some work up at the Manor last year. Repairing the front wall. I was only there for a couple of days but I could tell she was a nasty piece."

"How do you mean?"

"For a start, the way she humiliated her son in front of us."

"Go on."

"He was stood chatting to us one morning. Just passing the time of day and she came over, fluttering her eyelashes at us, saying how nice it was to see *some* people hard at work. I can't remember exactly what she said, not word for word, but it was something about people being useful. How she admired anyone with a trade unlike *some* she could name. She was looking right at Hampton when she said it. You could tell what she meant."

"How did he react?"

"He didn't. Perhaps he was used to it. Anyway, so much for her appreciation of hard work. We didn't get a single bloody cup of tea and it took her weeks to pay the bill. And to top it all off, she went and told her hairdresser, who happens to be my wife's second cousin, that her builder kept staring at her suggestively and made her feel uncomfortable. It got back to my wife who luckily saw the funny side of it." Linton watched him shudder and repressed a smile. "I know she used to be a model, but come on! I mean, it's embarrassing, isn't it?"

***

Brown was back at his desk by the time Linton had finished the interview. She filled him in what the builder had told her.

"Don't you think it's odd that Hampton nearly knocked someone off his bike on the way back from the theatre?" she said. "Do you think it could be the same person?"

"That was over an hour later," Brown said, looking unimpressed. "It must've been someone else."

"But out at that time of night?" she persisted. "It just seems too much of a coincidence."

"What are you thinking? That it was the killer hanging around?" Brown sounded dubious.

"We've had it before. People coming back to the scene of a crime to see what's happening." She paused, then said, "I'd like to ask Hampton if he can describe the person he saw on the bike."

Brown looked over and grinned. "I bet you do."

"What's that supposed to mean?"

"It's a good excuse to talk to him."

"You're not still on about that, are you?"

"*Are you a skydiver?*" he said, putting on a high voice and fluttering his eyelashes at her.

Before Linton could answer, Hooper shouted across the room excitedly.

"Brown? Linton? Have you got a minute?"

"Here we go," said Brown under his breath. "Better get the paper bag ready for when he starts hyperventilating."

Hooper scuttled over and stood jiggling up and down in front of their desks. "It's the neighbour, next to Sheila," he said excitedly. "He's phoned. He's been away with work and he's only just got our message…"

"And? Does he know if Sheila was at home or not?"

Hooper shook his head vigorously. "He says she definitely wasn't. He remembers he went out just after eight to put out his recycling. He was surprised that hers still wasn't out. For a minute he thought she might be ill but then he saw her lights were out and her car wasn't on the driveway."

"How can he be so sure of the time?"

"He says it was straight after the *Channel 4 News*."

"Right. Ring her up and ask her why she lied," he said turning to Linton. "Find out where she really was and…" He stopped midsentence and sighed. Linton turned to see The Toad stomping towards her desk for the second time that day.

"Looks like it'll have to wait," she said.

"Right, you lot," Hargreaves yelled. "Gather round. We've got some results at last."

***

JULY 27TH

I should have hidden Angela's gift. When I went to collect my presents from the drawing room this morning, only one of the earrings was there. I didn't even attempt to look for the other one. Wherever mother's put it, she'll have made sure I never find it.

JULY 29TH

Bored, bored, bored, bored, bored. All of my friends have gone back home for the holidays and I have nothing to do. There are a couple of other day pupils, who live close by, but Mother doesn't like their parents and so I'm forbidden from seeing them. I'm counting down the days until I'm back at school!

***

"Right," said The Toad, as everybody gathered round. There was sudden rustling of paper and Linton glanced to her right. It was Hooper, oblivious to The Toad's amphibian stare, unwrapping a Kit Kat chunky.

"Put that sodding chocolate away and listen!" Hargreaves barked.

Hooper's skinny body seized up, his hand frozen in mid-air. He slowly moved it down towards the table then gently laid the chocolate on it.

"Thank you," said The Toad at a more normal volume. "We've got the result back from the autopsy. No surprises. Lauren Hampton died from suffocation. The carrier bag was pulled over her head, held tightly against her face until she stopped breathing."

"Any prints on it, Sir?" asked Brown.

"Hold your horses. Christ, you're as bad as our eager beaver," he said nodding at Hooper. "I'm coming on to that. Prints were found, but they haven't yet run them for matches against the ones SOCO collected for elimination or against the national database. As usual there's a sodding backlog. It could take a couple more days."

Hargreaves put up his hand to stop the grumble and groans that had broken across the team.

"SOCO also found minuscule traces of skin under three of Lauren Hampton's fingernails, so it looks like she tried to fight back." *That wasn't surprising,* thought Linton. She remembered the woman's long, perfectly manicured fingernails. Skin would've become easily trapped underneath them which meant that somebody, somewhere, might have some frenzied scratching on their arm.

"How long 'til we get the results back from the fingernails, Sir?" she asked.

"Again, a couple of days. I feel like going up there and doing the sodding tests myself. Brown!" he said suddenly turning his unblinking glare on the DI. "What have you got from her computer?"

"She was a big online shopper," he replied. "Mainly clothes and shoes. A couple of the big department stores. A few boutiques in London I've never heard if. We've gone through her emails for the last few months, but there's nothing of interest so far. Our next job is looking at her Twitter account in more detail. See what she's posted; find out who's following her."

"Twitter," The Toad grunted, his face revealing exactly what he thought of the social networking site. "Aptly named. For twits with too much time on their hands. Who wants to read about their latest bowel movement or what they've had for breakfast? Hooper?" he snapped, before anyone could disagree.

The trainee detective sat up straighter in his chair, his expression alert, like an affable dog waiting to be thrown a stick.

"Brown tells me you've been checking her jewellery against the insurer's list. Anything missing?"

Hooper shook his head slowly. "No, Sir." He paused. "There's nothing missing."

"Come on," said Hargreaves impatiently. "What aren't you telling me?"

"It's just that…" He stopped obviously unsure whether to continue, no doubt fearful of annoying The Toad with what might turn out to be irrelevant information.

"Chop-chop," Hargreaves said, tapping his watch. "I haven't got all day."

"I'm not sure if it's relevant, Sir. It's just that we seem to have gained something."

"Let me guess. The purple earrings."

Hooper's eyes widened with surprise. "Yes, Sir. They weren't on the list. But how did you know?"

"I was just about to come on to that. Very strange. No fingerprints at all. In fact they've been wiped clean. With surgical spirit. What do you reckon to that then, Hooper?" His tone was challenging.

The trainee detective frowned. "It doesn't make any sense, Sir. She would've put them on, so they'd have had her fingerprints on. Unless of course she was wearing gloves. Or," he said excitedly, his whole body perking up again, "are you thinking the killer put them in her ears? Made sure they were wiped clean before…"

"But that doesn't make any sense either," Brown interrupted. "Why wipe them clean but leave fingerprints on the bag? And why put them in her ears in the first place?"

"That's what you get paid for, Brown," said Hargreaves. "To make sense of the senseless. Right you lot. Get on with it."

He leant over the desk, grabbed at Hooper's chocolate and

threw it across the room. It landed in the metal bin with a loud thud.

***

Sheila was doing the crossword when the phone rang. The caller display came up as private number, presumably someone trying to sell her something. She almost left it to ring, but decided she'd enjoy reprimanding someone, telling them she was on the caller preference service and that they shouldn't be ringing. But when she picked up and heard the deep voice on the other end, she wished she hadn't.

It was DI Brown. That smarmy detective. The one who thought he was God's gift, trying to charm her, stupidly unaware that his mock flirting was insulting. He launched straight into what he had to say.

"Mrs Martock," he said. "We've spoken to one of your neighbours. He said you weren't home on Monday night. Your lights were out and your car wasn't on the driveway."

For a moment she considered lying. Telling him her car had been in the garage and she'd been watching television in the dark, but what was the point? Why hadn't she just invented something at the time? She could've said she was shopping; or round at Heather's visiting her grandson.

"Mrs Martock? Are you still there?"

"I didn't think it was any of your business," she said tightly.

She could hear the exasperation in his voice as he answered. "This is a murder enquiry. Everything's our business. Now. Are you going to tell me where you were on Monday evening between eight thirty and eight forty-five?"

She sighed and closed her eyes.

***

As the headlines on Radio Five *Live* came to an end, Elizabeth Hampton turned down the volume and clicked on the BBC News home page again. It had only been a few minutes since she'd last checked and as she'd suspected its contents remained the same. There was nothing new about Lauren. No mention of any leads or any suspects. She'd check again in a few minutes, just to be certain.

She picked up the remote control that lay on the table beside her laptop and aimed it at the flickering TV in the corner, holding down the button until the assured tones of a well-spoken man filled the tiny room. The *News 24* presenter was asking an exhausted-looking woman why she thought the German economy had started to shrink. Elizabeth let the answer wash over her, watching the headlines running along the bottom of the screen, waiting until they'd gone full circle but again, there was nothing new about Lauren.

She picked up a tumbler from the bedside table, raised it to her lips and took a long, greedy sip before refreshing the BBC home page again. She glanced at the clock on the corner of her screen. Only ten more minutes and Radio Five *Live*'s headlines would be on again.

***

"Come on Sheila," pressed the detective. "I haven't got all day."

"I was at Avalon College," she said resignedly.

"Doing what exactly?" The suspicion was apparent in his tone.

"A course. In creative writing. You can ring them. The woman who takes the class is called Miranda Fouracres."

"What time was that?"

"From six thirty to eight thirty. I got home just before Mr Hampton rang at quarter to nine."

"It's a five-minute car journey from the college to yours. So why did it take you fifteen minutes to get home?"

"The class overran by about five minutes. And I'd had to park at the far end of the campus, near the new sports hall. It took me a few minutes to get back to my car."

"So why didn't you tell us that in the first place?" he said, not bothering to hide the exasperation his voice.

Because she'd felt embarrassed, she thought. Convinced that the detectives would laugh at her, wonder why someone like *her* was doing something like *that*. She could imagine Henry's scornful voice in her head. *A creative writing course? Don't make me laugh. Who the hell do you think you are? You're a bloody cleaner, not an intellectual.*

"I didn't think it was important," she said.

There was pause then she heard him sigh deeply. "Sheila. From now on you need to be honest with us. Do you understand?"

She thought about the other lies she'd already told. Except that one of them wasn't really a lie. More of an omission. And she'd only said it to protect him. The more she thought about it, the more convinced she was he'd done it.

"If that's all…" she said hurriedly.

"Wait," he said, obviously sensing she was about to hang up. "There's something else."

She winced, knowing what was coming. Thinking how long she'd waited for a policeman to utter the words she was certain she was about to hear. How long she'd dreaded it.

"The purple earrings that Lauren was wearing the night she was murdered. They weren't on the list of jewellery that was insured."

Earrings? Was that it? Sheila felt suddenly lightheaded, as her body flooded with relief.

"Sheila?"

"Sorry. What did you say?"

"I asked you if Lauren owned any jewellery that wasn't on the insurance list."

"Possibly. But you must be mistaken about the earrings," she said as his words caught up with her thinking.

"What do you mean?"

"They couldn't have been purple."

She could hear the impatience creeping back into his voice. "I've seen pictures of them myself," he said. "They were definitely purple. Maybe they were new and you hadn't seen them."

"No. You don't understand. She detested the colour. With a passion. She said it was only fit for hippies. She wouldn't even allow purple flowers in the garden..." she faltered, then stopped.

"What if someone had given her the earrings as a present?" said Brown. "She might have worn them out of politeness."

Lauren doing something out of politeness? That was a joke. But someone putting them on her, as a way of taunting her, bringing her down a peg or two. Having the last laugh. That was something she could imagine. *Oh God! He really had done it.*

"I expect you're right," she said.

***

Linton had waited until Brown was on the phone before she rang Hampton. She would've felt self-conscious talking to Mark in front of him, knowing he'd be listening for anything he could tease her with.

"The man you saw on the bike on Monday night," she said, after he'd asked if there'd been any developments, "the one you nearly knocked over…"

"Oh God," he interrupted. "Has he put in a complaint? I shouldn't have been driving, should I? I was in shock. I'm surprised I didn't kill the poor bastard."

"It's not that," said Linton. "We've got a witness who saw a man cycling away from Elmtree Manor around the time your mother died."

"Really?" She heard a perk of interest in his tone. "Do you think it was the man who killed her?"

"We can't rule anything out at this stage."

"But it can't be the same person that I saw? I mean that was ages after. Surely he wouldn't have hung around."

"You'd be surprised," she said. "Could you describe him?"

He was quiet for a moment; all Linton could hear was his steady breathing.

"I'm sorry," he said eventually. "It was just a flash. And to be honest I was in such a state…" He hesitated and Linton wondered if he was reliving the humiliation of fainting in front of her.

"Can you remember what he was wearing?"

"It was dark. But I'm certain he had a helmet on."

"What about clothes?"

"I'm not sure."

"Close your eyes. See if you can picture him."

He was quiet for a moment then said, "Possibly a Barbour? Don't ask me why, but I thought he might've been on his way back from fishing."

Linton felt a tremor of excitement. It fitted with their witness statement. A helmet. And fishing clothes. Was it possible that it was the same man? That he'd come back to watch the police activity? "Did you recognise him?"

"No," said Hampton slowly.

"You sound uncertain."

"This is going to sound crazy but I initially thought it was a woman dressed in men's clothes."

"What makes you say that?"

"It was just something about the way the person was sat."

"Our witness thought he remembered the person being broad across the shoulders."

"Some women are though, aren't they? I mean look at..." He stopped again.

"Go on."

"I was just thinking about Elizabeth. My ex-wife. She's a swimmer. She used to compete at county level."

"Are you saying it could've been her?"

He laughed. "Riding a bike dressed in fishing gear. In the dark. In January. I can't really see it somehow, can you?"

***

"It's odd about those earrings," said Linton, as she prepared to leave for the evening, tidying her desk as she always did. "Especially after what Sheila told you. About Lauren hating purple."

"This whole case is starting to do my head in," said Brown, glancing at his watch. "Thank God I'm doing a 10K with my mate tonight. That should help me let off a bit of steam. By the way," he said, not bothering to disguise his smirk. "How's your running going?"

"Great," said Linton airily, as she dropped her mobile into her handbag. "In fact I might go out again tonight."

"Not alone?" he said, suddenly serious. "Not with that sick fucker on the loose."

"I'll be fine Brown. I won't go near any supermarkets and I'll stick to the main roads."

"Linton," he said his face so uncharacteristically serious that she almost laughed, "Please. Promise me you won't go out on your own."

***

When Linton finally arrived home, all she wanted to do was lie on the sofa, watch TV and finish off the bottle of wine and packet of chilli peanuts she'd opened the night before. It was only out of sheer stubbornness that she went; to show Brown she was capable of looking after herself. And running as fast as he could.

It took her half an hour to find her trainers. They were hidden in a box at the back of her wardrobe. She didn't have the first clue about sports fashion, even if such a thing existed, but she hoped that the shoes were so old they were retro. She rummaged around in her bottom drawer and pulled out her only pair of tracksuit bottoms, the ones she'd bought when she decided she was going to start Pilates, and dragged them on.

Christ, she thought studying herself in the mirror. What a state. She was glad she'd managed to book the last appointment for Saturday afternoon at Aphrodite's. Her long brunette hair was a mess and her eyebrows desperately needed shaping. She wouldn't have time for a facial, but a couple of long runs before the wedding reception and her skin would be glowing.

She pulled on her Puffa jacket and was about to leave the house when she remembered Brown's warning. She ran upstairs, picked up a can of deodorant and shoved it in her coat pocket. It wasn't exactly Mace, but it was the next best thing.

***

He was thinking about the other night. The air was frigid, burning his cheeks as he walked briskly towards his car, but he didn't care. He embraced the cold; he embraced anything that made him feel something.

He remembered the warmth of her smile. The smile that hadn't been for him, that had turned to a suspicious frown when she'd sensed him watching her carefully as she pushed her trolley hurriedly along the aisle. How dare she grimace at him like that! How dare she think she was better than him!

He shivered, reliving the thrill as he'd watched her cross the supermarket car park, still pushing her trolley, knowing instinctively that she was the one.

***

Linton was off. Pounding the pavements. Her long hair fanning out behind her as she leant headlong into the refreshing wind. No wonder Brown was so into it. She felt free. At one with everything. Maybe it wasn't too late to enter the half marathon. Perhaps they could even run it together.

The biting air was revitalising, uplifting. And she was glad it had started raining. The moisture was welcome; it would cool her down, although next time she might wear a coat with a hood. Something more lightweight. In retrospect, a Puffa jacket was probably a bit too warm for running.

Apart from a few cars and a couple of vans that had hooted and the odd lorry whizzing past, there was nothing except for the sound of her breathing. Why hadn't she done this before? This was what she'd been missing in her life. It was great. Wasn't it?

No. It bloody wasn't. *Christ!* Was this normal? Her lungs were burning. And her legs. What the hell was wrong with her legs? They felt so heavy. Like they'd been stuffed with wood or something even heavier. Concrete?

Oww. Now it was her left knee. It was starting to twinge. Perhaps she should stop. Before she caused any serious damage.

She thought of Brown. His seven-minute miles and his smug, grinning face. No. She had to keep going. She couldn't stop yet. Maybe if she had a goal. Yes! She needed a goal. If she could make it to the next lamp-post, then the next lamp-post after that then before she knew it, she'd have run at least a couple of miles. Which wasn't bad for her first time. Was it?

The next lamp-post. That's all she needed to do. Just get her head down and move her arms like pistons. She could make it. Yes! *She was going to make it.*

Actually. No. She wasn't.

"Christ," she cried out, pulling to a sudden halt. She bent over, clutching her knees, her breathing ragged.

A van tore past, beeping its horn. She managed to use her last kilojoule of energy to give the retreating driver the finger.

When she finally got her breath back she pulled out her phone to check her distance. *Shit.* She'd run a quarter of a mile. She could picture the self-satisfied expression on Brown's face if he ever found out.

And then she had an idea.

TEN

The following morning, Brown was already in when Linton arrived. She walked into the Incident Room to find him hunched over his desk, rubbing his arms briskly.

"Bloody heating's gone down," he said. "But the good news is I've found something on Twitter."

"Go on," she said, placing her handbag and mobile onto her desk, not bothering to remove her coat and scarf.

"It's easier if I show you."

She wheeled her chair round to Brown's desk and positioned it so she could see his computer.

"Lauren's Twitter account," he said, nodding at the screen. "Look at one of the tweets she posted a couple of weeks ago."

Linton read the three sentences aloud. "Hey Tweetie Pies! I'm in the Feb edition of *Country Living*! Here's a sneak preview."

"She's attached a photo of her front room," said Brown, clicking on the attachment to reveal a picture of her drawing room, looking like an antiques showroom.

"I don't get why this is important."

"There's a chance someone saw this on Twitter and decided to break in."

"But that goes against everything we've said. About it not being a robbery."

"There's nothing wrong with keeping an open mind. I'll print it off," he said, "and take it with us when we go to see

Hampton. We can compare it to the actual room. See if anything's missing."

"We're meeting Hampton?"

"It's your lucky day! I've got Hooper to arrange it. There are a couple of things I want to ask him."

"Such as?"

"Why he didn't tell us that Lauren changed her will because they'd had an argument. And whether there's anything in Lauren's story that Henry Martock's death wasn't an accident."

"Why not just get him in here?"

"Because it's bloody freezing. And have you seen The Toad? He's got a face like a smacked arse. I just want to get out of here."

"Talking of getting out," she said casually, as she picked up her phone from her desk, "I went for a run last night."

"On your own?" said Brown crossly.

"Don't worry," she said clicking on the running app, "I put a can of deodorant in my pocket. To spray in any would-be assailant's face."

"As if that's going to help."

"Anyway, that's not the point, she said tapping on *History*. "Look," she said, passing him the phone.

He studied it for a second then said with genuine awe, "I'm impressed. Four miles in thirty minutes. Eight-minute miles. Not as fast me. But that's good."

"I know."

"Hang on a minute," he said, looking up, suddenly suspicious. "What did you do? Drive?"

"Not quite," she said sheepishly. "I went out on my bike."

***

"It's bloody freezing," moaned Linton, pulling her coat tighter as she and Brown cut across Elmtree's lawn towards Mark Hampton's cottage.

"At least it's warmer than at the station." Brown's hands were clutched underneath his armpits, his head bent against the icy wind. He turned slightly towards her with a smirk and said, "So are you excited?"

"About what?"

"Finally getting to see inside Mark Hampton's residence."

"It's hardly a cottage, is it?" she replied, choosing to ignore the jibe, warm air escaping from her mouth like puffs of cigarette smoke. "It's twice the size of my house."

"At one time it would've housed the manor's servants…"

"By the way," she interrupted before he had a chance to launch into an episode from the History Channel, "any more news on his finances? Evidence he might've paid someone to kill her?"

"Hooper's still digging," said Brown. "Literally probably. If there's anything to find, he'll find it. Oh. And I forgot to tell you. Wells had a look at the CCTV footage from the theatre car park."

"And?"

"Mark's Saab was there from about six thirty until just after ten. But before you say anything," he said, putting up his hand, "he could've taken someone else's car."

"Do you *really* think Hampton did it?" she asked, lowering her voice as they reached the front door of the cottage.

"All I know is it's not the sort of money to sniff at," he murmured. "Once he sells the house and he's paid someone off that leaves a fair amount for him."

"But why bother? It looks like he's living comfortably already. And don't start with the skydiving comment. It's getting boring now."

As Brown put his finger out to ring the doorbell, there was a sharp whistle to their right. They turned to see Hampton striding towards them wearing a heavy-knit, navy jumper with its sleeves rolled up, dabbing at his forehead with the back of his right arm. Despite the cold, he looked sweaty and dishevelled. It suited him, thought Linton.

"Any news since we spoke?" he asked eagerly.

"Not yet," said Brown. "We've got a couple of things we hope you can help us with."

"No problem," he replied, glancing down at his clothes. "You'll have to excuse the state of me. I've been having a bit of a tidy up. Our new gardener was supposed to start today, but I've had to put him off until next week. Your lot rather pulled the garden to pieces. Not that I'm complaining of course," he added quickly. "I know it's their job. Apparently they're down in the arboretum today with a sniffer dog."

"They're still looking for trace evidence. Footprints, fibres, that sort of thing," Brown said.

"I was worried they might have to dig up our cemetery, but they said it wasn't necessary."

"Your cemetery?" said Linton, a sudden image of a hole being dug in the middle of the garden. Ready to receive Lauren Hampton.

"Our pet cemetery," said Hampton, nodding in the direction of the cottage. "A cat, a couple of my hamsters and all Lauren's dogs. She had six of them over the years. It's a shame she didn't still have one. It might have protected her."

"What breed were they?" asked Linton, noting Brown's distaste. Mainly due to his phobia of canine faeces, she knew that the idea of dogs in general disgusted him.

"Border terriers," Hampton replied. "Lovely, gentle things. But she hasn't had one for years. Winston was the last one. He died when I was a teenager. She refused to replace him. She didn't like the idea of having to go through all that grief again."

"She was an animal lover then."

He shrugged. "They love you unconditionally," he said simply. "Why don't we go inside?" he said, nodding towards a path that disappeared to the rear of the cottage.

As they followed him, Linton thought about what Sheila had said; about Hampton doing his own gardening. His mention of a new gardener suggested there must've been an old one. She must remember to ask why their stories didn't match.

"Here we go," said Hampton, leading them across a large stone patio and through the back door of his house. It led straight into a typical cottage kitchen with wooden sideboards and a rustic stone slate floor. The walls were painted a warm yellow, which matched the cushions scattered along an unpainted wooden bench beneath the window. Linton cast her eyes around appreciatively, thinking how clean and tidy it was. She could imagine herself living here.

Hampton gestured towards the farmhouse table in the centre of the room. It was piled high with paperwork. As Hampton pushed it to one side, Linton noticed some long red scratches on the inside of his right arm.

"Bloody thorns," he said, noticing she was studying them. "Can I get either of you a drink?"

"We're fine," said Brown.

"I hope you don't mind, but I'd rather like to go and change if it's OK with you."

Linton watched him cross the kitchen, pulling off his jumper. His shirt got stuck in it, revealing his long, naked back, tanned and surprisingly muscular. She glanced at Brown, but he'd already pulled his iPhone out of his pocket and was tilting it backwards and forwards.

"Monkey ball," he said, sighing contentedly. Linton knew the game. Her six-year-old nephew had a Wii version of it.

She leant back in the chair and closed her eyes, enjoying the warmth of the Aga. She must've briefly nodded off, because she started at the scraping sound of Hampton pulling a chair back to sit down. He was wearing a white polo shirt and a fresh pair of jeans and smelt of aftershave and soap. He smiled at her, his eyes soft and warm. She hadn't noticed how unusual they were until now. They were light brown with tiny flecks of gold.

"So," he said, slapping his hands on his knees. "How can I help?"

"Linton spoke to your solicitor yesterday," said Brown. "He said that you and Lauren had an argument. And that's why she left most of her estate to charity. Why didn't you mention that to us when we last spoke?"

Hampton sighed. "Because I didn't think it painted my mother in a very good light. You see she only did it to upset me. To get a reaction."

"And did she get one?" asked Brown.

Hampton's eyes narrowed. "What do you mean?"

"Were you angry with her?"

"Angry enough to kill her, you mean? Look, I know you don't know me from Adam, so of course you're going to be suspicious. But talk to anyone who knows me. I don't care about money, I never have. Perhaps it's because I've always been surrounded by it."

"What about principle? The fact she was taking away something that was rightly yours."

"I was upset, not angry. She had this way of making me feel worthless. But I could see her point to be honest."

"Which was?"

He looked down at the table, fiddling with the ring on his finger, twisting it nervously. "Between you and me, I'm a huge disappointment to her. After all the sacrifices she made, devoting all those years to bringing me up, I could've at least repaid her and become a doctor or a lawyer."

"Mums are supposed to make sacrifices," said Linton, thinking sardonically of her own mother, a woman who'd never forfeited anything for her children.

"It doesn't matter anyway," said Hampton, "because Lauren was about to alter her will so that everything was left to me again. She told Jonathan a few days ago."

"Why did she pick Rape Crisis as the charity?" Brown asked. "It's an unusual choice. Most people go for children or animals."

"It simply was her way of having the last word."

"I don't follow."

"The argument we had," said Hampton. "It was about those local women who were raped. I said how awful it must've been for them, but Lauren said they'd probably brought it on themselves. Called them sluts, if I remember rightly. I got cross, as you can imagine, so she said if I cared so much about them, they could have my money."

Christ, she really was a vicious cow, thought Linton. "Apart from you and Sheila," she asked, "is there anyone else who may have expected to be left something?"

Hampton's eyebrows knitted closer together. He shook his head. "As I said before, she had no family. There was Sally Hughes and the rest of the book club. But they weren't close friends."

"What about your ex-wife?"

"Elizabeth?" he laughed. "She knows she's the last person

Lauren would have considered. As I said before, they couldn't stand each other. Lauren could see how manipulative she was."

Poor Mark, Linton thought, he hadn't had a chance. Moving from a relationship with one domineering woman straight into another one.

"I didn't tell you everything the other day," Hampton continued. "About why Elizabeth went to Lauren for money."

"You said she was in debt," said Brown.

"But I didn't say why."

"Go on."

He paused for a moment then said, "The thing is, you'll see for yourself if you ever meet her."

"See what?" said Brown, beginning to sound impatient.

Hampton looked down at the table, obviously uncomfortable. "My ex-wife is an addict."

"What sort of addict?"

"Cocaine, mainly. That's why I refused to give her any more money. And why she went to Lauren. I suppose she was desperate. The thing is she's an unstable person as it is. The drugs make her even worse. She becomes aggressive and paranoid. When we were together, she constantly accused me of things I hadn't said or done and made up the most awful lies about me to my friends." He paused then said, "Again, this may sound strange, but in a way, it was her instability which attracted me to her. I suppose I thought I could somehow rescue her."

Linton thought back to what the woman at CDA had told Brown. That she'd been erratic at work. It sounded like the behaviour of someone who took drugs.

"It's not really her fault," Hampton continued. "She had a terrible upbringing. Her father was a violent man; served time for GBH. Her mother was an alcoholic. Elizabeth didn't stand a chance with that sort of background."

"And you're sure you don't know where we can find her?" said Brown. "You're not protecting her."

"I swear, if I knew I'd tell you, but if you're thinking Elizabeth killed her because she blamed her for our marriage breaking up…"

"Nobody's suggesting that, Mr Hampton," Linton interrupted, but he carried on oblivious.

"I mean she wouldn't have gone that far. She's got a nasty temper, I'll say that much for her but…" he stopped. He'd gone bright red.

"She hurt you, didn't she?" said Linton. "I mean physically."

"I don't want to talk about it."

"But if she was violent…"

"As far as I know, it was only ever towards me."

"And you're certain you don't know where she is. You're not telling us because you don't want all this out in the open."

He shook his head. "I promise you. I've got no idea. After I left her, she made herself scarce. Partly, I think, because she stole a lot of valuable items from me. A couple of days after I walked out, I went back to collect my belongings, but she'd already gone and taken everything with her. Including some antiques I'd collected over the years. The only things she'd left behind were my photos."

"Perhaps that was her way of showing some remorse," Linton said.

"I wouldn't say that." He stopped again.

"What?"

"It's nothing. Just something I've remembered. It's only disturbing in the light of what's happened."

"Go on."

"There was a photograph of Lauren and she'd cut her head

off. But please, don't think it meant anything. You've got to understand, she wouldn't have hurt my mother."

Linton noticed Hampton was fiddling with the ring on his little finger again.

"My wedding ring," he said, looking up to meet her eyes. "Elizabeth was so thoughtless she didn't even bother finding out my size. I should've known then. I wear it as a daily reminder that I did the right thing in leaving her."

Before Linton had time to think of a sympathetic reply Brown said brusquely, "Tell us about Henry Martock's death."

If Hampton was thrown by the sudden change of subject, he didn't show it. "He tripped over and shot himself," he said. "By accident."

"Did you know that Lauren told Michael Fenn there was more to it? Insinuated that he was murdered."

He shook his head. "She's unbelievable. She'd do anything to get a bit of publicity. That's absolute rubbish. I got to him seconds after the gun went off. I was so close; I'd have heard someone running off."

"You were very young at the time," said Linton. "Sheila said you were back from school."

He smiled his lop-sided smile and said, "I don't know what she said about that, but it was all a horrible misunderstanding."

Brown looked confused. "What was?"

"My expulsion from school," said Hampton.

"I think we're talking at cross purposes here. No one mentioned anything about expulsion."

"Oh. Well, it's not important. I got the blame for something I didn't do. Anyway, going back to Henry's accident, I was old enough to know nobody else was involved. And what whisky smells like. He was drunk as a lord. It's not surprising it happened."

"Just one other thing," said Brown, opening his briefcase with a loud click. "The earrings that Lauren was wearing the night she died. I've got a picture of them here. I wondered if you recognised them."

He riffled through his case and eventually pulled out a photograph, placing it on the table in front of Hampton.

"They must be new," he said, his brow furrowed in concentration. "I don't recognise them."

"Are they the sort of thing she'd normally wear?" asked Linton.

"Possibly, although they look rather cheap."

"Sheila said your mother wouldn't have worn them because she hated purple."

Hampton looked confused. "I wasn't aware of her aversion to any colours."

"Before we go," said Brown, as he put the photo away and snapped his briefcase shut. "We'd like to go back into the main house and look at the living room. We've got a copy of a photograph that Lauren posted on Twitter a couple of weeks ago which we'd like to compare it to."

"That's no problem," said Hampton pushing himself up from the table. "I'll come over and let you in."

***

It didn't take the long for Brown to spot that something was missing from Lauren Hampton's drawing room.

"This silver pot," he said, pointing at the photo he was holding. "It's not on that table over there."

He passed the picture to Hampton who studied it for a second before looking across at the table that Brown had indicated.

"You're right," he said, his eyes sweeping round the room. "It's not in here."

"Perhaps it's somewhere else in the house?" said Linton.

"It won't be," said Hampton confidently. "Lauren was very particular. This was definitely a drawing room object. She wouldn't have moved it elsewhere."

"Do you know much about the pot? Whether it's valuable?" asked Linton.

"It's worth a couple of grand. I know because I bought it for her birthday last year. I got it from Sotheby's."

"And you don't know how long it's been missing."

He shook his head. "I don't come in here very often. Lauren and I tend to sit out in the kitchen. Sheila would know though. You'd better ask her."

As they came back out of the house, a small bird swooped down and landed in nearby bush.

"A black cap," said Brown.

Hampton nodded in agreement. "I've seen a lot of them since I've been looking after the garden. They seem to like the insects in the shrubs."

"Which reminds me," said Linton, "you mentioned earlier that you're getting a new gardener. Presumably that means you had somebody working for you before."

"That's right," he said, nodding again. "Until very recently."

"It's just that Sheila told us you didn't have a gardener because you liked doing it yourself."

"Ahhh," he said, awkwardly. "Well, I'm afraid she would say that."

"Why would she?" said Brown sharply.

Hampton hesitated, chewing on his bottom lip. "I expect she's embarrassed."

"About what?"

"The fact that Brandon was our gardener."

"Who's Brandon?"

"Her son."

"And why is that embarrassing?"

"Because Lauren sacked him."

"For God's sake," said Brown angrily. "Why the hell didn't you tell us before?"

"I suppose I assumed you knew," answered Hampton, looking at Linton helplessly.

She smiled reassuringly and said, "Why did he sack her?"

"Lauren said he was stealing jewellery from the house."

"You sound uncertain."

"To be honest, I think she made it up because she wanted to get rid of him."

"Why?"

"I've got no idea, but it was simpler to let him go than argue with her."

"So Brandon's a gardener like his father," she said, "following in his footsteps."

"I suppose so," said Hampton, pausing before he said, "and in more ways than one." Linton waited for more. "Didn't you know? Lauren sacked Henry too. For stealing."

"When exactly did you sack Brandon?" asked Brown.

"A couple of weeks ago."

Two weeks, thought Linton. Wasn't that how long Hampton said Lauren had been acting anxiously?

"Has he been back to the house since?" she asked.

"Once," said Hampton. "Just to collect his stuff from the shed. He used it a bit like a staff room. He'd put a gas heater in there. Used to eat his sandwiches in there."

"Did you see him?"

He shook his head. "Lauren did though."

"Did she seem upset afterwards?"

He paused. "It wasn't in Lauren's nature to get upset. And she certainly wouldn't tell me if she was. She was far too proud. But now you mention it, she seemed a little distracted that day."

"When you sacked Brandon," said Brown, "how did he take it?"

"To be honest," replied Hampton, "he was absolutely furious."

***

"We need to speak to Brandon Martock and find Hampton's ex-wife," said Brown, as they walked back to the car. "They both could have killed her for that silver pot. Brandon's got a history of theft…"

"Allegedly," Linton interrupted.

"And Elizabeth Hampton's got a drug habit to fund."

"Do you think a woman would be capable of killing her?"

"Easily. Elizabeth's a lot younger than Lauren. And didn't Hampton tell you she used to be a swimmer? She'd have good upper body strength."

It was bitter in the car. Brown started the engine and turned on the heating, blowing icy air onto Linton's face.

"It'll heat up in a minute," he said as she winced.

"I hope it's a bit warmer for Saturday."

"Why? What's happening?"

"The wedding reception," she said, feeling her heart plunge into her stomach. "The one you said you'd like to go."

He grinned. "I'm winding you up. Of course I haven't forgotten."

"If you don't want to come it's fine. I mean you're the one

that invited yourself. To stop me going on about it. So, if you've changed your mind I'd rather you just said and I can ask someone else."

"Linton. I just said, I was winding you up. I want to go. Anyway, like you said, anything to stop you whining about having no one to go with."

As Brown pulled out of Elmtree's driveway onto the road he said, "I'm convinced Sheila didn't tell us Brandon was sacked because she believes her son killed Lauren. I think she's protecting him. She knew if we found out he'd lost his job, we'd put two and two together. Ring her. Find out when she last saw the silver pot."

Linton was about to reach for her mobile when he said, "Hang on. That can wait. Doesn't Sally Hughes, the woman from the book club, live along here? Why don't we pay her a visit whilst we're here? I'd like to hear what she's got to say about Lauren Hampton."

***

JULY 30TH

I spent the day helping Henry tidy up the Arboretum. Mother is having one of her garden parties next week. It's unlikely anyone will even venture in there but of course everything has to be perfect. I like Henry. I can talk to him about Mother. When I tell him some of the things she does, he laughs which makes her seem less foreboding. It's harder to be afraid of someone when you can make fun of them. He asked me why I didn't stand up to her, but I can't. I tried to explain it and then he hit the nail on the head. He said she'd spent so long putting me down, I wasn't able to trust my own judgement. I think he is right.

ELEVEN

Linton recognised the woman the moment she flung open the front door and greeted them with a hearty, "Good morning."

"Miss Hughes!" she blurted out.

The woman looked at Linton quizzically. "Do I know you?"

"You were my headmistress at school. You probably don't remember me. Kate. Kate Linton. I'm DS Linton now."

Miss Hughes pushed her glasses down the bridge of her nose and peered over the top.

"Good grief," she nodded vigorously. "I recognise your face. Oh dear. I feel terribly old now."

Linton laughed. "You don't look any different." She meant it. But then, the woman with her brunette, curly hair piled high onto her head and her streak of coral-coloured lipstick had probably looked the same in her teens. Linton had forgotten how tall she was; an inch or so taller than Brown. She was still attractive and dressed as flamboyantly as she remembered.

Brown introduced himself, holding out his identification card. Miss Hughes didn't look at it, merely shook her head and said, "You must have hated me when you were at St Crispin's. I was a dragon."

Linton flushed. "You were quite strict," she replied, as diplomatically as possible.

"A complete dragon," Miss Hughes said, turning to Brown with a look of amusement on her surprisingly unlined face. "It was all for show, you know. You've got to get respect from the kids or they'll walk all over you." She shook her head as though throwing off a memory and then said, "You're obviously here about Lauren."

"If it's convenient we'd just like to ask you a few questions."

Miss Hughes stood back and waved her arm in the direction of her hallway. "Of course. Please come in. As a matter of fact your visit couldn't be timelier. Serendipity, don't they call it? I was about to ring, you see. I pulled the cushions off the sofa, so I could get the dust buster in behind them and I found Lauren's appointment book. She must've left it behind on Monday night."

She led them down a long, narrow hallway. Linton wasn't surprised to find the walls painted in a bright turquoise and decorated with a selection of David Hockney prints. She ushered them into her sitting room, and Linton smiled at the hotchpotch of shapes and colours; the art deco fireplace, the red and blue rug, the bright crimson sofa. Reflecting the colourful personality she remembered from school.

"Sit down, sit down," she said pointing towards the sofa. "Here's Lauren's appointment book." She picked up a slim black diary from the mantelpiece and passed it to Linton.

"Were you and Lauren Hampton good friends?" Linton asked, as they struggled to find a spot amongst the plethora of brightly patterned cushions.

Miss Hughes tilted her head to one side. "It depends on how you define friendship," she said slowly. "We spent time together, but I was under no illusion about how she felt. I was acceptable society because I was an ex-headmistress, but as far as she was concerned, I was still beneath her. I think she kidded herself I somehow looked up to her."

"But you didn't."

She laughed, more of a snort than a chuckle. "Not in the least. I swung from finding her amusing, all those airs and graces she put on, to feeling sorry for her and to... well, hating her."

"That's a strong word to use," said Brown.

Miss Hughes shrugged. "I suppose it is, but she was a bully."

"In what way?"

"There's a lady in our group called Marion. She's a lovely person, but she was definitely at the back of the queue when God was handing out looks. Lauren was very nasty to her." She signed and shook her head sadly. "Bullies. They destroy people's lives. I used to see it all the time in my job."

"And was Marion here on Monday night?"

"Oh no, she's missed the last couple of meetings. She's up in Scotland. Her mum died a couple of weeks ago and she's settling her dad into a care home."

"How was Mrs Hampton on Monday evening?"

"The same as ever. Supercilious, condescending, arrogant." She must've caught the expressions on their faces because she said, "I'm not going to pretend I liked her just because she's dead. That would be dishonest, wouldn't it?"

Neither Linton nor Brown answered so she continued, her tone becoming noticeably more strident as she spoke. "To be honest I've been thinking for a while it was time to ask her to leave. She ruined the atmosphere. Generally upset everyone," she faltered, and then came to an abrupt stop.

"How was her mood on Monday evening?"

Miss Hughes shrugged. "Her mood was always the same."

"And what was that?"

Hughes shook her ahead impatiently. "It's hard to explain. I never saw her worried or upset or moved by anything. Things didn't seem to affect her like other people. She was like a viscous waxwork. Horrible, but almost unreal."

"Not anxious?"

She pulled a face and shook her head. "Not in the least. That's not a word I'd ever associate with her. She wouldn't want to show any weakness in front of others."

"What do you think of Mark Hampton?" asked Linton.

"I've only got to know him since he moved back, but he seems very sweet. And he's thrown himself into the local community. Joined the theatre group. That sort of thing." She picked up a cushion and pulled it onto her lap. "It's funny," she continued, fiddling with the cushion's tassels absentmindedly, "when he was younger, I always thought he was rather cold and stuck up. He was sent away to school at seven. Didn't ever mix with the local kids in the holidays. Looking back, I think he was probably shy. Or more likely Lauren didn't let him."

"Did Mrs Hampton mention if she was planning to meet anyone after the book club ended?"

Miss Hughes shook her head. "She wouldn't have told me even if she was. We didn't talk about anything personal."

"What time did she leave?"

"Around the same time as everybody else. At about eight twenty-five. Of course she had to leave first because she'd blocked everyone else with her car. That was typical of her as well."

"Just out of interest, what did you do after everyone left?" asked Brown, as they got up to leave.

Sally didn't hesitate with her answer. "I had supper and watched that programme about the safari park. I went to bed just after nine and read."

***

Linton started flicking through Lauren's appointment book as soon as they were back in the car.

"Do you reckon she bats for the other side?" said Brown, as he pulled out of the lay-by opposite Miss Hughes' house.

"Why? Because she's attractive and never married," she tutted disdainfully. "She probably just likes her independence."

She wasn't about to tell how at school they'd nicknamed her Magnus Pike, cockney slang for dyke. She was a miss, therefore she was obviously a lesbian.

"Well, you're the expert," he said, grinning, "what with your mum…"

"Brown," she said, "I've told before, I don't want to talk about it."

"Is she still with whatevername?"

"It's not funny."

Bloody Brown. He still thought it was hilarious that her mum was living in Amsterdam with a woman. Even funnier that Linton's ex-boyfriend had had a one-night-stand with her mother's lover on his mate's stag do.

She carried on flicking through the book until she found the page for the day that Lauren was murdered.

"Listen to this," she said. "The day Lauren was killed, she had an appointment at 2.15."

"With who?"

"I don't know. She's only put their initial. B."

"Brandon Martock," he said.

"I'll ring Sheila now," said Linton, pulling out her mobile. "Ask her why she didn't tell us he was Lauren's gardener. And how we can get hold of her son."

***

Sheila recognised the voice immediately.

"Mrs Martock?" she said, in that annoying, bouncy way she had of speaking. "It's Detective Constable Kate Linton. Is now a good time to speak?"   *Sergeant*

"As good as any, I suppose."

"I'm just looking through Lauren's appointment book and it looks as though she was planning to meet someone on Monday whose name begins with the initial B. Do you happen to know who it might've been?"

"I told you. Monday was my day off."

"But did you know she had a meeting arranged? An appointment with someone."

"I'm not her secretary."

She heard the policewoman sigh. "The initial B," she said in a less lively tone. "Can you think who it might be?"

Sheila paused for a few moments to give the impression she was thinking. "No," she said eventually.

"So are you saying you don't know anyone whose name begins with B?'

"I'm saying I can't think of anyone Lauren knew."

"What about your son? Brandon. She knew him, didn't she?"

Sheila paused and then said as evenly as she could. "Why would she be meeting my son?"

"When we last spoke you told us Mr Hampton did his own gardening."

"Well, he does at the moment," Sheila said, knowing exactly where this was leading.

"But what you didn't say was your son gardened for Mrs Hampton up until recently and that she sacked him because he stole from her."

"Allegedly stole," she said sharply. "He didn't take anything."

"Mr Hampton said…"

"I don't care what Mr Hampton said. I know the truth. A case of outright snobbery," she said hurriedly. "That's what. Just because he's got a record."

"A record?" *Damn*, thought Sheila. Her and her big mouth. She'd assumed they'd have known. "For what?"

"Not theft."

"What then?"

"Selling alcohol. Smuggled in from France. Just a bit of wine. It was no big deal."

"So he's not the most honest of people."

"It's typical," said Sheila angrily. "When something goes missing, blame the staff. There was no proof my son stole anything. Things were always going missing from Elmtree. Half the time they turned up and Lauren had mislaid them. And half the time she made it up for a bit of drama."

"So why didn't you tell us Lauren had sacked your son? You must've known we'd find out eventually."

"Because, as far as I'm concerned, it's not relevant. He didn't steal anything, he didn't do anything wrong."

"Do you happen to know what Brandon was up to on the night Lauren Hampton was murdered?" Sheila was silent. "Mrs Martock? Can you answer the question please? And the truth this time."

"I haven't lied to you."

"There's such a thing as lying by omission."

"I don't know where he was and that *is* the truth. You'll have to ask him if you want to know."

There was a long pause before the policewoman said, "When was the last time you cleaned Lauren's front room?"

"Sunday."

"Do you remember seeing the silver pot? The one that her son bought her from Sotheby's."

Sheila hesitated. "Yes. I dusted it like I always do."

"And when was the last time you spoke to your son?"

"A couple of weeks ago, after he got sacked."

Actually, they hadn't talked. He'd sworn and shouted at her. He couldn't believe she'd taken the Hamptons' side. *You should have walked out,* he'd yelled at her, *to show your support.*

"Where does your son live?"

"He shares a flat," she said. "Ninety-seven Magdalene Road. But if he's not there, he'll be working. Heather said he's started at the The Rowan Tree. As a prep chef."

"Heather. That's your daughter, isn't it? I don't suppose she ever worked for the Hamptons and perhaps you've forgotten to mention it?"

Sarcastic bitch. "The Hamptons never employed Heather." *Well, not officially,* she thought. She used to help out in the school holidays when she was younger, but there was no point mentioning that, it didn't count. And anyway, Lauren soon put a stop to it after she'd got that ridiculous crush on Mark and started following him around like a little lap dog. He hadn't helped matters by being so nice to her.

Bloody children, she thought after she'd said a curt goodbye to the Detective Sergeant. What a couple of let-downs they were. She was desperate for them to go University, so they'd have the chance she'd never had. Neither of them had though. Heather had worked in dead-end jobs for years and then went and got herself pregnant.

As for her son, well, in the words of her husband, "You can't make a silk purse out of a sow's ear." Except he *wasn't* stupid. He only thought he was because he'd spent his whole childhood being told that.

She sighed. Perhaps she was wrong to expect so much from her children. She knew she should be kinder to them. Just when she thought she was making progress, she found herself back on the same page, of the same predictable script that composed of her nagging and judging and criticising.

Maybe it wasn't too late to help them. Or at least Brandon. She picked up the phone. The least she could do was warn him.

TWELVE

Linton liked The Rowan Tree. She'd eaten there with Ben a few times and the food was wholesome and tasty. The lunchtime rush was coming to an end when she and Brown arrived. The restaurant was busy but there was an air of unhurried repletion, people chatting idly and sipping at coffees.

A waitress greeted them on their way in. Brown showed her his card and asked for Brandon Martock. She pointed them in the direction of the kitchen.

As they made their way through the obstacle of oak tables and chairs, they passed an older woman with bright pink hair. Linton recognised her as one of her mum's cronies. She could hear her talking to her companion about the town's forthcoming psychic fair and it reminded her of the complaints they'd had one year from its organisers. Someone had crossed through every advertising poster and written, 'Cancelled, due to unforeseen circumstances'. They'd all had a laugh at that one.

There were two people in the kitchen; a tall, willowy man with a mass of dreadlocks tied back into an enormous ponytail and an older, shorter, stockier one with closely shaven hair.

"Brandon Martock?"

The smaller of the two men turned to look at them quizzically. "Yeah?"

"Police," said Brown, holding out his ID again. "We've got a few questions about Lauren Hampton."

Martock looked across at the taller, dreadlocked man. They exchanged a glance that Linton couldn't decipher before the other man turned back to lift the large saucepan from the hob.

Brandon turned and said to Brown, "We can talk out the back. We've been flat out for two hours and I'm gasping for a fag."

They followed Martock to the rear of the kitchen. He pulled open a fire door, turned to Linton and said with a lascivious grin, "After you." She could feel his eyes on her, knew that he was looking her up and down. She moved as quickly as she could through the open door and out into a small, dank courtyard. It was a miserable looking space with a couple of overturned red plastic crates and a scattering of cigarette ends, a combination of roll-ups and straights.

Brandon strolled across to the furthest wall then leant against it, studying Linton through slitted eyes. He moved his hand to his pocket. She could see the shape of a box of cigarettes through the material of his trousers, but as he went to pull it out he stopped suddenly, a brief look of panic passing his face.

"I've, err, just remembered. I've run out," he said awkwardly. "Hold on."

He disappeared back into the kitchen and reappeared a couple of seconds later holding a bulky pouch of tobacco and some Rizla papers. He took his place again against the damp stone wall and set about constructing an emaciated-looking cigarette.

"You don't seem surprised to see us," said Brown, after a couple of moments.

"I know why you're here," he said, licking and lighting his creation with practised ease.

"Go on then," said Brown. "Enlighten us."

"It's about me being sacked, isn't it? From the Hamptons' place."

"Partly."

"I know how these things work. You look around for someone with a motive…" For a moment no one spoke as Martock executed a couple of perfect smoke rings. Linton watched them float away, suppressing an urge to flick them with her finger.

Then Brown said, "And what would yours be?"

"What?"

"Your motive? For killing Lauren Hampton."

"She gave me the sack, didn't she? For stealing some jewellery. Which I didn't."

"Where were you on Monday night?" asked Linton. "Between the hours of eight and nine p.m.?"

Brandon nodded in the direction of the kitchen door. "Here. I started bang on six and, by the time I'd cleared up and had a beer with Jools, it must've been after eleven when I left."

"Jools?"

"The chef. Old Mop Top in there," he said, nodding towards the open door. He exhaled a long, loud breath and said, "Look. Lauren Hampton pissed me off, especially seeing as I was innocent, but I'm not the sort of bloke to knock off an old woman. However much of a bitch she was."

"Why would she accuse you of something you didn't do?" asked Brown.

Martock shrugged and the action reminded Linton of Sheila. "She did the same thing to my dad. She obviously had something against our family. God knows why."

He took another deep drag on his cigarette and, as he exhaled said, "Do you know what? She didn't even have the nerve to sack me herself. She got Mark to do it, not that I hold it against the bloke. He was only acting on her say so. He was very apologetic. I think he believed me, he almost said as much, but he reckoned it was better if I left otherwise she'd get the police in." He stopped and sniffed. "Anyway, he paid me a month's wages as an apology and wrote me a brilliant reference. I deserved it, mind. I worked bloody hard up there. Not just in the garden. Odd jobs round the house. Sometimes I'd be up there well into the evening. Ironic really. If she hadn't sacked me, I might've been up there that night. Maybe she wouldn't have been killed."

"So if you didn't steal the stuff from her house, who do you think did?" asked Brown.

Brandon flicked the grey caterpillar of ash from his roll-up and said, "I dunno. Nobody ever seemed to go up there. At least not from what I could tell. Perhaps she made it up for a bit of fun. That would've been her all over. She loved a bit of drama." He yawned, as though bored with the conversation, pulling his muscular arms up above his head, the movement bringing with it the stench of stale body odour.

"What were doing at quarter past two on Monday afternoon."

Brendon's eyes narrowed.

"I was at my flat. I'd gone back to bed. I'd worked late and I was in again that evening."

"You didn't happen to have anything arranged with Lauren?"

"Yeah, I had her over for lunch. Just the two of us. Lobster and champagne. It was very romantic."

"It's not really a joking matter, is it?" she said. "Lauren Hampton's dead."

"Look," he sneered. "I just told you. I was asleep."

"Can anyone vouch for you being home?" asked Brown.

He shrugged. "I doubt it."

He blew another smoke ring, this time in the direction of Linton. As he finished blowing, he licked the top of his lip with his tongue, then slowly smiled.

"So you didn't ever see anyone suspicious hanging around Elmtree?" she asked, trying to keep her voice calm, determined not to be intimated by him.

He shook his head slowly. "Nope."

"And have you got any idea who might have wanted to kill Lauren?"

He shrugged and flipped his cigarette onto the floor, grinding it out with the heel of his black rubber clogs. "Anyone who ever met her. She could be a spiteful cow when she wanted to be. I can't say I'm sorry she's dead. It's like she had this hold over mum. She treated her like shit, but it's never entered her head to leave, even after she accused me and dad of stealing from her. Mind you, she's always been a bloody victim."

"How do you mean?"

"She used to let dad push her around. She never stood up to him either. I reckon she enjoys the suffering."

He put his hand to scratch his head, and as he did, the sleeve of his sweatshirt rolled down. The bottom half of his right arm was bandaged.

"What's that?" asked Brown sharply.

Brandon shrugged. "A burn. Hazard of the job. It's a right pain in the arse cause I can't have a shower. Gotta have a bath instead and stick my hand over the side."

"We're going to have a quick word with your chef," Brown replied. "See if he can vouch for you being in on Monday night."

"Be my guest. I'm leaving in a bit anyway. I've got the

evening off for a change." He winked at Linton. "I'm looking forward to having a bit of fun tonight."

They left Brandon in the courtyard rolling another cigarette and went back into the kitchen. The chef was near the door, busy ladling an aromatic concoction onto a plate of brown rice.

"Sweet potato and coconut curry," he said, with a toothy grin, as they approached him. "Lunchtime's over, which means I get to eat. And I'm bloody starving."

"You're Jools?" said Linton.

He nodded as he opened the lid of a jar of mango chutney and spooned a generous dollop onto the side of his plate. "What I can I do for you?"

"Were you working here on Monday night?"

The man nodded again, causing a clattering of beads in the dreadlocked hair he'd tied behind his head. "I'm in every night this week."

"And Brandon Martock was working as well, was he?"

"Yep." He picked up a fork and shovelled a large lump of food into his mouth. Still chewing he said, "It was a mad night. We had a large party in from Millbank School."

He tipped his head in the direction of a blackboard. It had the days of the week and the bookings next to it, written in white chalk. *Monday – 8pm Millbank School – 23 people.* "Their Christmas party got cancelled 'cause of the snow so they'd postponed it until January. They took over the whole restaurant."

"What hours did Brandon work?"

"He started at six and finished about eleven."

"Did he have a break?"

"At about half nine I let him go for a fag."

"Where?"

"Only out the back. In the courtyard."

"So he didn't leave the premises."

Jools shook his head. "No way. Like I said, it was mental."

"He didn't stop before that. Between say eight and nine?"

"We didn't get a breather all night. I didn't even to go to the toilet. I was knackered come the end of the shift."

***

"Bollocks," said Brown, as they left the restaurant, "Look like the smarmy git is off the hook."

"What now?"

"Ring Hampton. See if he can think of anyone whose name begins with B. He might know who his mum was planning to meet on Monday."

She called his mobile but he didn't answer so she left a message. "I wonder where he is."

"Fuck knows. Skydiving off the Eiffel Tower for all I care."

***

AUGUST 3RD

I helped Henry again today. Mother was busy with one of her charity groups. She amazes me. She seems to be able to go to any length to help the poor or abused, but she never seems to have any empathy whatsoever for the people around her. Henry says she doesn't really care about her charities; she only does it because it makes her look good and that's all she worries about. I asked him what he and Sheila did on their day off. He said 'not much'. He didn't sound very enthusiastic. We didn't talk a lot after that. He's the sort of person you can spend time with and not have to speak.

***

She pushed the unwieldy trolley across the supermarket car park, wondering how her husband was getting on with putting Ollie to bed. She prayed their son would be asleep by the time she got home. She didn't want him tired tomorrow. And he was bound to get up at five o'clock, screeching his cockerel-cry of "Is-it-time-to-get-up-yet?" before bounding into their bedroom to tear the Power Ranger paper off his birthday presents.

The mornings were bad enough at the moment without that. Nibbling on a ginger biscuit when she woke up to stop the nausea completely crippling her. The other day she'd had to pull over on her way to work to throw up.

She hoped she wouldn't be sick at the party although she could always blame it on a hangover. They wanted to wait until the twelve-week scan before they announced their news. She hadn't got past week nine with the other baby she'd lost. She didn't want to jinx it, although she knew that telling people had had nothing to do with the miscarriage.

She loaded the shopping bags into the back of the car feeling guilty about the food she'd bought. She'd had to stop herself from telling the cashier she didn't normally buy as much junk as this.

It's a kids' party, her husband would say. *That's what they're supposed to eat.*

Still, she'd bought some carrots to peel and a cucumber to slice and she'd chop up some strawberries as well.

She left the trolley in the nearest shelter and, as she walked back to her car, she mentally revised what they'd need to take to the hall tomorrow. Food, tablecloth, balloon, party bags, pass the parcel. Paper towels in case anyone spilt anything.

Some bin bags so they could clear up afterwards. And a lighter. She mustn't forget the lighter for the cake she'd picked up earlier from the baker's. *Happy birthday, Ollie! Four today!*

She climbed into her Range Rover and turned on the engine, drove out of the car park and on to the little slip road, which eventually took her up to the main road. She stopped at the junction and indicated right, waiting to make sure it was safe to pull out.

In weeks to come, this was the point in her head she referred to as *before*. When everything was still normal. Before she became too afraid to go shopping. Before she was afraid to go *anywhere* on her own. Before she made her husband put a deadbolt on the front door and two locks on their garden gate and insisted on sleeping with the lights on. Before the slightest whiff of Imperial Leather soap caused her heart to beat so fast, she was convinced she was going to die.

In the weeks to come she tried not to think about what happened *after*. Although of course from now there would only ever be *after*. She could never get back to before.

Night times were the worst. In every sweaty, tussled dream she'd feel the sharp notch of a knife and his hot, minty breath on her neck. She'd wake up screaming, convinced he was in their room, staring at her through his balaclava with his cold, dead eyes.

***

"You got off with Mark Hampton!" Linton couldn't believe she didn't know this piece of information about one of her best friends. She was out with Lisa for a drink. Gemma, who normally made up their weekly threesome, was busy.

"It was years ago, before I even knew you."

"How old were you?"

"About fourteen. Dad was running for council, so we got invited up there for dinner. Mark was back from school."

"So what was he like?"

"Good looking and very aloof, which made him even more of a challenge. And he'd been expelled from school. You know what I'm like. I can't resist a rebel."

Linton tried to marry this description with the Mark Hampton she knew. Aloof and rebellious were the last two adjectives she'd have used to describe him.

"What was he expelled for?"

"I dunno. I didn't ask. He went to a posh school. Probably caught smoking or snogging one of the local girls."

"So what happened? The night you got off with him."

"Not a lot. My dad went outside for fag and caught us snogging." She stopped suddenly, a look of alarm passing across her face and for a second Linton wondered if she was reliving her dad's discovery. "Shit," she hissed. "Whatever you do, don't look behind you."

Linton immediately did, instantly regretting the action. *Fuck.* She couldn't believe who it was. Her ex, Ben and he was walking towards the empty table next to them, with a woman in tow. An exceptionally pretty woman.

She turned back to her friend and grimaced.

"Look like you're enjoying yourself. He's coming over," whispered Lisa. Of course he was. If nothing else, her ex-boyfriend had manners.

"Kate!" he said in that faux-jolly voice she'd heard him use when he was talking to one of his more demanding students. "How are you?"

"Ben!" she trilled, smiling broadly. "I'm great. How are you?" She continued to grin as she spoke, feeling like a ventriloquist's dummy.

"This is Kiera," he said, turning to the woman. Linton half-expected him to say *da dah!*

Of course it was. There was no other name for her. She was slim, beautiful and elegantly dressed. Linton scanned her face and body for something she could criticise. *Her neck.* It was a bit on the scrawny side. And her skin looked delicate. She probably wouldn't age well.

"Hi," said Kiera brightly. Well, at least she didn't do the whole, 'I've heard all about you' routine, so that was a *small* point in her favour.

"We're getting married," said Ben quickly. "In a couple of months. Just a small ceremony." He spoke as though he was in a competition, to see how many words he could get out without taking a breath.

"Congratulations." Linton could taste bile at the back of her throat, from where her heart felt like it had lodged itself.

"Kate," said Lisa suddenly, grabbing at her coat. "We'd better get going. Or we're late for our double date with Jamie and, um, Pete."

"Right. Of course."

It was the most preposterous piece of acting she'd had ever witnessed, but she wanted to hug her friend for trying.

"Uhhh," said Lisa, when they were safely out on the pavement. "Did you see her neck? It looked like a chicken's."

***

It had taken Linton fifteen minutes to make Lisa understand that there was *no way* she was going to Joker's. Yes, she agreed, she could do with some excitement in her life, but she didn't think a mirrored cavern full of drunken idiots was the place to provide it. She finally left Lisa outside the entrance to the nightclub and got a taxi home.

Now as she sat slumped at the kitchen table, too spent even to take off her jacket, she reached into her handbag for her mobile. She needed to talk to someone about her encounter with Ben. But who could she phone?

Gemma's husband went to bed early, so she couldn't risk ringing her. Her sister Jasmine would be asleep by now as well.

Her thoughts turned once more to Ben. She wasn't even angry with him any more. Just depressed about the whole thing. But then, wasn't that what depression was? Anger turned inwards.

She was livid with him back when they split up. Once she'd got past the humiliation of what he'd done. Perhaps if she'd vented her anger when it had happened she wouldn't feel like this. She would've 'moved on', 'had closure', wouldn't have felt like curling into a ball and sobbing at the thought of him spending his life with someone else.

There were loads of things she could've done back then. Lisa had been full of them: 'Slice his ties in half. Cut holes in the crotch of all his trousers. Hire a plane with a banner saying "Ben Simon's a twat".'

No, she'd decided to take the moral high ground, but it was getting lonely and boring up here. Lisa was right. What she needed was some fun. Something to give her ego a well-needed boost. And maybe Brown could be the one to give it to her. Literally.

It was simple. No more analysing everything to death, making things more complicated than they were.

She would seduce him on Saturday night. They would go to the wedding, have a few drinks and she'd invite him back to her house for a nightcap and some mindless sex. She would kill two birds with one stone; prove to herself she still had it and finally get him out her system once and for all.

And then she could leave the tossers behind for good and concentrate on finding someone decent.

***

He sat in the bath, thinking about how much he'd enjoyed his evening. How lucky he'd been to have had a choice. He smiled to himself as he closed his eyes, remembering the feeling of excitement building inside him as he'd watched the two women, trying to decide which one he would choose as he waited for them outside the supermarket.

Eeeny meeny miny moe.

THIRTEEN

The following morning the heating still wasn't working and the temperature in the Incident Room appeared to have dipped below freezing.

"Has Hampton got back to you yet?" Brown said irritably, rubbing his hands together to keep warm. Linton shook her head. "Well, ring him again. Ask him who Lauren might've known with a name beginning with B."

She tried his number a few times but just kept reaching his answerphone.

"Perhaps the fucker's had a parachute accident," mumbled Brown. "Broken both his legs."

"God, you're a miserable sod. I'm making a cup of tea to warm up," she said. "D'you want one?"

It was whilst she was returning to her desk that Linton overheard something that almost caused her to drop the mugs of tea she was clutching.

She knew another woman had been raped the previous night, more viciously even than the last time. The news had circulated the station first thing, but until she heard Wells talking to Brown, she hadn't known the victim's name.

"Gemma Dorland," she heard him say. "She was in my sister's year at school."

Gemma Dorland.

Oh my God.

It couldn't be, she thought. She must have misheard.

But in case she was in any doubt, Brown turned to her and said, "Shit. That's your best mate, isn't it?"

***

Linton got the rest of the details from Keen.

"It was brutal," he said. "She's got a fractured cheek bone. He slammed her face into the ground when she struggled. She'll need surgery for it."

"Whereabouts was she attacked?" Linton asked, still numb with shock.

"Baltonsborough. In a field. She gave us exactly the same spiel as all the others. Reckoned she'd finished her shopping and fancied a drive along the moors. Then when she reached the turning to the village, a bloke ran out in the road. Told her his wife had gone into labour and he needed her help. The bloke obviously forced his way into her car at the store. Got her to drive out there."

"Surely someone would have noticed *something*. What about CCTV?"

"Her car was out of range. Just like the others."

"Are you putting out another warning?"

"It's going on the local news again today. We're asking women to stay extra vigilant when they go shopping. Park in spaces as close to the entrance as they can."

"What about surveillance?"

"We haven't got the manpower to station officers at every supermarket, every night. There are seven in Street and Glastonbury alone. The most we can do is to send a patrol car round to each of them once an evening. We're hoping when he hears we've put out another warning, he'll be too scared to try it again." He paused. "Although it hasn't deterred him so far."

"He might just go further afield."

"There is that danger."

"Gemma was supposed to come out for a drink with me last night," she said. "But she couldn't. She was busy…" She let the sentence fizzle out as she thought about what her friend had been going through while she sat in the pub getting drunk with Lisa. "Did you get anything from her?"

"She reckons she didn't see his face, can't remember how tall he was, and has no idea of his build. Oh, and she had a shower when she got home and chucked all her clothes on a 90 degree wash so there's no forensic evidence either."

"What about the car?"

"Luckily her husband drove her to the station in his own car, so apart from her driving it home after the attack, no one's touched it. When we told her we needed it for forensic evidence, she went mad and said there was no need 'cause he didn't get in it. She's obviously terrified that if we track him down, he'll think it was her fault because she's grassed him up. Anyway, we collected it this morning, but we don't know if we'll find anything." He paused and then asked, "How good a mate is she?"

"We've known each other since school."

"Do you think she might talk to you?"

"That's exactly what I was thinking."

***

Linton didn't tell Gemma she was going round. She knew she'd only try and fob her off.

She rang the doorbell, giving it an initial short burst, followed by a couple of longer trills, but there was no answer. After knocking a few times, hard enough to make her knuckles sting, she peered through the front window into the living room and could see the flicker of the television through the net curtains. Someone was definitely home.

It was only then it occurred to her that if her friend was in there alone, she'd be too scared to come to the door. She pushed the letterbox open and shouted, "Gemma. It's me. Kate. I came round to see how you are." A few seconds later and the door opened to a slither. Gemma must've been standing behind it, praying whoever was there would go away.

Linton stepped into the dark hallway and gasped involuntarily. Gemma, normally so fresh-faced and pretty, looked distorted, like a surrealist portrait. Her left eye was a painful slit, the skin around it purple and puffy. She had stitching across the bridge of her nose and the left side of her face was bruised and swollen. Her neck was covered in patchy blue bruises, as though a hand had tightly gripped it. Linton was used to seeing injuries like this, but not on someone she knew, someone she cared about.

"Christ."

Linton followed her friend into the living room. Gemma slumped onto the sofa. A black and white film was flickering silently on the widescreen TV.

"Where is everyone?" Linton asked, picking up a Lego dumper truck from the cream armchair and placing it on the coffee table before sitting down.

"It's Ollie's party today," she said, nodding at the cards on the mantelpiece. Linton spotted hers halfway along. "I didn't want him to miss it. It wouldn't be fair. Nick's over there with mum."

Gemma's eyes were darting all the over the place, not settling on anything as though she didn't even trust inanimate objects. Linton knew she should tread gently; ease her into the conversation before she asked the big question. Except that when she opened her mouth to say something else, she blurted it out.

"So what *really* happened then?"

"Kate, please. Just leave it."

"They all know the story you've told isn't true."

"Look, I've made a statement. There's nothing else I want to say."

"Come on, Gemma. You must have an idea of what he looked like. You know we can't catch him unless you tell us."

"Please, Kate."

"Did he threaten you?"

"No."

"Did he tell you he was going to come and finish you off if you told us anything? You know we wouldn't let that happen."

Gemma didn't answer. Instead she picked up an embroidered cushion and pulled it onto her lap.

"I spoke to one of the officers on the case. He said you'd showered so they couldn't get anything from you. Why didn't Nick stop you?"

"I told him I was going to the loo. I locked the bathroom door, so he couldn't get in."

"Did he tell you to do that? The man who attacked you? Did he tell you to clean yourself up before you went to the police? We could've got fibres from his clothes, collected saliva or sperm."

Silence.

"He told you to shower and change your clothes, didn't he? He's obviously intelligent, someone who's forensically aware. Did he wear a condom?"

Gemma's answer was a hoarse whisper. "Yes."

"Gloves?"

Gemma nodded, twisting a cushion tassel around her little finger, staring down at the carpet in front of her. She was chewing on her bottom lip, something she did was she was under stress. It reminded Linton of Mark Hampton.

"Did he tell you he'd come after you if you described him to the police? You know he's trying to scare you Gemma. He doesn't know where you live."

"He said he'd come after Ollie," she said looking up, her eyes wide with fear.

"How did he know you had a son?" Linton pressed. "Did you tell him?"

Gemma shook her head.

"But did he actually say Ollie's name? Do you think he knew who you were before he attacked you?"

"He didn't say his name. But he knew I had a son. How could he have known that if he didn't know me?"

"Unless he was inside your car."

She saw her flinch.

"He was, wasn't he?"

"No."

"He forced his way in at the supermarket, didn't he?"

"No!"

"He would've seen the car seat. And there are always toys all over your back seat. Boy's toys. He made an educated guess and he used it to get to you."

"Look, Kate. Thanks for coming round, but I'm tired. If you don't mind I'd…"

"Gemma. Please. He's going to keep attacking women. You need to tell us what happened so we can stop him."

Gemma had shut her eyes as though it might help block out Linton's voice. A single tear seeped out from under a swollen lid and made its way down her face.

"Kate, you haven't got any children. You don't know what it's like. He's already responsible for killing my baby."

"Baby?" said Linton taken aback. "What are you talking about?"

"I'm ten weeks, Kate. At least I was until I started bleeding this morning. Another miscarriage."

"Oh God, Gemma. Look, I'm sorry. I shouldn't have…" Linton stopped, feeling herself morphing from detective into friend again. She pushed herself out of the armchair and said, "I'll let you get some sleep. Take care and I'll give you a ring. And I promise I won't go on about it again."

"Kate?" Gemma's voice was trembling. Linton looked down at her hunched shape on the sofa and saw the helplessness in her eyes.

"What is it?" she asked gently.

"Why do you think he did it?"

Linton felt a sudden surge of anger. How could someone have reduced her friend to this shaken, beaten mess? "I don't know Gemma. Different men rape for different reasons. Some of them hate women and want to hurt them. For some it's about the feeling of power it gives them."

"It's like he wanted to punish me." Gemma's hand moved towards her ring finger then stopped and pulled sharply back. She always fiddled with her wedding ring when she was stressed except now it wasn't there.

"Where's your ring?" asked Linton, aware of the suspicion in her voice.

She watched her friend's expression change to one of fear. "It fell off," Gemma said quickly. "In the field. Nick wants to go back and look for it."

"How could it have just fallen off? That's never happened before."

"It was when I was struggling."

"He took it, didn't he?"

"No!" She knew she was lying.

Trophies, thought Linton. Serial killers and rapists often took something from their victims. Clothing or trinkets without obvious value, except to the perpetrator. In his sick fantasy world, he'd see it as a symbol of his achievement; a little souvenir to remind himself of the crime. If he'd taken things from the other women, it might be a way of finding him. They could alert the public to the missing items; someone might have seen him with them. That's if they could find out what the other trophies were. His previous victims might be too scared to tell the police he'd taken anything.

Linton left Gemma's house feeling dark and leaden, completely at odds with the bright winter sunshine that had finally broken through the grey clouds.

When she reached her car, she pulled her mobile out of her bag and leant against the passenger door. She found Keen's number and dialled.

"I've just come from Gemma's," she said, when he answered on the second ring.

"Did she tell you anything?"

"I think you're right about the rapist getting into her car at the supermarket. When I suggested it, she clammed up. He's obviously told her not to tell us because he knows we'll be over it with a fine toothcomb. What happened with the other victims' cars?"

"The first two had them valeted. Obviously under his instruction."

"And am I right in thinking all the women have got young kids?"

He paused. "Funnily enough they've all got at least one."

"So they'd all have car seats?"

He hesitated. "As far as I know."

"That's how he knows they've got children."

"What d'you mean?"

"I think he's using them as a threat. Telling the women he'll come after their kids if they tell us anything. What mother would risk that?" *Not even mine*, she thought. "And another thing. I think he might be collecting trophies. I noticed Gemma's wedding ring was missing. She said she dropped it in the field but I know she was lying."

"I'll go back to our victims and see if they'll talk. If we can get a description of any missing jewellery we can out it put in the media. Someone might spot him with it."

Linton hung up and got into her car. She flicked on the radio but the DJ was too flippant so on a whim she turned to Radio 4 and found herself half way through a programme about gardening. She smiled as she thought about Mark Hampton and his gentle, cultured manner. The complete antithesis to the lowlife scumbag who'd attacked Gemma. Linton felt instinctively that talking to him would make her feel better. And she had a good excuse to go and see him.

***

AUGUST 5TH

It was mother's garden party today and as usual we had all the theatrics before it started, with her screaming at me because I dared to choose my own outfit and refused to change out of it. I think my talk with Henry the other day had emboldened me. However, I soon discovered I'd made a big mistake by going against her wishes. She did everything she could to undermine me in front of everyone; the drink I got her was warm; the joke I told was met with a stony silence; my lack of a boyfriend and propensity to put on weight was discussed at length. In the end, I went off to hide in the arboretum.

Henry must have followed me there. He found me crying, so he put his arms around me to comfort me. He is the kindest man I know.

**

She should've rung first, Linton thought, as she pulled up outside Elmtree Manor a couple of minutes later. Lauren Hampton's Mercedes sat forlornly on the gravel, the sun glinting off its polished paintwork. Mark's Saab was nowhere in sight.

But instead of turning round and driving back up the long driveway, Linton cut the engine and got out of her car, knowing as she did she was simply delaying going back to work and having to talk to anyone about Gemma.

She stood for a few moments looking up at the large house wondering how it would feel like to live in such an imposing building. As she traipsed slowly back to her car, she heard the sound of a car engine and looked up to find Mark's Saab racing down the driveway towards her.

He braked abruptly and jumped out grinning broadly, obviously pleased to see her. Linton couldn't help smiling back.

"What a nice surprise," he said warmly. "Have you got some news for me?"

"Nothing like that, I'm afraid. I've just got a couple of questions I need to ask. I've left a few messages on your mobile."

"I'm so sorry. I stupidly left my phone in Taunton yesterday.

At the skydiving centre. I've just been back to collect it and it's out of battery."

"Don't worry. But if you've got time now…"

"Do you mind if I just grab my shopping first?"

"Of course not."

He turned and opened the rear door of his car. "My boot's full of stuff for the dump," he said. "So I had to stick the shopping in here."

Linton could see a couple of carrier bags on the back seat.

"Damn. One of the bags has tipped over. I think a tin's rolled under the seat." He climbed into the footwell and stuck his hand under the seat in front. "There's no room in the back of these cars. I could do with something a bit bigger, to be honest."

As he said it, something churned and crunched in Linton's brain. *There's no room in the back of these cars.* Gemma had a four-wheel drive. She had plenty of room in the back of hers.

"There," he said, interrupting her thoughts as he pulled out a tin of chopped tomatoes and held it in the air triumphantly. He grabbed the two shopping bags from the seat then turned to Linton.

"Are you OK?" he asked, pushing the door shut with his hip. "You look like you've seen the proverbial ghost."

She shook her head, "I was thinking about work."

"I could do with some tea," he said, nodding towards the cottage. "Fancy a cup?"

As they walked, Mark chatted about the garden, pointing out various plants and shrubs. Linton answered with the occasional 'oh!' and 'lovely', not really listening, thinking about the conclusion she'd come to about the rapist. She was certain she knew how he was getting into the victim's cars without anyone noticing.

This time Hampton led her straight into the living room. It was as clean and tidy as his kitchen had been, every surface gleaming and there was a faint trace of furniture polish in the air. The room looked like it had been styled and cleaned to be photographed for a magazine. Its walls were painted a light grey, but rather than seeming cold, they looked sophisticated, creating a perfect backdrop for the colourful paintings that hung round the room. There was a cluster of chairs in striped burgundy and cream and a long, squishy looking sofa, covered with deep red cushions. She could imagine spending the evening curled up on it with a book in her hand, a fire roaring in the open grate.

"I'll make some tea," said Hampton. "Make yourself at home."

As soon as he disappeared into the hallway, Linton rang Keen. His phone was engaged. She tried a couple more times and finally got through.

"Not you again!" he said. "What is it? Do you want to transfer to investigations or something? Have you finally had enough of Brown?"

"I think I know how the rapist is abducting his victims without being seen," she said quietly.

"Go then," said Keen. "Let's hear it."

As she opened her mouth to speak, Hampton appeared at the living room door carrying a large, wooden tray.

"I'll have to ring you back," she said.

"So, how can I help?" he asked, placing the tray on the oak coffee table in front of the sofa.

"Did your mother mention meeting anyone on Monday?" asked Linton as she moved over to the sofa and sat down at the opposite end to Hampton.

He picked up the teapot and frowned. "Why do you ask?"

"We found Lauren's appointments book," she said. "She was supposed to meet someone on Monday at quarter past two. Only a few hours before she was killed. Someone with the initial B. Have you got any idea who that might be?"

"Brandon?" he said slowly, as he poured tea into one cup and then another. "Although I can't think why she'd want to meet him. As I said, he didn't exactly leave on good terms."

"Is there anyone else?"

He shook his head. "I can't think of anyone with the initial B. Apart from Betty of course, but…" He tapered off, as though he'd said too much.

Linton felt her heart tugging at the bottom of her throat. "Betty?"

Mark picked up a small white jug. "How do you like your tea? White? Sugar?"

"Just a drop of milk," she said, trying to keep the impatience out of her voice. "You were saying? Someone called Betty."

He gently tipped a small amount into one of the cups then passed it to Linton and settled back in the seat opposite her.

"My ex-wife," he said. "That's what Lauren called her. She hated the nickname. Thought my mother did it to make her less, what's the word, *significant*?"

"Do you think Lauren might've been meeting her?"

He laughed uneasily. "Certainly not socially. As I said before, they hated each other."

"You told us Elizabeth asked Lauren for money in the past. Perhaps she was trying again."

"She must be pretty desperate by now," he conceded. "She's left her job and she hasn't got me supporting her. And I suppose she may have thought she had some leverage this time."

"What do you mean?"

"Lauren wouldn't want any sort of negative publicity. Not when she's trying to persuade people to publish her book."

"Negative publicly?"

"I could imagine her threatening to go to the papers about the way my mother treated me if she didn't pay up. I told her things I've never admitted to anyone before."

"Are you saying your mother abused you?"

"She wouldn't have called it that."

"What did she do?"

"It was mainly emotional. Constant criticism, sarcasm, withdrawal of affection," he paused. "On the odd occasion it became physical."

"Did she hit you?"

"Among other punishments."

"Such as?"

"Being made to sit in a cold bath. Or stand in a corner for hours at a time. It depended which punishment she fancied that day. It was generally one or the other. It's amazing I turned out as well-adjusted as I have. Nowadays social services would probably have got involved."

Linton thought about her own mother. She may not have been there for her, but at least she'd never been cruel. Not in the way that Lauren had.

"And there's no one else you can think of whose name begins with B?"

He cocked his head to one side. "Maybe someone from the book club? You could ask Sally Hughes. She might know."

"Thank you," Linton said, moving forward to pull herself off the sofa. "You've been very helpful."

"Before you go…" he stopped.

"Is there something else?"

He cleared his throat nervously. "I was just wondering." He

stopped again and swallowed. "Would you like to go out for a drink one night?"

It was the last thing she'd expected him say and for a moment she couldn't speak. "I, um, I'd love to," she said eventually, "it's just that…"

He looked down at the coffee table, obviously embarrassed. "I understand. Sorry. You've got a boyfriend. Of course someone like you wouldn't be single."

Linton could feel herself flushing. "It's not that," she said, "it's just that, well, you're involved in the case."

"But surely I'm not a suspect, am I? I mean I've got an alibi."

"But the rest of the team wouldn't see it like that." Or at least Brown wouldn't. And as far as he was concerned the alibi wasn't watertight.

They sat in uncomfortable silence for a moment. Linton was reluctant to leave immediately in case it looked as though she was going because he'd asked her out. She racked her brain, desperately trying to think of something to say.

"So, um, have your family always owned Elmtree Manor?"

As Hampton opened his mouth to answer, a phone started ringing from another room.

"It's probably my broker," he said, jumping up quickly. "He said he was going to ring this morning. And he wouldn't have been able to get me on my mobile. I ought to take it."

"Don't worry," she said, forcing a smile. "It's not a problem. I'll see myself out."

Hampton mirrored her expression with his own lop-sided smile, before turning abruptly and hurrying out of the room.

Linton let a deep breath before pulling herself slowly up from the sofa. *God, that had been awkward.* She was anxious to leave but was suddenly conscious of all the tea she'd drunk.

She wondered if Hampton would mind if she used his bathroom before she left.

Out into the hallway she could hear Hampton's low, reassuring voice coming from kitchen.

"… we've got no choice but to sit it out. The worst thing one can do is panic. With these things it's all about patience and…"

Linton tapped loudly on the kitchen door, uncomfortable about listening in on his conversation.

"Just a second," said Hampton. "Can I help?" he called out more loudly.

"Sorry," Linton said, pushing the door open, feeling herself flushing again as he turned to look at her. "Can I use your loo?"

"Of course. It's down there on the right." He nodded at the phone, "My broker's trying to persuade me to sell some shares." He let out a short laugh. "This could take a while."

"It's fine. I'll be off in a sec."

The cloakroom looked exactly how Linton had imagined it. It was a country gentleman's room complete with green wellies, a well-worn Barbour hanging on a hook in the shape of a Labrador's head and a watercolour of a black horse. The toilet had a chain flush. Pulling it reminded her of school and in turn Miss Hughes, her ex-headmistress. It was odd how everything was connected. People and events all linked together.

She moved over to the sink to wash her hands. Hampton had proper soap, not the squirty disinfectant stuff she always bought; the same brand her granny had always bought because she thought it was posh. She glanced at herself in the mirror as she washed her hands, aghast at how flushed she looked. She rinsed the suds away then splashed cold water on her face, trying to lessen the blush that had spread across her cheeks.

She could hear Hampton still on the phone when she came out of the bathroom so she went back to the front room, grabbed her coat and then hurried out through the back door.

Outside the cold air hit her and with it the realisation of what she'd just done. She was single and she'd turned down a date with a kind-hearted, good-looking man. As she walked back towards her car she wondered what would happen if she turned round now and told him that she'd changed her mind. That she'd love to go out for drink. *No.* That would be stupid, irresponsible. And besides, what about her plan to seduce Brown?

One thing at a time. Talking of which, she hadn't finished her conversation with Keen. She pulled her phone out of bag and rang him for the third time that morning.

"That makes a lot of sense," he said, when she finished her theory. "It would certainly explain how he's not drawing attention to himself. SOCO are still working on Gemma's car, but they've already collected some trace evidence. We're about to send it off. Let's hope the FSS get something back."

Linton shoved her phone back in her bag, pulled out her keys and pointed the fob at her car. As she pressed it, it made a loud clunk and she realised she'd locked it. For a second she was confused until she remembered she hadn't locked it when she'd arrived. She hadn't seen the point, not when it was at the bottom of a long driveway, a few hundred yards from a quiet road.

Which was exactly what Gemma, and the other rape victims, must've done after unpacking their shopping. Left their cars unlocked while they took their trolleys back to the trolley rack. Linton did it all the time.

The rapist must've opened the back door of the car and slipped in; no one would think it odd if they saw a man getting into an unlocked car. They'd assume it was his.

He could've knelt in the large footwell; rested his head on the back seat. As long as he stayed deathly quiet, Gemma and the other women wouldn't have known he was in there. Until he wanted them to.

She climbed into her car and pulled on her seatbelt. As she pulled away, she automatically checked her rear-view mirror and felt her blood spike as she imagined the horror of discovering the face of a man staring back at her.

"There's nobody there," she said aloud.

Of course there wasn't. She was acting ridiculously. Even so, she felt the hairs bristling on her arms and the back of her neck, rising up in fear. She thought of Gemma and her ruined face and her dreadful bruises, not only the ones she could see, but the ones in her mind that would take much, much longer to fade.

***

Mark had told Sheila whilst she was cleaning the cottage. Of course she hadn't let on that it bothered her, but the truth was she was seething, imagining her own hands on that carrier bag, pulling it down over Lauren's head, making her fight for every last breath of air. *Oh, she was a clever bitch.* This was what was meant by talking from beyond the grave. No, not talking, taunting. Letting Sheila know that she could never get away from her.

"Sorry, what did you say, mum?" Heather asked distractedly, when she rang her daughter to tell her. She could hear Toby in the background, *playing up again.*

"She's left me a painting," she said, more loudly this time, carefully accentuating each word, tasting the bitterness in them. "A portrait of *her*. The one that's hanging in her bedroom."

"Well that's good, isn't it?" said Heather, mirroring the rise in her mother's voice, in an obvious effort to be heard over her whinging son. "It's probably worth something."

She just didn't get it, did she? thought Sheila. *She never had.*

She could hear Toby more clearly now. Heather must've bent down because he sounded closer to the mouthpiece. He was whining about being hungry. *Again.* Heather would probably give in to him. She usually did. It was no wonder he never ate his meals properly. He was always snacking on something.

"What's up with him?" she asked curtly.

"He's always like this when I'm on the phone. He's doing it for attention."

What about giving me some for once? Sheila wanted to shout. "What he needs is some discipline," she said.

"Here we go again." Sheila could hear the anger and frustration in her daughter's voice.

"We all know what happens to boys who aren't disciplined."

"Are you going to start on about how he takes after his father? That no good will come of it? Because we all know what happens to boys who get too much."

"What do you mean?"

"Well look at Brandon," said Heather. "Fat lot of good dad's discipline did for him."

"There's nothing wrong with Brandon."

"Come on, mum. I know what you're thinking. Don't pretend you're not. Because I've been thinking the same thing myself."

"I don't know what you mean."

"You know what his temper's like," Heather scoffed.

"It's not that bad."

"Well if he hasn't got a bad temper, then why have you never let me tell him the truth about Toby's dad? It was because you knew Brandon would go after him. That he'd kill him. Just like he killed…"

"Don't be so bloody ridiculous," screeched Sheila, interrupting Heather before she could finish her sentence. "He's my son. I know what he's capable of and it isn't that."

She slammed the phone down. It started ringing a couple of seconds later. Sheila ignored it.

FOURTEEN

"How's Gemma?" Brown asked, as soon as Linton entered the incident room.

"Not good. But I called in on Hampton on my way back," she said, quickly changing the subject, not wanting to talk about her friend.

"And? Does he know who the initial B stands for?"

"Apparently Lauren used to call his ex-wife Betty. Hampton wonders if she was blackmailing Lauren and that's why they met on Monday."

"Blackmailing her? With what?"

"Threatening to tell the papers about the way she treated him as a child if she didn't give her money to fund her drug habit."

"I've been thinking," said Brown. "There's every chance she could've left the country. It might be why we can't find her."

"Do you think we're going to have to widen the search?"

"If we don't get anywhere in the next day or so, we'll see if we can track her through customs."

"That's going to be expensive. Do you honestly think The Toad will sanction it?"

"He might not have a choice if we don't come up with any other firm leads. By the way," he said, rummaging around on his desk until he eventually pulled out a piece of paper. "Hooper's been busy." He leant across his desk and passed it to Linton.

"What is it?"

"The list of all the calls made to and from Elmtree Manor

the night Lauren was killed. The one made *to* the house at 8.45 is interesting."

Linton scoured the typed sheet. There were a number of calls from the same mobile between 8.35 and 8.40. According to the sheet, they were made from Mark Hampton's phone, presumably when he was ringing to ask Lauren if she'd come across his wallet. She looked further down the list until she found the call made to Elmtree at 8.45.

"It says it was made from Sally Hughes' mobile," she said.

"It's odd she didn't mention ringing Lauren when we spoke to her."

"Maybe she forgot. I expect she was just phoning to tell her she'd found her appointment book."

"She couldn't have," said Brown. "She'd only just discovered it. Remember? She said she'd just been hoovering behind the cushions on her sofa." He snorted. "Who bothers with stuff like that? Apart from you of course. Perhaps you and Sally should get together. You could invite Sheila along. Set up your own little group."

"You know what they say, Brown. Cleanliness is next to godliness."

He grinned. "I thought that it was a spotless house is the sign of a misspent life."

"I'll ring Sally, shall I? And once we've swapped cleaning tips, I'll ask her why she rang Lauren and didn't bother mentioning it."

Linton dialled the number but it went straight to answerphone so she tried again, this time more slowly to make sure she didn't make a mistake.

"That's odd," she said. "She's got it turned off."

Brown shrugged. "She's probably like my mum. Only uses it in emergencies. Or rings me then switches it straight off."

"So why use her mobile on Monday night? Presumably she's got a landline."

According to the online directory, she did. Linton rang the number and Sally Hughes answered on the third ring.

"I don't remember ringing Lauren," she said, when Linton explained why she was phoning. "You must have it wrong."

"But I've got the list of calls in front of me. Someone definitely rang Lauren's house at 8.45 using your mobile. Unless it wasn't you."

There was a slight pause and then Sally said, "Oh, of course. You're quite right. I'm getting confused. It's old age I'm afraid. I'm becoming terribly absent-minded." Linton thought of the sharp eyes and keen wit Sally had greeted them with the previous day. Somehow she doubted it.

"So why did you ring her? You'd only seen her ten minutes before."

"I, um, I wanted to double check she'd got home all right."

"Why wouldn't she have? She only lived just up the road and she was driving."

"She seemed a bit shaky when she left, that was all."

"You didn't mention that when we first spoke."

"Why? D'you think it's important? I thought she'd died from suffocation, not low blood sugar." She said it lightly enough, but Linton could detect a wariness in her tone.

"So did Lauren Hampton answer the phone?"

"No. It rang and rang and went straight to answerphone. I didn't bother to leave a message. I didn't see any point."

"Why not?"

"I thought she'd probably gone to bed. She wouldn't get the message until the morning."

"That was thoughtful of you. To ring to see if she was OK. Particularly as you said you weren't fond of her."

Sally Hughes cleared her throat then said, "Whatever my personal feelings are, I believe it's our duty to look out for one another."

"So weren't you concerned when she didn't answer?" Linton pressed.

"Um, not really. I, err, assumed she was too busy to pick up. On her mobile perhaps. Or having a bath."

"Didn't you think she might have collapsed? Especially as you said she was a bit shaky."

"I decided I was being silly. After I put the phone down, I didn't give it another thought."

"Whilst we're on the phone," said Linton. "Is there anyone in the book club with the initial B?"

"Um, no. Not that I can think of."

"Did Lauren ever mention anyone whose name began with B? Either first name or surname?"

"I don't think so."

"Did she ever talk about Mark's ex-wife?"

"Elizabeth? But that begins with E."

Linton jumped as she felt a sudden tap on her head. A rolled up ball of paper bounced onto her desk. She looked over at Brown, his raised arm confirming him as the culprit. He mouthed "mobile" at her and stuck up his thumb.

"Just one other thing before I go," said Linton. "According to the phone records, you called Lauren from your mobile rather than your landline. Why was that?"

"I was upstairs and the landline was downstairs. I was being lazy. I always have it with me."

So if Sally had her mobile with her all the time, thought Linton after she hung up, why hadn't she picked up when she'd called her earlier?

"What did she say?" asked Brown.

Before Linton had a chance to answer, she heard Hooper calling Brown's name. She looked up to see him hurrying across the Incident Room. As he reached Linton's desk, he tripped over a wire, almost pulling her laptop off the table.

"Sorry," he said, reaching forward and grabbing at the computer.

"What's up?" she asked.

"I've just got off the phone with Karen. I didn't get a chance to speak to her yesterday. It's such a massive cast, you see. And there's only me and Wells, so it's taking forever. Anyway, she didn't answer when I phoned yesterday, so I left a message and she's just rung back…"

"Christ, Hooper," Brown interrupted. "Take a breath will you? Who the hell's Karen?"

"She played one of the plates. In *Beauty and the Beast*."

"A plate?" said Brown. "Have you gone mental?"

"You mean you don't know the story," said Linton, triumphantly. "At last! Something you're not an expert on."

"I'd rather stick a blunt pencil in my eye than watch a pantomime."

"So what did this Karen say?" she asked Hooper.

"That Hampton wasn't with Baines the whole time."

"What? How does Karen know that?" Brown was instantly interested, all thoughts of the absurdity of plates put to one side.

"At eight forty, five minutes before the interval finished, she knocked on Hampton's dressing room door. He was due on stage ten minutes into the second half, at eight fifty, and she wanted to check he was ready. She asked him if he was OK. He shouted 'fine', but she was leaning against the door and it swung open. He was sat in there on his own."

"Where was Baines?" asked Brown.

"She doesn't know."

"Perhaps he went to the loo?" said Linton. "Where are they?"

"There's some backstage. Just along the corridor from Hampton's dressing room."

"And Karen was certain it was Hampton she saw?" Linton asked.

"Definitely. She said…"

"Shhh," said Brown, putting up his hand to stop him from going any further. "I need to think it through. Hooper, go and make us both a cup of tea, will you?"

As they watched the trainee detective lope off dejectedly in the direction of the kitchen, Brown said, "I want to go through this, see if we can get the timings to fit. Let's go backwards."

"OK," said Linton, sceptically.

"Let's say for sake of argument Baines nipped to the loo giving Hampton twenty minutes."

"But…"

"He was seen on his own in his dressing room at eight forty."

"Brown, we don't know that…"

"Stop interrupting me," he snapped, "or I'll lose my train of thought. Lauren was killed some time after she got back from her book club at eight thirty. The theatre's only a couple of minutes away by car. Just say Hampton left the theatre at around eight twenty, which was still during the interval, he could've easily driven there, killed her and been back in his dressing room by eight forty."

"But according to the CCTV, his car didn't leave the car park."

"He could've…" he stopped.

"What?"

"I was about to say he could've taken Baines' car from the car park but that's not possible. Baines isn't driving at the moment. He's lost his licence."

"Anyway, if he drove, surely he'd risk someone spotting him."

"Perhaps he ran there."

"Brown! You're completely missing the point. It wouldn't have taken Baines twenty minutes to nip to the loo!"

"It could if he was having a shit."

"You're vile," she said wrinkled up her nose involuntarily. "And anyway, it's still pushing it." She shook her head, as she caught Brown's grin. "That wasn't meant to be a pun. Even if he had twenty minutes, which is a random number you seemed to have plucked out of the ether to fit your theory, I don't think it's long enough get to the manor, suffocate Lauren and come back again and act as though nothing had happened. Besides, it's too risky. Baines could've come back at any moment and found him gone."

Brown grunted. "So why did they both lie and say Baines didn't leave the dressing room?"

"Maybe they just forgot."

"Ring them and find out. And then I'm going to carry out an experiment. See how long it takes me to run to Elmtree Manor and back from the theatre."

"Run? Just because you can do seven-minute miles doesn't mean everyone else can."

"Hampton's a fit bloke," he said with a wink. "Or hadn't you noticed?"

***

Linton phoned Hampton first, acutely aware of the recent conversation she'd had with him. She hoped it wouldn't be awkward.

On the contrary, he sounded pleased to hear from her.

"Of course," he said, when she told him one of the cast remembered seeing him alone in his changing room. "I completely forgot. Jonathan nipped to the loo during the interval. I'm so sorry I didn't mention it before."

"Do you know how long he was gone for?"

"Not very long at all. Probably only five minutes. Ten at the very most."

She rang Baines next. He sounded confused at first; he couldn't remember leaving the changing room at all.

"One of the cast popped her head round the door," said Linton, hoping to jolt his memory. "She saw Mark in the dressing room on his own. At around twenty to nine."

He paused, then said awkwardly, "Of course. I, um, must have nipped out."

"Where did you go?"

"Just a moment please," he said. There was silence for a few seconds, then he came back on the line. "Sorry about that. My secretary needed to ask me something. What were you were saying?"

"You nipped out of the dressing room. During the interval."

"Ah. Yes. Of course! I went to the loo. But I was only gone for about five minutes. Ten at the most."

"About five minutes. Ten at the most, they both reckon," she said to Brown when she finally put the phone down. "In fact their estimation of the timing was identical. I'd like to see you get to Elmtree Manor, commit a murder and get back to the theatre in ten minutes."

***

It was late afternoon when Linton and Brown arrived at the Avalon Theatre. Brown parked as close to the building as possible and they made their way round to the side of it, stopping at the unmarked door which led backstage. There was another door a few metres along with a green fire exit sign attached to it.

"Hampton's dressing room is behind there," said Linton, pointing at the sign. "I remember Baines saying that if it hadn't been for the fire door, they'd have boiled alive in there."

"Hampton could've used that exit to get out without anyone seeing him. He wouldn't have had to go out into the corridor or out through the main backstage entrance."

"I suppose so," said Linton grudgingly.

"Right," said Brown, pulling off his coat and then his jumper and handing them to Linton. "Let the experiment begin."

"Are you going to be able to run in those?" she said, pointing to Brown's trousers.

He shrugged. "It's not ideal, but I'll manage. Luckily I've got a t-shirt under my shirt," he said. "It's so bloody cold at work I've been layering up."

She watched as he slowly unbuttoned his shirt revealing a crisp, white t-shirt. His taut stomach muscles were visible through the thin material. She swallowed hard as she took the shirt from him, resisting an almost overwhelming urge to hold it up to her nose and bury her face in it.

"I'll start from here," he said. "I reckon it's less than a mile each way. I'll use my Roadrunner app. See you in a sec."

She watched as he sprinted off and quickly disappeared around the corner. He looked surprisingly light on his feet, despite his heavy build.

With nothing to do, except pace up and down in a useless effort to keep warm, it felt like Brown was gone for hours. She counted paving stones, the number of cars in the car park, anything that might distract her from thinking about Brown's stomach muscles and toned biceps as he'd handed her his shirt.

By the time he returned, he was deep red. His t-shirt clung to him and sweat was pouring from his face.

"Seventeen minutes and twenty seconds," he panted, as he pulled his mobile from his pocket and studied it. "Six minutes each way. And I waited at the gates to Elmtree for another four."

"So he couldn't have done it," said Linton.

"Why not?" Brown grunted. He was stretching now, putting one leg behind him and pushing down hard on the other, his fists clenched.

"Because Baines said he was only gone for ten minutes at the most. And Hampton agreed."

"Of course he bloody did! He needs an alibi. Anyway," he said standing on one leg and pulling his other one up behind him. "It's easy to misjudge time. How long did you think I was gone for?"

"About half an hour. At least," she said grudgingly as Brown changed legs. "How come you don't fall over when you do that?"

"Because I'm brilliant," he replied grinning. "Hey!" he said suddenly, "I've just had a thought. He could've run it much quicker. If he cheated."

Linton frowned. "What d'you mean?"

"You managed it."

"Brown. I don't know what you're on about. Oh! Shit!" she said smacking her forehead, as she realised what he meant. "He could've cycled." She paused, thinking. "The bloke on the bike! You think it was Hampton after all?"

"It could've been."

"But hang on. What about the other bloke on the bike that he almost knocked over. He was wearing identical clothing: a helmet and fishing gear."

"What if he said that to confuse us? To throw us off the trail. What if there was no other bloke on a bike?"

"But Lauren was about to change the will in his favour. I still don't get why he'd want to kill her now?"

"For fuck's sake Linton. All you ever do is defend the poncy tosser."

"It's called playing Devil's advocate," she said, ignoring the expression of scorn on his face.

Brown mumbled something under his breath.

"What?"

"Nothing," he grunted.

"So what do we do now?"

Brown sighed. "Well we can't arrest him, can we? Not without any evidence. The Toad'll go nuts."

"The results should be back soon," said Linton. "I guess we'll just have to wait until then."

Brown nodded and looked at his watch. "Right, I'm off home for a shower. Let's call it a day. And I'll see you bright and early tomorrow."

FIFTEEN

Brown was in with The Toad when Linton got in to work the following morning.

"Are the results back from the FSS?" she asked Hooper, who was squinting at his computer screen, his face tired and pasty-looking in the unflattering light.

"Maybe," he said, looking up eagerly. "D'you reckon Brown's right? And that it's Hampton?"

She shrugged. She'd lain awake the night before thinking about it and she just couldn't see it. And not just because she couldn't imagine him carrying out such a vicious crime. There were too many things that didn't make sense. The will that was about to be altered in his favour, his alibi from a solicitor who had no reason to lie, Brown's fabricated timings that didn't really fit.

Brown emerged from The Toad's lair a couple of minutes later, looking alert and handsome in a crisp white shirt and pair of dark jeans.

"They found Sophia's diary," he called across the incident room. For a moment, Linton's mind went blank; the name meant nothing to her.

"Lauren's dead daughter," he said, as he reached her. "It's from the year she got pregnant and killed herself. SOCO found it when they were going through the garden."

"Where?"

"In a pigeon tower. Down in the arboretum. It was pushed up inside the chimney."

"Have you got it?" she asked, glancing over at his dishevelled desk.

He shook his head. "It's still with SOCO. They're going to copy it before they send it off for analysis. We should get it later today."

"Shit," she said sitting down. "So we might find out who got her pregnant."

"And who might have a possible motive for wanting Lauren dead."

"So you've changed your mind about Hampton?" she said, taken aback.

"No. I still think it's him. But just in case I'm wrong, which I don't think I am, at least we'll have another avenue to explore. And then if nothing comes of that, we go wider with our search for Elizabeth Hampton."

"OK."

"By the way. How's your friend Gemma?"

Linton shook her head. "Not good. I rang last night but she didn't want to speak to me."

"I hope they find that sick fucker," he said. "And when they do, I'd like to punch his fucking lights out."

***

Sheila picked up Mark's dry cleaning at nine thirty as she did every Saturday morning and had done for more years than she cared to remember.

The fact that Lauren was dead wasn't going to change that. Mark still had to wear clothes, didn't he?

Angela Martin, who worked in Mr K's Cleaning Service, was clearly desperate to know every detail of Sheila's discovery at Elmtree Manor. The woman reminded her of a dog, panting in the hope that Shelia might throw her a scrap of information.

She was determined not to give her a morsel.

"You're not going up there this morning, are you?" she said, in a loud whisper, despite Sheila being her only customer. Her dried-out, wrinkled face was looking even more furrowed than usual.

"I haven't got a lot of choice, have I?"

"Ohhh," she exclaimed, shuddering dramatically, causing her large hoop earrings to tap against her face. "I wouldn't want to go anywhere near that place."

As Sheila drove towards Elmtree Manor it seemed as though her surroundings had taken on a new clarity. The road, the trees, everything she passed looked overly bright, as though someone had taken a highlighter pen to them. She remembered it had happened after Henry died. Was it some sort of delayed shock?

As she reached Sally Hughes' house she had to pull into the lay-by opposite to let a van go past. Sally must've been watching out of the window because just as she indicated to drive away, the woman's front door flew open and she ran out onto the flagstone path.

"Sheila? Sheila?" She could see Sally mouthing her name but she ignored her and pulled out of the lay-by and continued driving. *Silly stuck-up cow.* She'd never once asked her to join their stupid book club, even when they'd bumped into one another at the library and had had a short conversation about their mutual love of Jane Austen. But then Sheila was only a cleaner; the ex-headmistress probably didn't think she was clever enough.

Whatever it was that Mrs Hughes wanted to say, she wasn't giving up. As Sheila pulled up outside Elmtree Manor and opened her car door, she heard the crunch of gravel and turned to see the woman's car racing up the driveway, her wheels spitting tiny pebbles as it moved.

"Sheila!" she called out of her open window. "Can you hang on a second? It's important."

Sheila waited as Mrs Hughes came to a halt and clambered out of her car. She was dressed in a long scarlet coat, her red hair loose, hanging down her back in long tendrils. She could've got away with being twenty years younger Sheila thought resentfully.

"Thank you for waiting," said Sally breathlessly. "There's something I'd like to talk to you about. If you don't mind of course."

Sheila eyed the taller woman suspiciously. Apart from their brief chat in the library, they'd barely exchanged more than five words in the time they'd known each other. There had been the occasional forced 'hello' at parents' evening if she happened to pass her in the corridor, a few choice words from Mrs Hughes at the end of Brandon's school report summing up his school year. He hated the woman, reckoned she had in for him but Sheila knew he probably deserved every punishment she'd meted out to him.

She watched Sally lick her painted lips nervously, enjoying the woman's awkwardness as she waited for her to speak.

"I wanted to ask you something," she said, eventually. "Something rather, um, delicate."

"Go on then," Sheila replied, aware that she was relishing this shift in power. Knowing it was wrong, but taking pleasure in it all the same. "You'll need to be quick though. The house isn't going to clean itself."

"Did Lauren ever say anything? About me. Anything about, well, about my, um, personal life?" Sally said hurriedly, the words tumbling out of her as though she'd been turned upside down and shaken.

Of course she hadn't. Lauren hadn't ever told Sheila anything except what to do, what she'd done wrong, what she could do better. Well, that wasn't quite true. She'd told her something deeply personal once, but that had only been to upset her. Still, there was no need for Sheila to let Mrs Hughes know that. She didn't want the stuck-up cow thinking Lauren hadn't valued her.

"She might've done," she said.

"It's just, well, I was going to ask Lauren not to say anything. You know what it's like round here. How malicious people can be and, well…" She faltered and came to a stop, looking flushed and uncomfortable. Perhaps the rumours that had surrounded her for years were true after all. What was it Brandon had called her when he was at school? Something that rhymed with dyke? Perhaps Lauren had found proof that Sally Hughes was a lesbian. No wonder she was so embarrassed.

"Why didn't you then?" she said coldly.

"What?" Mrs Hughes looked confused.

"Say something to Mrs Hampton."

"Oh, well, I tried to, you see," she continued, the colour of her face deepening as she spoke. "I wanted to speak to her face to face so I walked up here after the meeting on Monday. When she didn't answer the door I tried ringing from my mobile but she didn't pick up. The thing is Sheila. I wondered if, well, if you'd keep what you know to yourself as well. Please?"

"Hello, ladies!"

Sheila jumped, aware that Sally had done the same. They both turned to see Mark Hampton, appearing suddenly from round the corner of the manor house.

"You gave me a fright," Sally admonished him. She paused and Sheila watched as she rearranged herself into an expression of sympathy before saying, 'I'm so sorry to hear about Lauren."

False cow, she thought, *Sally Hughes had probably hated Lauren Hampton as much as everybody else did.*

"Thank you," said Mark, nodding gravely. "Now ladies, if you'll excuse me…"

"Actually Mark," said Sally, anxiously. "Whilst you're here. I, um I wondered if I might have a word with you. In, um, private."

"I'm so sorry, Sally," he said, jangling his car keys. "I'm in a terrible hurry. I've got a meeting I have to get to. I could pop round later if you like?"

"Thank you," said Sally, called out to his retreating back, the relief obvious in her voice. "I'll be in all day."

Sheila turned and began to walk towards the path to the back door.

"So can I rely on you, can I, Sheila?" Sally called after her. "Not to say anything to anyone?"

Sheila carried on walking and didn't answer.

***

A copy of Sophia Hampton's diary was delivered to the incident room later that morning marked for DI Rob Brown's attention.

"This should be interesting," he said to Linton as he pulled the photocopies out of the manila envelope with a flourish. "I might as well start reading them now."

The Toad, however, had other ideas.

"Brown!" he warbled, sticking his head outside the door of his office. "A word please. Now! Come on, chop-chop."

"Bollocks," he said, stuffing the paper back into the envelope. "What now?"

Linton waited until Brown was out of sight then grabbed the envelope from his desk. Sitting back in her chair, she began to read.

It was fascinating, seeing Lauren Hampton through her daughter's eyes. She felt desperately sorry for Sophia and was so engrossed in reading about her treatment on the night of her birthday party that she wasn't aware of Brown until he was standing next to her desk.

"Linton!"

She jumped. "What?" She looked up guiltily, about to apologise for taking the diary without asking but stopped short, suddenly unable to speak. In that moment Brown looked so implausibly sexy, his dirty-blond hair dishevelled, as though he'd just rolled out of bed. She felt her heart squeeze and let go, leaving her momentarily breathless as she thought about the evening ahead, the possibility that something might finally happen.

"Good news."

"What?" she said again.

"We've got some results," he replied, his face breaking into grin. "The FSS came back with the fingernail tissue. And guess who it belongs to."

She knew immediately but all she could think was *thank God* she'd turned down his offer of a drink.

"Mark fucking Hampton," he announced triumphantly, when she didn't answer. "It matches the DNA they took from him for elimination." He did a little victory dance in front of her desk, moving his hips from side to side, clicking his fingers in time. A move that would've made any other man look like an idiot; Brown however, still managed to look cool.

"Ye of little faith," he said, coming to standstill. "I told you. And there you were trying to pick holes on my timings. It looks like he managed to kill her at eight thirty and get back to the theatre by eight forty."

"He'd have had to be back way before eight forty," said Hooper, appearing with two mugs of steaming tea.

"What?" said Brown.

"Karen said he was in full costume when she saw him. He had his beast suit and mask on. So he couldn't have *just* got back from Elmtree."

"Why didn't you say before?" said Brown sharply.

"I tried to tell you but you sent me off. You said you needed to think."

"Well, he must've just chucked it on as soon as he got back."

"I dunno," said Linton, doubtfully. "He wasn't just wearing a beast suit. He had to put on a mask and a wig. Plus a pair of high heeled boots. It would take a few minutes at least. Could he really have killed her and got back to the theatre in about seven minutes? Even on a bike?"

"This Karen woman might've got the time wrong," said Brown. "We've only got her word she saw him at eight forty. It might've been much later."

"Listen to you," said Linton. "You're starting to sound desperate. Why are you so certain it's Hampton?"

"And why are you so certain it's not?" Their eyes met and locked until Linton flushed and looked away.

"Let's get him in," said Brown gruffly, "and none of this eliminating him from our enquiries crap. As far as I'm concerned he's a suspect now."

***

"What I'd like to know, Mr Hampton," said Brown an hour later, as they sat opposite him in one of the interview rooms, "is how someone with a so-called watertight alibi managed to get his skin under our victim's nails."

"I'm sorry?" answered Hampton, looking genuinely confused.

"We've had the results back from forensics," explained Linton. "The thing is, the tissue sample we found underneath Lauren's fingernails, well, it matches your DNA."

"I don't understand."

"No, neither do we."

Hampton laughed. "Well, at least you're honest."

"Those marks you had on your arm," said Brown. "The ones you said were caused by brambles. I want to know how they really got there."

Hampton was silent for a moment. Linton studied his expressionless face, trying to decipher what he was thinking, shifting uncomfortably in her seat. She'd dressed with extra layers, expecting the station to be cold again but the heating had started working and the small room was unbearably hot.

"I'm sorry," he said, eventually, "I should've told you. The thing is I felt terribly guilty after what I'd said to you. About how Lauren could be critical. It was disloyal. She's not here to defend herself and I didn't want to damage her reputation any further."

"Cut the psychobabble crap," said Brown coldly. "And just tell me how you got those scratches on your arm."

"It was nothing. Really. Just something that happened on the morning of the day she was killed. Before I went skydiving."

"I'll be the judge of whether it was nothing. Go on."

Hampton sighed heavily then said, "I called round to the

manor house first thing like I always do, to check that Lauren
was OK."

"And?"

"We were talking in the kitchen and she said something
slanderous about Sally Hughes. I defended her. Lauren was
absolutely furious that I'd contradicted her." He paused then
cleared his throat. "We were sat at the table," he continued,
"and my arm was resting next to hers. She went for me. She
scratched me all the way down my arm, badly enough to draw
blood."

***

"Bullshit," said Brown, the minute they stepped out of the
interview room, leaving Hampton staring after them with a
bemused expression on his face. "His skin wouldn't have stayed
under her fingernails for that long."

"Why not? You saw Lauren's nails. They were like talons.
And we're talking miniscule amounts of skin."

He shook his head. "I'm going to speak to The Toad," he
said decisively. "I want Hampton charged so we can keep him
in for further questioning." He turned and started walking
away in the direction of the incident room.

"What do I tell Hampton?" she called after him.

"Nothing. He can stay there for the time being and sweat
it out. Come on."

"About tonight," said Linton tentatively, as she followed
him back down the corridor, struggling to keep up with his
long strides. "Is it still OK?"

Brown turned and looked at her blankly.

"The wedding reception?" she said, holding her breath.
"Remember? You promised you'd go with me."

"Come on Linton. You're not serious are you? I don't think either of us will be going now do you?"

When they reached the incident room Brown disappeared into The Toad's office. With a sigh, Linton picked up Sophia's diary and started reading again.

***

AUGUST 8TH

The last few days have been agony. All I can think about is Henry, but he's always working in the garden under Mother and Sheila's gaze and I've felt too self-conscious to go over and talk to him. I've spent hours watching him from my bedroom window, willing him to look up, but he never does.

AUGUST 9TH

I couldn't stand it anymore. I made myself a cup of tea and asked Sheila if I should take one out to Henry. I expected her to look at me oddly, but she just said, "That's kind of you," and carried on sweeping the floor.

Henry looked pleased to see me and said he hadn't stopped thinking about me. He's supposed to be playing skittles tomorrow night, but instead he's arranged to meet me in the arboretum in the old dove tower at eight o'clock.

AUGUST 10TH

What an incredible evening!!!

AUGUST 11TH

I don't understand it. I saw Henry today and he completely ignored me.

AUGUST 12TH

I hate him! I took a cup of tea out to him and I asked him what was wrong. He said nothing. I asked him if he was feeling guilty about the other night because of Sheila, and he said he didn't know what I was talking about. Was he feeling guilty, I said again, about making love to me? He looked at me with disgust and said I obviously wasn't right in the head. Why else would I invent something like that? He said he knew I had a crush on him and I was obviously getting carried away with a childish fantasy. He said if I kept making things up like that, then he'd have to tell Mother. He said there were special places for people like me, people not right in the head, and that's where I'd end up.

OCTOBER 8TH

I went to the Doctor today and he confirmed the worst. I will have to tell Henry.

OCTOBER 9TH

Henry laughed when I told him. He said I was going too far with the make-believe. He said I was sick in the head and that if I didn't leave him alone he'd go to the police and report me for harassment!

OCTOBER 29TH

I did it. I finally told Mother. I didn't know what else to do.

I waited for her to go completely crazy, to stand up and slap me or call me a tart, but she said nothing. Instead, she sat staring at the ceiling for the longest time. The silence was worse. Finally she asked me, in a frighteningly calm voice, whether I'd told Henry. I said yes, but he was denying everything. She said that was good as she would hate anyone to find out that her daughter had slept with a gardener. She made me promise not to tell Father I'm carrying Henry's child.

I know I've got off far too lightly. She is planning something.

OCTOBER 31ST

Mother has sacked Henry for theft. Apparently some jewellery went missing from her room after she asked him to change a light bulb in her study. I'm certain she made it up so she had an excuse to get rid of him.

Then this evening I heard Mother and Father arguing. Mother said she wants me to go to London, to have the baby terminated.

Father thinks I should be allowed to decide whether I want to keep it. He also thinks the baby's father should have some say in the matter. He said that if Mother would only tell him the man's name, he could speak to him and perhaps persuade him to marry me. Mother just laughed at him and said he was being ridiculous.

Then she said something so disgusting, I could hardly believe it.

She said if that he tried to talk me out of aborting the baby she'd tell everyone that he raped me. I sometimes wonder if my Mother is mentally ill.

NOVEMBER 1ST

Yesterday was the worst day of my life. I know I'll never get over it.

It was Sheila who found him, when she went to clean his study, slumped over his desk. They can't be sure until they carry out a post-mortem, but they think it was probably a heart attack.

Mother says it was the stress of my pregnancy that brought it on. That it was all my fault.

I HATE her. She is a hypocrite. She acts distraught, breaking down in front of Dr Hunter, falling into the arms of friends who come round to comfort her. But when there is no one else here, she carries about her business as though nothing has happened.

***

The rest of the diary was blank. Linton laid it on her desk, feeling despondent, knowing that only a few weeks later and Sophia would be dead. If only the girl had had someone to talk to, someone who could have helped her.

She knew it wasn't just the diary that had left her feeling so down. It was only now that the evening wasn't going ahead she realised how much she'd been looking forward to it.

SIXTEEN

When Brown came storming out of The Toad's office a few minutes later, the only word Linton could think of to describe his expression was stunned.

"What's up? Not enough evidence."

"What if I said yes?" he snapped. "Would you give me another lecture about dodgy timing and lack of motive and the fact that he's a posh country twat who couldn't have done it because you fancy the arse off him?"

"I take it he said we can't keep Hampton in."

"He's just spent the last five minutes ranting at me."

"About what?"

Brown let out an odd noise, a cross between a grunt and laugh. "We're arresting someone else."

"What?" said Linton, completely taken aback. It was the last thing she'd expected him to say. "Who? Elizabeth Hampton? Has Hooper tracked her down?"

"I can't believe we could have been so fucking stupid!"

"Brown! Who are we arresting?"

"Brandon Martock. That's who." Linton opened her mouth to say something but Brown put his hand up to silence her. "The Toad had a call, while we were in with Hampton."

"And?" she said.

"According to the FSS, Brandon Martock's fingerprints are on the carrier bag."

"So? He's got an alibi. He was at work the night she was killed. He had Millbank School in for a meal. Remember?"

Brown snorted. "Do you know what The Toad said? 'You've spent all this time trying to disprove Hampton's alibi. I hope you put the same effort into disproving Martock's'."

Despite his serious face, Linton couldn't help laughing. He'd imitated The Toad's warbling voice perfectly.

"You're laughing now, but you won't be when…"

"Brown!" They turned to see The Toad storming towards them. "I am pissed off," he yelled. "And that's putting it mildly." He put his hands either side of his head and squeezed, and then in a slightly calmer voice said to Brown, "I hope you don't mind, but I took the liberty of making a phone call. No, actually, I'll rephrase that. I took the liberty of doing your job for you. But before I tell you who I rang and what I discovered, perhaps you could go through something with me point by point."

Linton sensed she was watching a firework, waiting for the flame to travel slowly up the wick before it exploded.

"Sir?"

"Now, let's see," said The Toad in a frighteningly calm voice. "Brandon Martock. He's got a criminal record. He was sacked by Lauren Hampton a couple of weeks ago for allegedly stealing some jewellery. You had him in your sights as the possible perpetrator. Am I right so far?"

Brown nodded, licking his lips nervously. "Yes, Sir."

"But according to your investigation, he couldn't have carried out the crime. And why that was? Come on, chop-chop."

"Because he was at work that night, Sir. He didn't leave the kitchens all evening because they were. busy. They had Millbank School in for a meal."

"And how do you know that? Apart from him telling you?"

"We saw it written up on the board in the kitchen, Sir." Linton could hear Brown's voice falter.

"A board. What sort of board?"

"A blackboard, Sir."

"And explain how a blackboard works."

"You write on it with chalk."

"And when you want to write something else what do you do?"

"You rub it out."

"You rub it out." The Toad paused, then said in a low voice. "I phoned Millbank while you were in with your so-called suspect. They went to The Rowan Tree on Sunday night. Not Monday. Brandon Martock obviously changed the board. And you took it at face value."

"But it wasn't just the blackboard, Sir. The chef backed up his story."

"I don't give a monkey's what the bloody chef said!" he yelled, a glob of saliva exploding from his mouth. "For God's sake! You know you can't take alibis at face value…" He paused and grabbed hold of the back of a nearby chair. His face was the colour of claret and he was breathing heavily.

The Toad's voice was chillingly quiet when he next spoke. "You'd better get Brandon Martock in and find out what he was really up to that night." He turned, staggered slightly, before stomping back towards his office. "And if I hear anymore crap about bicycles and five-minute miles," he barked over his shoulder, "or how long it takes someone to have a shit, I'm going to kill someone."

"Is he all right?" said Linton, under her breath. "He looks terrible."

"It's that bloody diet," said Brown. "Low blood sugar. Shit," he said slumping down at a desk. "You better ring The Rowan Tree. I'll go and tell Hampton he can fuck off home."

***

According to the restaurant manager, Brandon had the weekend off and had gone away.

"Somewhere up north," was the only answer Linton could get. He couldn't be any more specific.

"I need to speak to Jools then."

"Sorry, love. It's not a good time. He's getting everything ready for tonight and..."

"It'll take five minutes," she interrupted. "Or I could ask him to come into the station, in which case you won't have a chef for the evening."

A couple of minutes later, Jools came on the line.

"You lied," she said.

There was a long pause. "About what?"

"The Millbank party coming in on Monday night. They didn't, did they?"

She heard a long exhalation of breath. "I did it as a favour. He's a good mate. And it's not like he did it or anything."

"How can you be so sure of that?"

There was noticeable pause. "It's obvious. You just need a culprit and he fits the bill. You're setting him up."

"Who changed the blackboard?"

"That was Brandon's idea."

"So was he with you all evening on Monday? And you'd better tell the truth this time."

"We were quiet," he said reluctantly. "He had a couple of things to do, so I let him pop out."

"For how long?"

He paused, "Not long. About half an hour."

She estimated the distance to Elmtree from the pub. A minute or so by car. Ten minutes walk, if that. A much more acceptable time frame than the ridiculous one Brown had tried to squeeze Hampton into.

"What time did he *pop* out?"

"About quarter past eight. Look," he said, hurriedly, "he's not a murderer. I've known him for years."

"So if he's not a murderer, what was he doing for half an hour?"

The chef sighed deeply. "He's gonna kill me."

"You're doing him a favour. If he's got an alibi, he can't be charged with murder."

"He's dealing in contraband tobacco. He went back to his flat to meet a delivery and he asked me to cover for him. I could hardly say no, could I? Not when he's been giving me free fags."

Linton remembered Brandon in the courtyard, about to pull the packet out of his jeans and stopping. They were probably fakes and he was worried they'd spot it.

"Where is he now?"

"I dunno exactly. Somewhere up north."

"Can't you be more specific? Bristol? Manchester? Liverpool? He must've said."

"I didn't listen. I never do when he talks about fishing. All I know is he's got a mate who lives next to a river. He's got the fishing rights to it."

"Fishing," she said, thinking back to the man the builder and Hampton had spotted on bike that evening, near Elmtree Manor. "Does he own a pushbike?"

"He rides it to work. It's not against the law, is it?"

"I wouldn't get cheeky if I were you. We may still have you in for perverting the course of justice."

"It was just a favour to a mate. And he's innocent anyway, so what's the harm?"

"What's his mobile number?"

"You can have it, but you won't get an answer. I've tried him before when he's fishing. He'll either be out of range or he'll just ignore it."

***

Jools was right. Brandon's phone was turned off.

"He's probably one of those twats who sits around all weekend waiting for the big one," said Brown.

"By the way," said Linton. "It was Brandon's dad. Henry."

"What was?"

"The man who got Sophia pregnant?"

Brown shrugged. "So it wasn't a blast from the past after all. Anyway, are you still on for tonight?"

"What?"

"There's not much we can do until Martock comes back," he said. "I could do with a few drinks."

***

Linton made it to the salon just in time. She'd booked an eyebrow shape and tint, but was persuaded by Andrea, the beautician, to have her eyelashes dyed as well.

As she lay waiting for the colour to take, she answered Andrea's predictable questions.

Had she had a nice Christmas? Was she going out somewhere nice that evening? What did she do for a living?

"Wow," said the woman, sounding impressed, when Linton told her she was a detective. "That must be fascinating."

"Sometimes."

"You're not working on the Lauren Hampton murder, are you?"

"Er, no."

"Oh," replied Andrea, obviously disappointed. "I've been following it closely on the news. Not in a morbid way," she added hurriedly. "It's just that I knew her quite well. She was one of my clients. She was in here quite often for one thing and another."

A couple of minutes later Linton's eyelashes were ready. The girl handed her a mirror so she could see the result.

"Lovely," said Linton, not even looking at the lashes, only noticing the thin lines around her eyes. The beginning of crow's feet. She'd seen the ad for Botox when she came in. Give it a few years and she'd definitely need some of that.

***

By seven Linton felt like she'd completed a half marathon. She'd left the salon at six, was home by ten past and in that time she'd showered, moisturised, deodorised, blow-dried her hair, eaten a banana, put her make-up on, took it off, put it back on again, eaten a packet of Monster Munch, cleaned her teeth, re-did her lipstick, put her dress on, took it off, changed her bra, put her dress back on again, gulped down a glass of wine, cleaned her teeth again, flossed and gargled with mouth wash.

At seven o'clock she rang Lisa.

"I'm feeling guilty."

"About what?"

"Going to this wedding reception with Gemma the way she is. Do you think I'm bad?"

"Will it make any difference to Gemma if you go? Will it turn back time and stop her from being raped?"

"Well, no, but it seems wrong going out and enjoying myself."

"Well go out and don't enjoy yourself then. The best of both worlds."

She couldn't help laughing. "Thanks, Lisa."

At five past seven her mobile rang. She looked at the number and considered smashing the phone against her bedroom wall.

It was Brown. Bastard! She knew why he was ringing. To give her some shit-poor excuse for why he couldn't make it. Deep down she'd known all along he'd do this, that he'd let her down at the last minute. She could feel a tight, hot lump building in her chest. She'd told Sam she had a date for the night. Now she'd look like a sad cow turning up to the party on her own. Not only that, she'd have to put her plan to seduce Brown on hold and once she'd made a decision, she hated having to go back on it. She wouldn't admit it to anyone, not even Lisa, but she was so sure tonight would be the night that, to put it crudely, she'd shag Brown out of her system once and for all. She was sick of dangling on the edge of this sexual precipice. It was time she threw herself off and got on with her real life.

"Go on then," she said crossly, as she pressed the answer button. "What's your excuse?"

"What d'you mean?"

"For not coming. I know you're ringing to say you can't make it."

"Actually, Mrs Bloody Know All. I was wondering what I'm meant to be wearing."

"Oh." She took a deep breath. "Well some clothes would be good."

"You're hilarious, Linton. What kind?"

"I don't know. Whatever blokes usually wear to evening dos. Smart but casual I suppose." She could hear a phone ringing in the background. No. Surely he wasn't. She felt the tidal wave of relief that had swept through her body promptly recede.

"Where are you?" she asked.

"At work."

"Work?" she screeched involuntarily. "I thought you said there wasn't anything to do until Brandon came back."

"Calm down. I'm going home in a sec."

"It's gone seven. The taxi's supposed to be picking you up in less than an hour."

"Linton, it'll take me five minutes to get changed. I'll see you in a bit."

No, he wouldn't, she thought, flinging her phone across the bed. She knew what would happen. He'd get held up at work. Then he'd ring and say he wasn't coming. And she'd end up arriving late and have to spend the evening explaining why she was at the party on her own.

The doorbell went at three minutes to eight. She yanked it open, expecting the taxi driver, but found Brown instead, leaning against the wall of her porch, looking handsome and relaxed in a dark suit and tie. He looked her up and down and whistled.

"You scrub up well."

"What are you doing here?" she asked confused. "The taxi's supposed to pick you up on the way."

"I thought I'd call on you instead. So it would feel like a proper date." He laughed and then said in a more serious tone, "Honestly Linton. You look stunning."

She felt disorientated, as though she'd opened her door to a parallel universe, where Brown was a charming gentleman and not the irritating big-head who drove her up the wall. It was all wrong, she thought, looking up as the short honk of a horn announced the arrival of their taxi. Well, not wrong exactly, it just wasn't how she'd played out the evening in her head. She hadn't expected him to say anything about the way she looked, let alone pay her a compliment, and had been prepared to secretly fume all the way to the party, annoyed he hadn't noticed her efforts.

Was he serious when he said he wanted it to be like a proper date? She couldn't ever be certain with him, she thought, as he took her arm and guided her down the front path. What she *was* certain of was that she didn't want him to be *too* nice, because then she'd be in danger of actually liking him and that would only complicate things. Sleeping with him had to be about closure, not the start of something new.

She felt unexpectedly self-conscious sitting with him in the back of the taxi. By the time they'd reached the end of her street and pulled out onto the Wells road, neither of them had spoken. She sensed the space between them was more than a physical one, and she could feel it growing as the journey continued. She stared intently at the back of the driver's head, wondering why she wasn't aware of any gulf between them before, and realised they normally filled it with work. Tonight though, it didn't feel right to bring it up and besides, surely they had other things they could talk about? She riffled through her mental filing cabinet, desperate to find a topic, but couldn't. She felt suddenly panicked. Maybe they didn't have anything else in common. Perhaps this evening was one big mistake.

Brown was the first to break the tense silence. "So who's getting married again?"

"I've told you, Debbie and Sam."

"What? Are they lezzers or something?"

"No! Sam's a bloke. I went to college with him."

"Where's the do again?"

"Don't you listen to anything I tell you? They've rented Huntsford House for the evening. It's a disco."

"Is it a proper wedding?"

"What d'you mean?"

"Did they get married in a church?"

"There's a chapel in the grounds of the house. Why d'you ask?"

He grinned and winked. "I just wondered if there were going to be any bridesmaids."

Good, she thought, feeling the gap between them shrink, things felt back to normal.

***

Linton was drunker than she'd anticipated being so early on in the evening. As she crossed the busy dance floor, clutching a drink in each hand, she had to concentrate on navigating the short distance in her heels. She dodged a sweaty-looking usher playing air guitar, stepped around a small, sticky-looking boy skidding to a halt on his knees and decided it was, as Brown had put it, a proper wedding.

He was sat at a table in the corner of the ballroom, nodding his head in time to the music, his tie loosened and shirt sleeves rolled up. He was easily the best-looking man in the room and she felt a jolt of pride and anticipation as she approached him. She handed him his pint and sat down opposite. 'Manic Monday' started playing, accompanied by a bawdy cheer from the gaggle of middle-aged women lined up in front of the DJ, like a row of ailing cheerleaders.

"I love this song," she said. The alcohol had numbed her lips and she was talking like she'd had a dental injection, pronouncing the last word of the sentence as 'shong'.

Brown didn't seem to notice. "Cheers," he said with a smile. He took a long swig of lager and then leant forward, conspiratorially.

"What?" she asked, studying his eyes. His pupils were dilated and she tried to remember if this was a good sign.

"Did you know Prince wrote this?"

"No," she said, shaking her head. "I didn't."

"He fancied Susanna Hoff, so he gave her the song as a present."

"Really?"

Brown nodded earnestly. "It was The Bangles' first hit single."

"I don't suppose you know where it got in the charts?"

"Number two."

"What year was that?"

"Eighty-six."

"Month?"

He paused and rubbed his bottom lip, looking thoughtful. "I'm not sure. Around the beginning of the year, I reckon. Either February or March."

Linton laughed.

"What?" he asked.

"Nothing," she said and took a sip from her drink.

Maybe it was the vodka working its magic, but tonight his infuriating habit of fact-spouting had transformed itself into an endearing trait. She smiled as she imagined him at the dinner table in years to come, filling their children's heads with useless information, as she looked on affectionately.

She was about to ask if he fancied a dance, when his phone rang. It was the fourth time she'd been treated to the *Mission Impossible* theme tune since they'd arrived. She hoped his new choice of ring tone wasn't some sort of omen for the evening ahead. He grabbed it from the table, flicked it open and glanced at the number. Just as he'd done the other four times, he grimaced and quickly flicked it shut.

"It's not work, is it?" she asked again.

He shook his head hurriedly. "It's no one important."

"Why don't you switch it off then?"

"I'd better not."

She shrugged. She'd turned hers off before she'd even left the house, determined nothing would interfere with what she had planned for the evening ahead.

"It's sweltering in here," he said suddenly. "D'you fancy getting some fresh air?"

"OK. Why not?"

As they collected their coats from the cloakroom, a cat sidled out from behind a table and began rubbing its cheek against Brown's ankle.

"Bloody cats," he said, shaking his leg and causing the cat to slope away with a disappointed miaow.

"Is there any animal you actually like, Brown?"

He paused and said, "Seahorses."

She laughed. "That's a no then," as she slipped her arm into her coat.

"I'm being serious," he said earnestly. "They're amazing animals. Did you know they mate for life?"

"How romantic."

"It is! Once they've found their lifelong partners, they link their tails together and stay like that forever." He paused, then said, "Do you know one of the saddest things I've ever seen?" She shook her head. "It was at the Plymouth Aquarium. There was this seahorse swimming round clutching a bit of rope in his tail. He'd lost his mate and they'd put it in as his substitute. To stop him getting depressed."

"God, Brown," she said and laughed. "You're going to have me in tears in a minute."

"I tell you what," he said seriously, buttoning up his coat. "I nearly was. It was only because I had my niece with me that I held it together."

"Christ," said Linton as they stepped outside. "It's bloody freezing."

"We could go back in if you like?"

"No, I could do with a bit of air to clear my head."

"Let's walk down there," said Brown, pointing past a group of wedding guests puffing furiously on their cigarettes, towards a small chapel overlooking the lake.

Instead of marching ahead, he let Linton set the pace, keeping in time with her stride.

"Late eighteenth century, I reckon," he said, as they approached the chapel. The stone path leading to the entrance was still strewn with pieces of paper confetti and dried rose petals from the ceremony earlier.

Brown mounted the uneven stone step in front of the wooden door, grabbed at the hooked metal handle and pushed hard against the door. A sudden vision flashed across Linton's mind, of them naked and writhing on a cold, stone floor.

"It's locked," he said, turning to look at her and his disappointed expression made her wonder if he was thinking along the same lines.

"Do want to go back to the party?" she asked, hoping he'd say no.

"Why? Are you cold?"

She shook her head, hoping he wouldn't notice her teeth were chattering.

"Look," he said, "there's a bench over there. You can put my coat on over yours," he said, unbuttoning it from the top.

The seat overlooking the water was crafted from a tree trunk. They sat down and Brown took off his coat and wrapped it round her, then handed her the bottle of sparkling wine he'd minesweeped from a table in the dining room. She took a greedy gulp and handed it back to Brown.

In front of them a pair of swans glided majestically along the water, leaving lengthy ripples in its wake.

"What about swans?" she asked. "Do you like them?"

"Nah. They're horrible, vicious things."

"So only seahorses?"

He turned to her and grinned. "Only seahorses."

Somewhere in the distance she could hear the low rumble of an aircraft, no doubt heading to some exotic location, but for once she wasn't envious. At this precise moment, she thought, there was nowhere else she'd rather be.

Brown passed the bottle back to her. They were close, but not quite touching, and she could hear the steady rise and fall of his breathing. She carried on watching the swans, but hardly taking them in. All she could think about was how he might feel against her. She experienced a throbbing ache of lust and was seized by an urge to push him off the bench onto the damp grass and climb on top of him. She sensed him shifting on the seat and felt his thigh press against hers. Her coat fell open and a moment later she could feel the heat of his leg through the thin material of her dress. She carried on staring ahead, but she knew he'd turned his head and was looking at her.

"Kate," he said. *Kate? He never called her that.* His voice sounded low, gravelly, as though he'd struggled to get the word out. But just as she turned to face him, *Mission Impossible* rang out again.

"Fucking hell!" he said and jumped up from the bench, pulling his phone roughly from his pocket.

"Just answer it! Then they might leave you alone."

He put the phone to his ear and walked away.

Linton could hear him mumbling, but couldn't make out any actual words. He edged closer to the lake and began to pace up and down. It was funny, she thought, as she took a large gulp of wine. Instead of breaking the mood, his moving away had merely made things more exciting, added to the anticipation. Now she couldn't wait for him to come back to the bench.

Except that when he did his face looked white and pinched; like someone had kicked him in the stomach or worse. He looked like he was in shock.

"Shit? What's happened?" *Please don't let it be a death*, she thought. She was crap with stuff like that.

"You're not gonna believe this," he said.

***

Sheila caught herself doing it again, staring at the TV, not taking anything in, tormenting herself instead with all the 'what ifs' and the 'if onlys'.

Conversations from the past would rise up from the depths of her mind, like bloated bodies bobbing to the surface, too buoyant for her to force them under again. More often than not, it would be the one she'd had with Henry, after she'd shown him the letter from Bristol University, telling her they'd accepted her on to their English Literature course.

"What d'you want to go for?" he'd asked, tears welling up in his eyes.

"Because it's what I've always wanted to do," she'd replied gently. "You know how much I love books."

"More than me, you mean?"

"No. Of course not."

"Please don't go, Sheila. I love you more than anything in the world. And I thought you loved me. I don't know what I'd do without you."

"Look, I'll still be able to see you every weekend."

"It's not the same though, is it? People will try to change you. They'll fill you up with ideas."

If only she'd told him she was going, that nothing he said or did was going to stop her then maybe the heated exchange wouldn't have taken place two weeks later.

"What have you done? You said you'd stop before you…"

"I'm sorry. I got carried away."

Nor would they have had the inevitable conversation, two months later.

"Henry. I'm pregnant."

"So why are you crying? That's brilliant news, Sheila."

"But what about my place at Bristol?"

"What about it? We'll get married. It'll work out. You'll see. And Mrs Hartry is retiring soon. They're going to need a housekeeper. We'll be all right."

Sometimes Sheila had a picture of a woman in her head. She looked like her, only happier. She was the woman who'd never met Henry. The one who'd gone off to University and gained a first in English Literature, the one who'd got a job working for a publishing firm in London and gone on to publish her own novel to worldwide acclaim. She lived in a house that was bright and colourful and lively, full of loving grandchildren and exciting friends. Sometimes it disturbed Sheila how much she hated this woman.

For having the life that was rightfully hers.

***

Brown was sitting on the bench, his head in his hands, the stereotyped recipient of bad news. "I don't fucking believe this," he mumbled.

"Brown. Please! Just tell me. Who was on the phone?"

"Kelly. Kelly Turley." It took Linton a second to remember who she was. PC Turley. She'd been seconded from Devon to work with them on the Ley Line Strangler case. She'd had a thing about Brown and he'd taken her out for a drink the night after the case ended.

"What's happened to her?"

"She's pregnant."

Linton was about to ask what that had to do with him, when the realisation hit her. The night he took Turley out. The same night he'd phoned Linton from the nightclub.

Christ! Talk about having a bucket of cold water thrown over you. Brown may as well have picked her up and chucked her head first into the lake.

"So, is she…?" she faltered.

"Keeping it?" he said nastily. "I dunno. She says she wants to think about her options."

"I was only asking."

She picked up the bottle of wine and put it back down on the bench again. The thought of the sweet, flat liquid made her feel nauseous.

"And it's definitely yours."

"She's not a slag, Linton."

"I never said she was."

He mumbled something but she couldn't catch it.

"Didn't you use something?"

"I'm not fifteen, Linton. Of course I bloody used something, it must have split."

"What are you going to do?"

He stood up suddenly and glared at Linton. His face looked twisted, ugly even.

"For fuck's sake, Linton," he said, spitting the words out, like they were pips in a grape. "You're not my mum."

"Hey," she said, standing up, not liking the way he was towering over her. "There's no need to get shitty with me. I'm not the one who fucked up."

"No. You never do though, do you? Mrs Fucking Perfect, always in control of everything."

"What's that supposed to mean?"

"You and your fucking high standards. It's no wonder you're on your own."

"Hang on a minute. I've just got out of an eight-year relationship so I'm hardly…"

"And why was it you split up? Let me think. Oh, I know, it's because he didn't match up to your… oww!" he squealed. "What the fuck d'you do that for?" he bent down, clasping his shin.

"You fucker," she hissed, clutching at her toes, hoping she hadn't broken any when she kicked him. "What Ben did was wrong."

"Yeah, it was. But he was drunk. He made a stupid mistake…"

When she found her voice, it sounded unnaturally sharp and high.

"A mistake? You know what, Brown? You're the one who's going to end up on your own if you think what Ben did was part and parcel of being in a relationship with someone. You've got some fucked-up views. I pity Turley. She hasn't got a clue what she's let herself in for."

"Fuck you," he hissed. "You don't know anything about it," and with that he turned and began to storm off in the direction of the house.

"Where d'you think you're going?" she shouted after him.

"Home. I'll get a taxi."

"Good. Maybe now I can finally start enjoying myself, you misogynist pig."

He didn't bother looking round, just stuck his hand in the air and gave her the finger.

"Go swivel on it," she shrieked at his departing back.

Fucking, fucking, fucking fucker! She wasn't going to let him get away with talking to her like that.

She started striding after him and then stopped. What would it achieve? She was drunk and she'd only end up saying something she regretted. She was going to have to face him at work as it was. She took a deep breath and realised she was shaking. She could feel hot tears running down her face. Where had they come from?

Her handbag was on the bench. She probably had some tissues in there. She went to grab it and noticed Brown's key ring on the grass, with its three keys attached. It must've fallen out of his pocket when he'd pulled his phone out.

Ha! she thought, bending down to pick it up. It was Saturday night and his flatmate always went out. With any luck he'd stay at Joker's until it closed at two. Linton had a fleeting, enjoyable vision of Brown sitting morosely on his doorstep, shivering in the cold, as he waited for Steve to come home so he could get in.

Good, it would serve the bastard right, and with that thought she raised her right arm and flung the keys as far as she could into the water, causing a ruffle of feathers and indignant honking from the swans.

She staggered back onto the bench, thinking about the clean sheets she'd put on her bed that morning in anticipation. She pulled her phone out of her clutch bag to ring for a taxi and switched it on. There was a message from Lisa, saying she'd gone round to see Gemma, who was still no better. *That's what she should've done*, she thought. She should've spent the evening with her friend instead of acting like a selfish cow and going to a party. Tonight's crappy outcome served her right.

The taxi picked her up from the top of the driveway. She was glad it was a different driver to the one who'd taken them. She didn't feel like having to explain why she was leaving the party early and alone. Sitting back in her seat, comforting herself once again with the thought of how incensed Brown would be when he realised he was locked out of his house.

"D'you mind taking a quick detour?"

As she approached Brown's house, she asked the driver to slow down. She wasn't sure what she was planning to do when she saw him; stop and apologise or give him the finger through the taxi window but in the end she didn't have to make a decision because his house looked dark and empty and he wasn't sitting waiting on his door step, as she'd expected.

When she got home she withheld her landline number and rang his mobile. He answered with an upbeat "Hello?" There was loud music and a cackling laugh in the background. Joker's. "Kelly? Is that you?" She hung up.

Brown's words came back to her. Did she really have impossibly high standards, expecting her boyfriend to be faithful? If that's what Brown thought, then she didn't want anything more to do with him.

Maybe tonight she'd got him out of her system after all, just not in the way she'd intended.

SEVENTEEN

It was almost midday and Sheila had just finished cleaning Mark's cottage. A routine had developed since he'd moved back to the Manor after splitting up with his wife. Lauren had insisted on a lie-in on Sunday, whereas Mark liked to be up, tearing off to the skydiving centre at some ungodly hour, so Sheila would take Lauren her newspaper and cup of tea in bed, then make her way over to Mark's cottage for three hours of cleaning before traipsing back to prepare Lauren's lunch and tidy the mess she'd invariably left from the evening before.

There would be no lunch to make today. Once Sheila had put the bin bag from Mark's kitchen into the dustbin, she was finished for the day. As she made her way round to the back of the cottage, her eyes were reluctantly drawn to the small grass-covered mounds and gravestones on the lawn just beyond.

Six small lumps.

She had known and loved all the inhabitants of those graves; still thought of them fondly. Bailey, Bella, Princess, Rusty, Zeus and poor, poor Winston.

She remembered the smell of burning fur and fat; Lauren running across the lawn, her face maniacal and distorted. She shuddered. She hadn't thought about it for such a long time, had buried the hideous memory in the depths of her mind along with everything else.

***

Brown was at his desk when Linton arrived.

"What are you doing in?" he said, tersely.

"Same as you."

"Not much point, is there? Brandon Martock's not back in town until tomorrow."

"I've got some stuff to catch up on."

"So have I."

"By the way. I brought your coat back in."

Brown took it from her with a grunt and chucked it on the floor in a heap. After ten minutes of tense silence, Linton couldn't stand it any more.

"Look, I'm sorry about what I said last night," she blurted out. "It's got nothing to do with me. I was pissed. And I spoke out of turn."

"It's fine," he said, his tone icy. He carried on typing, not looking up from his screen.

"I went back in after you left," she said. "Had a few drinks. And a dance. Caught up with my mates," she giggled manically then shut up. God, she sounded like a lunatic. "How about you?"

He shrugged. "Got a taxi straight home and went to bed. By the way," he said suddenly looking up. "You didn't come across any keys, did you?"

"Keys?" She shook her head vigorously.

He tutted. "I'm gonna have to break the lock on my shed now."

"That's annoying."

"I had visions of you finding them and chucking them in the lake."

"Give me some credit, Brown," she said. "I'm not that immature."

***

MONDAY NIGHT – SIX DAYS EARLIER

Lauren Hampton sat back in the saggy armchair in Sally Hughes' living room and surveyed the gathering of worn out, wrinkled faces, thinking how much she adored secrets. She had plenty of her own and knew plenty of other people's. One of them belonged to someone who was sat in this very room, entirely oblivious to how much Lauren knew about her sad little life.

"Secrets are like vicious dogs," she once told an interviewer, pleased with the sound bite she'd come up with to show the pompous git she was more than just a pretty face. "Let them out and you run the risk of them attacking other people. But if you don't and you're not careful, eventually they may turn on you."

She first became aware of their worth when she was eight. Intent on stealing a cake she'd tiptoed into the back of her father's bakery to find him running his hand down the stubble-pricked cheek of Jim, the delivery man. He sprang back, as though he'd scalded his hand on one of the baking trays, but it was the expression of horror on his face that told her she'd caught him red-handed.

Years later of course, she understood the reason for her father's reaction, but, as a child, all she knew was she'd witnessed him doing something he shouldn't have. That day she had a choice of any cake she wanted, even though there was only half an hour until lunch time.

"Don't tell your mother," he said. But she knew her father wasn't referring to the cream bun she eventually picked.

With his offer and her acceptance of the confectionery, an

unspoken deal was made; the caressing of Jim's cheek would be their secret.

And from then on, he could never say no to Lauren; he gave her whatever she wanted. All she had to do was look at him the way she had in the bakery. But most importantly the incident had taught her something invaluable. Secrets gave her power.

Over the years she'd become an expert at discovering them. She was rather like a ferret, she thought, amused by the irony, since she'd always hated the stinky little creatures her father insisted on keeping when he was alive. He'd loved their long, lean bodies and inquisitive nature.

"Nosey little buggers," he called them.

When she was older, anxious for knowledge, she'd read that their name was Latin for 'little thief', thanks to their instinct for secreting small things away in hiding places.

"Ferreting's an art," her dad would claim. And so was unearthing a secret. It required patience and persuasion. Once she had one in her teeth, it was up to her whether she kept it or released it back into the wild.

She was good at keeping them. Perhaps it was because she had what her mother called 'grit'. She preferred to call it 'resolve'. It's why she was still the weight she was when she first married, had given up smoking the moment a wrinkle had dared appear on her face and why she hadn't shed a single tear when those solemn policemen had rapped on the door of her Maida Vale flat all those years ago to tell her that her only child was dead. If it wasn't for all the publicity surrounding Sophia's death, she'd have kept the way she died a secret too.

Sometimes secrets were left carelessly out in the open, simply waiting to be discovered. Like the one she'd come across a couple of days ago.

"So how's your husband, Sandra?" Lauren asked, over the buzz and chatter of the other women crammed into Sally's ridiculously colourful mish-mash of a living room. It was Monday night and it was the weekly meeting of the book club, something Lauren enjoyed attending for her own amusement as much as anything.

Sandra looked up from the sofa surprised.

"Um, he's fine, thank you."

Lauren had never paid much attention to the woman before, had only thought of her as someone's wife. She'd barely registered on her radar. She was insubstantial, almost blurry at the edges. This evening though she studied her more closely; her bumpy, white legs, the hideous flesh-coloured top that did nothing to enhance her sallow skin tone.

Lauren looked down at her own sheer legs, crossed gracefully at the ankle. She was wearing stockings. Her matching lingerie set was black and lacy – the underwear of someone thirty years younger. And why not? She still had the figure of someone half her age.

"Keeping busy, is he?" she continued. "I've always thought he's such an attractive man."

Sandra looked up again and nodded. "Um, I suppose he is."

Lauren left a pregnant pause then said, "It's funny. I'd have never put you and Jon together."

"What do you think of our choice for next week, Sandra?" Sally interrupted hastily. "Have you read *The Time Traveler's Wife*?"

"Err, no I haven't." Sandra was looking flustered, unused to all this sudden attention.

"He was on the high street," said Lauren, continuing as though nobody had spoken. "But I didn't get a chance to speak to him. He looked so well, I thought. Glowing, if a man can actually do that. Have you been away somewhere?"

Sandra shook her head. "We're hoping to go to Majorca in September though."

"Majorca," said Lauren, careful to pronounce it properly, My-or-ca, like the locals. "It must be love that's responsible for his glow then. And after all your years together. Isn't that wonderful?"

"I don't know about the rest of you, but I'm parched," said Sally, standing up abruptly. "Why don't we stop for a cup of tea? Sandra. Do you want to give me a hand?"

The two women returned a few minutes later, both carrying a large tray, one with a teapot and biscuits, the other with an assortment of mugs and cups.

But Lauren wasn't finished yet. As Sandra helped herself to two biscuits from the plate being handed round, Lauren put her head to one side and said, "You are lucky, Sandra, being the sort of woman who's happy with a fuller figure and indulges her appetite. I've always had to watch what I eat, but I suppose years of modelling taught me to be disciplined. I wish I could have a more laissez-faire approach to the way I look. You're fortunate that your husband obviously likes women with something he can grab hold of, otherwise you'd be worrying that he might stray."

She smiled to herself as Sally jumped up and clapped her hands together. "Right, ladies. I think it's time we get back to talking about the book. Don't you?"

Of course Sally knew exactly what she was hinting at, thought Lauren. Sandra's husband was having an affair, and they both knew who with. Not that poor Sandra had any idea.

Secrets, thought Lauren. They could be such fun!

EIGHTEEN

Brandon Martock was brought in for questioning within minutes of arriving back in Glastonbury.

His skin looked pallid and greasy and there was a small, red lump on his unshaven skin that looked to Linton like the beginnings of a boil. He certainly didn't have the look of a man who'd been away on a fishing trip.

"I'll ask you again," said Brown, "how did your fingerprints get on the carrier bag used to suffocate Lauren Hampton?"

"And I'll tell you again, I don't know. But it's bloody convenient, isn't it? You find someone with a police record and their DNA happens to be on the murder weapon. It's a set-up."

"And why would we set you up?" asked Linton.

"Because you've got no one else for it."

"Tell me, Brandon," said Brown, leaning forward onto the table, so his chest was resting on his clasped hands, "if you didn't murder Lauren and you've got nothing to hide, why did you lie about Monday night? According to Jools, you left the restaurant for half an hour, around the time Lauren Hampton was killed."

Brandon pulled firmly on his index finger. It made a cracking sound, as though he'd snapped a bone. Linton winced. "I didn't kill her," he said.

"So why lie?"

Another crack. "I knew if I told you where I really was that I'd be in the shit."

"So you've got an alibi?"

Linton watched him about to pull on another finger and snapped, "For God's sake, can you stop doing that?"

Brandon let go of his hand and shrugged. "I can't say who I was with."

"Jools told us you were meeting someone. About some contraband tobacco, is that true?"

Brandon swore under his breath.

"So, come on. You might as well tell us who you were with."

"My life won't be worth living if I tell you."

Brown leant forward even further and said in a low, menacing tone, "Or is it because your alibi doesn't actually exist?"

"He does," said Brandon, leaning forward himself. Linton wondered how long it would before their noses actually touched across the table.

"Then you'd better tell us. Come on, Brandon. Is it worth going to prison for something you didn't do?"

"Like I said, my life won't be worth living if I tell you. And anyway. I didn't kill Lauren, so I've got nothing to hide. And all you've got to go on are some fingerprints on a bag. Anyone could have picked it up. It was lying round the house. Circumstantial. You'll never get me on it." He sat back in his chair with a look of triumph.

"You're a fisherman, aren't you?" said Brown.

Brandon's eyes narrowed suspiciously. "What's that got to do with anything?"

"And you own a pushbike?"

He shrugged. "I don't use it much."

"How about on Monday night? Did you cycle to work?"

"I might've done," he said cagily.

"Yes or no? We can check easily enough."

"It was late and it was quicker than walking."

"And did you happen to be wearing your fishing gear when you popped out that night?"

Brandon's eyes narrowed. "I was wearing my work clothes. And I'm not stupid. I can see where this is going."

"What about a helmet?"

He laughed. "Give me a break. They're for kids. I suppose the bloke who killed Lauren was wearing fishing gear and riding a bike. I can't be the only bloke in Glastonbury that fits the bill."

"But as far as we know, you're the only bloke in Glastonbury who was sacked by Lauren Hampton for stealing from her."

"I didn't steal anything," he said, emphasising each word. "She lied. I don't know why, but she did."

"I bet that made you cross. Being accused of something you didn't do."

"And I didn't kill her out of revenge. You can go on at me for as long as you like. I'm not going to admit to something I didn't do. I didn't kill Lauren Hampton."

***

"What do you think?" asked Linton when they left him.

"Opportunity, motive, forensic evidence, no alibi," said Brown gruffly. "You know what I think."

"But is it enough to charge him?"

"We've got another eighteen hours before we need to make that decision. And in the meantime, we've got SOCO taking his flat to pieces. They might find something. Even if they don't, I'm ninety-nine per cent certain we've got our man. It all fits. The carrier bag, the silver pot going missing. The bike and the fishing kit."

"But what about the helmet? Our witness said the bloke on the bike was wearing one. So did Hampton. I can't imagine Brandon wearing a helmet. Like he said, it's for kids."

The word hung in the air like a bubble, waiting to be ducked or prodded. Brown's mobile saved them from making a choice.

"SOCO," he said tightly, looking at the caller display as he picked up.

After a couple of second his expression changed, his jaw set in steely determination.

"They found something."

***

When they returned to the interview room, Brandon was still sitting at the table, picking at a piece of skin on his lip with a dirty thumbnail.

"We've found something in your shed, Brandon."

"So?" he said, continuing to pick.

"Aren't you going to ask us what it is?"

"I'm sure you're going to tell me anyway."

Linton and Brown took their seats opposite Brandon. Brown clicked open his case, pulled out a folder and took out a photograph.

"For the benefit of the tape recorder, we're showing Brandon Martock exhibit 6.1." He pushed the photograph across the table. "Have a look, Brandon, and tell me what you see."

Brandon glanced at it then looked up his expression defiant. "It's a picture of Lauren Hampton's living room."

Brown pointed at the photograph. "And tell us what you can see on that table over there."

"A silver pot. Look, I know where this is going. Before you start accusing me of anything, I didn't steal it."

"So why did we find one that looks identical in your shed? Hidden under a dust sheet."

"I live with a couple of druggies, so I'm hardly going to leave it lying around the place. I hadn't had a chance to get it valued. I've got a job you know, which is where I'm supposed to be now."

"So are you saying that the silver pot we found on your premises belongs to you?" said Linton. Brandon turned to her, his eyes narrowed with spite, a small bobble of blood on his ravaged lip.

"It was in my shed, wasn't it?" he said aggressively. "You do the maths."

"Where did you get it, Brandon?" said Brown tersely.

"You won't believe me if I tell you."

"Try me."

"Mark Hampton gave it to me."

Brown laughed. "What? For your birthday?"

"He felt guilty about having to lay me off. He knew I could sell it and make a bit of money from it."

"When did he give it to you?"

"One day this week. Maybe Wednesday? It was definitely after Lauren was found dead. That's why he gave it to me. He knew she wasn't exactly going to miss it."

"And you expect us to believe that."

"It's the truth."

"We'll just have to see what Mr Hampton says."

***

"You can ring him," said Brown sullenly, as they left Brandon in the interview room still picking at his bloody lips.

Hampton answered on the second ring.

"We found the silver pot that's missing from Lauren's drawing room," she said. "I just want to double check something. Did you give it to Brandon Martock?"

His laugh was all the proof she needed. "Why on earth would I do that?" He sounded genuinely amused.

"He says you gave it to him because you felt guilty. About Lauren giving him the sack."

"I gave him some cash when I had to let him go. A month's wages. Nothing else." He paused. "So I'm guessing you found it on him. Do you think he killed her for it?"

"We don't know yet."

"But have you arrested him? For her murder?"

"I can't say."

"I take that as a yes. Christ!" he said taking a deep breath. "I know he was angry when he got the sack, but I wouldn't have expected this. Look," he said quickly, "before you ring off. I know I've asked you before, but I don't suppose you've changed your mind about going out or that drink."

She glanced over at Brown's surly face. "I'd love to," she said.

NINETEEN

The following morning Brandon Martock was charged with murder.

"There's one thing that still doesn't add up," said Linton.

"What?" Brown snapped. She noticed there were dark circles under his eyes and she wondered how much sleep he'd had.

"The purple earrings," she said. "Why didn't they have any prints on them? It doesn't make sense."

"I've been thinking about that. I reckon Brandon swapped them over. Put some cheap earrings in her ears and took the more valuable ones after he killed her."

"Shouldn't we ask him? See if that's what happened?"

"Why? So he can say he knows nothing about them? Look, Brandon Martock did it. If he didn't, he'd tell us who he was with on Monday night. All that bollocks about being too scared. He's just covering up the fact he hasn't got an alibi."

"There's always a chance he isn't. What if he knows there's someone in prison, connected to the contraband tobacco? Someone who could hurt him. It happens."

"For fuck's sake! His prints were on the bag, the silver pot was in his shed. End of."

"But it's circumstantial. The bag could've been planted. What if the case falls apart in court? We're back where we started."

"Linton," he said. "I'm tired and I'm pissed off and I don't want to talk about this any more."

"You're tired and pissed off because of what's going on in your personal life. I'm worried that it's affected your decision to charge him."

"Really?" Linton could hear genuine anger in his voice. "So who killed her then? Hampton? You've spent the last few days destroying any theories I came up with about him."

"There's no need to shout. Anyway I wasn't talking about Hampton. What about his ex-wife, Elizabeth? We could still track her down."

"Give it a rest, Linton. Brandon Martock killed Lauren Hampton. Now just leave it, will you?"

At five o'clock Mark Hampton rang Linton and asked her if she'd like to meet at The Rifleman's Arms that evening.

She said she'd love to.

***

Sheila sat at her classroom desk, watching nervously as her fellow students drifted in. She'd arrived early on purpose and constructed a no-go zone around herself, her handbag on one chair, her coat on the other, in the hope of avoiding having to speak to anyone. Thanks to the previous week's introductions, they all knew she was Lauren's housekeeper and the fear of being the centre of attention had made her question whether she should come tonight. But in the end she'd forced herself. Lauren had ruled over her life enough when she was alive. She'd be a fool to let her carry on now she was dead.

There were only two men enrolled on the course. The one with the leather jacket and greying quiff was yet to arrive. The other, who had aspirations of becoming a crime writer, sat two seats down from her. He leant over, garbled a quick 'hello' and said breathlessly, "I heard it was you who found her body. Was it dreadful?" Luckily the lively entrance of Miranda, with her cheery, "Evening, everyone!" meant Sheila was saved from having to answer.

"Tonight," announced their teacher, when everyone had finally settled down, "we're going to have a look at writing about what you *know*. As an exercise, I'd like you to draw on an event or a period in your life and think about how it may have helped to shape your present. Don't worry if you don't get it completed in class, you can finish it off for homework, and next week you can share what you've written with the rest of the class."

**

"I've finally given in," said Hampton as he placed his pint of real ale down on the table.

"To what?" asked Linton.

They were sat by the open fire, logs crackling in the hearth, giving off a mossy, woody smell. Hampton's face looked ruddy and glowing. He'd apologised when he arrived, for looking so formal in a suit and tie but he'd had a meeting that had overrun.

"An exclusive with one of the tabloids," he said pulling a face. "About my life with Lauren."

If Linton hadn't had two double vodka and tonics on an empty stomach, she might have covered up her disgust more effectively but she couldn't help saying. "God. That's a bit tacky, isn't it? Sorry," she said immediately. "I didn't mean it like that. It's just that…"

"It's fine," he said, smiling reassuringly, "whenever I read these things, I think it's rather tawdry. But they offered me so much money, I couldn't resist."

She must have looked even more affronted because he laughed and said, "Don't worry. I'm giving it all to a charity I support. It's called Comrades."

Linton shook her head. "I don't think I've heard of it."

"Not many people have. It offers advice and counselling to men subjected to domestic abuse."

There was an awkward pause, while they sipped from their drinks then she asked gently, "Mark, what exactly did your wife do to you?"

He put his drink down and looked around at the occupants on the tables either side of them. Obviously satisfied they weren't being observed, he began to unbutton his shirt.

"What are you doing?"

"Showing you."

When he got to the fifth button, he pulled it open revealing his naked chest beneath. She flinched. A patch of skin, the size of her palm, was puckered and scarred.

"Christ. What happened?"

"Boiling water. Elizabeth was cooking pasta at the time. I'd had a shower and was in the kitchen with a towel wrapped round my waist. She said she didn't want me going out that night, even though I'd planned it for weeks. She started screaming at me, saying I was hardly ever in, which wasn't true of course. Then she snatched the saucepan off the hob. I knew instinctively what she was going to do, so I grabbed her arm to try and stop her, but she flicked it at me and the boiling water hit my chest." He grimaced, as though remembering the pain. "It's lucky," he said. "I think she was trying to go for my face."

"Did you report her to the police?"

He shook his head. "Looking back now, I can't believe I didn't, but it had got to the point where I took her behaviour for granted. The worst thing was she didn't show any remorse afterwards. I had to drive myself to hospital. I couldn't even put my seatbelt on, it was so bloody painful. When I came back, she was sat watching television as though nothing had happened. She didn't even mention it."

They chatted for a while, the conversation moving easily from subject to subject. He was easy to talk to and Linton found herself telling him things she only reserved for her best friends, including the story of her bi-polar brother and how he'd recently tried to commit suicide.

"That's terrible," he said, when she finished the depressing tale. "When did you last see him?"

"A couple of weeks ago," she said, feeling guilty she'd allowed a fortnight to slip by so quickly. She'd promised herself she'd visit him once a week when he was sectioned. "But I'm going to see him tomorrow night," she said, making her mind up as she said it.

"Come on, it's late," said Mark eventually, with regret in his voice. "I'll walk you home." She looked around, surprised to find they were the only ones left in the snug.

"You don't have to," she said. "I'm only round the corner."

"I wouldn't dream of letting you," he said picking up his briefcase from the table. "I don't need to tell you there's a rapist on the loose."

She could've said she was a policewoman, that she was capable of looking after herself, that the rapist was targeting women at supermarkets so she was hardly under threat, but she didn't. She realised that she wanted him to walk her home.

"I keep hearing about it on the news," he said, as they slipped through the back gate of the beer garden that led out onto the pavement. "It's not the sort of thing you expect to happen around here. Are you any closer to finding out who he is?"

"It's not one of my cases. And even if it was, I couldn't tell you."

"Of course. Sorry. Well, I hope they get him. I know how terrible it can be. Someone I was very close to was raped and she's never really recovered from it."

As they turned into Linton's road, she saw a long, lean and unmistakable figure on his pushbike. *Bugger.* It was Hooper cycling towards them, his cue under his arm, evidently on the way home from an evening at the snooker club.

"All right?" he nodded, but Linton could see from his expression that was the last thing he thought about seeing her with Hampton. He looked embarrassed, like a pupil catching his teacher out on a date.

Would he tell Brown? She hadn't done anything wrong, but she didn't want him to know. She was still worrying about it when they reached her house, grateful Mark's skydiving monologue hadn't required much response.

"Would you like to come in for a coffee?" she blurted out, as they came to a stop at her gate, wincing at how clichéd it sounded.

He smiled. "I'd like that very much," he replied.

***

Half an hour later Linton was leaning against the inside of her front door, trying to work out which of the three possibilities were the most likely. One, that he'd simply taken her invitation for coffee at face value; two, he was too much of a gentleman to make the first move or three, he simply didn't fancy her. His parting words of, 'No doubt I'll see you soon', had hardly reassured her.

She wandered back into the kitchen, deciding some water

would be a good idea if she wanted to stave off a hangover and noticed he'd left his briefcase under the table. She rang his mobile, but it went straight to voicemail. She left a short message, drank some more water and decided to go to bed.

She was about to switch the kitchen light off when she caught sight of the briefcase again. She noticed it didn't have a combination lock, so it was easy enough to open. *No*, she wasn't the sort of person to snoop. Proud of her restraint, she went upstairs. She took off her make-up, undressed and got into bed, knowing as she did that until she looked inside that briefcase, she wasn't going to be able to sleep.

***

It had taken Sheila a long time to think of something positive she could write about, something she wouldn't mind sharing with the rest of the class. In the end she opted for the time she'd won the Puffin Short Story Competition when she was eleven years old. The prize had included an invitation to London to have her photo taken with the judge, Noel Streatfield, author of *White Boots*, her favourite book at the time. Her story was published in Puffin Post, the Penguin Books magazine for its young readers, and she was interviewed by the local press. 'This,' she wrote, 'was what had shaped my desire to write.'

But the exercise had stirred up more disturbing memories, ones already awakened by the events of the last week. The lid on the coffin of her memory had loosened and Miranda's instruction to think of the past had finally prised it off. Now, as she climbed into bed, she thought about the other occasions that had shaped her life. Of course, meeting Henry was one of them. And there was that other event, above all others, that had not only shaped her life, but effectively brought it to an end. She'd spent the last few years of her life living in an imprisoned hell, both of her own and of *their* making, because she needed to keep what had happened a secret.

Miranda had talked about how writing could be cathartic, 'a way of getting things out, perhaps bringing some sort of closure to an event.'

Sheila doubted whether she would even reach that state. Still, she would give it a try. She picked up the notebook she'd left by the side of her bed and began to write.

***

Mark's briefcase opened with a sharp click. A click that sounded more like a gun going off in the still silence of the kitchen. Linton jumped at the noise. It was ridiculous, she thought, the way she'd crept down the stairs and into the kitchen. How would he ever know what she was doing? It's not as if he was watching her through her kitchen window.

She'd finally given in, telling herself she was entitled to find out more about the man she might end up dating. It was no different to looking through his bathroom cabinet, she reasoned, to see whether he dyed his hair or needed cream for genital warts.

She admired his neatness, she thought, as she pulled the case open. He obviously only carried with him what he needed.

She pulled out the top piece of paper then froze, like a player in a game of musical statues. She could hear something outside the window, as though someone was moving around. She strained her ears and heard a faint tapping against the double glazed glass. Tap, tap, tap. There it was again. Tap tap

tap. Oh my God! Mark Hampton must've come back to get his briefcase and now he'd seen her going through it. The kitchen light was on, and she'd left the blind up so he'd be able to see everything.

She made an unglamorous dive for the light switch and as the room was plunged into darkness, she saw that the tapping was nothing more than the holly bush she kept meaning to cut back, beating at the glass in the wind. *Silly cow.* Why the hell would Mark Hampton have crept down the back path to spy on her?

She pulled the blind down, switched the light on again and looked at the piece of paper she'd pulled out of Mark's case. It was a form for donating property to charity and attached to it was a copy of a letter.

Dear Nick,

I hope you're well. As discussed at our meeting on Friday, I want to press ahead with donating Elmtree Manor to charity as quickly as possible. As you know, I would like to give the house to Comrades to enable them to set up a men's refuge. Domestic violence amongst men is low on the agenda and, as such, there are only two men's refuges in the entire country. This is something dear to my heart and a way of ensuring something good may come of my mother's untimely death.

Kind regards, Mark Hampton

Donating Elmtree Manor! That was beyond generous. The house was worth close to a couple of million, more if he applied for planning permission to build on the land. She had an urge to ring Brown, just to say *I told you so*, but instead went to bed with a smile on her face.

TWENTY

Now the Hampton murder was at an end, Brown's team were moved across to the rape case. Linton spent the day catching up on all the case studies. It was depressing, especially going over what had happened to Gemma.

Her evening didn't get any better. After promising herself she would the previous night, she arranged to see her brother.

His room at the rehabilitation centre displayed all the characteristics of a mid-range hotel room. It had a single bed with a beige duvet, a small desk and chair in the corner, a built-in wardrobe and a windowless bathroom with white fittings and a mildewed shower curtain. The only difference was that every fifteen minutes a nurse stuck her head round the door, and then shut it firmly without comment.

"Suicide watch," Linton's brother had said listlessly, the first time she'd come here.

This was her fifth visit and she was getting used to it. Getting used to the eighteenth century manor house, set in carefully landscaped gardens, which looked more like a venue for a wedding reception or a country retreat than a hospital for the mentally ill. Getting used to driving over the bridge, just inside the entrance, that was covered by a grilled fence, to prevent patients from jumping into the pathway of the unsuspecting traffic below.

"He reckons she might have Narcissistic Personality Disorder," Michael said.

She was getting used to this as well, conversations that

started half way through so she had to fill in the blanks. *He,* she guessed was Mr Edwards, Michael's therapist, *she* was their mum.

"Do you think he's right?" she asked.

He looked as though he was about to speak again but then simply shrugged, managing to make the movement look exhausting.

They didn't talk much after that. She promised she'd come again next week and left with the same feeling of guilt and helplessness she had every time she visited.

As she drove home, she thought about Mark Hampton. She smiled. Just thinking about him made her feel more uplifted.

"When's your next day off?" he'd asked, when he'd rung her at work that morning, in response to the message she'd left about his briefcase.

"The day after tomorrow."

"You can give it to me then? How about I take you skydiving? I remember you said you'd always wanted to give it a go."

"I'd love to," she said.

When Linton got home from visiting her brother, she made herself a bacon sandwich, checked her emails and typed 'skydiving' into Google. Fifteen minutes later she was wishing she hadn't. What the hell was she letting herself in for?

The first story she'd found was about a novice who'd had to guide himself and a dead body to the ground after his instructor died of a heart attack in mid-air. The next concerned a man who'd plunged to his death whilst taking part in a three-man jump at a skydiving contest in Ayrshire. The cords of his main and reserve parachutes were slashed, prompting investigators to believe he was murdered.

She decided it wasn't the best thing to read and was about

to switch off her laptop when she remembered what Michael had said. She searched for 'Narcissistic Personality Disorder' and clicked on the first website that came up.

"Narcissists put themselves before others and only form relationships for the purpose of advancing their purpose," she read. *"Hallmarks include the need for constant attention and admiration and the expectation of superior entitlement. They find it almost impossible to recognise the needs or feelings of others and are oblivious to the hurtfulness of their own behaviour or remarks. They are emotionally cold, have an arrogant attitude and are quick to blame and criticise others when their needs aren't met and can be physically and verbally cruel."*

No, she thought, her brother was wrong about their mother. Even she could see she wasn't as bad as that. Selfish, yes, and self-absorbed. But never cruel.

From what she'd read of Lauren's diary though, it seemed to describe the dead woman perfectly.

***

Linton's mobile rang half an hour later, waking her from the uncomfortable doze she'd fallen into on top of her duvet. The television was still on. She pulled herself up abruptly and felt around on her bedside table for the phone, her mouth dry and her neck aching. She flicked it open, half expecting it to be her dad as she'd been dreaming he was doing the Macarena in his dressing gown at her school fête. But it wasn't his number.

"Yes?" she whispered, managing to force the word out after her second attempt.

"Linton?" she immediately recognised Keen's voice. "You're not busy, are you?"

She cleared her throat. "Sort of," she said, more clearly this time. She could tell from the background noise he was in a pub.

"We're at the Castle. Is there any way you can come down? It's Brown. He's completely twatted and he's nearly picked a fight with someone."

"What?"

"Please, Linton. You could be here in a couple of minutes."

"Why me?"

"Because he listens to you."

"Since when?"

"He's being a complete nightmare. If he doesn't shut up soon someone's gonna punch him, and that someone might be me."

***

Brown was resting his head on the table when she arrived less than ten minutes later.

"He's calmed down now. I've never seen him like that. He was knocking everything back. Pints, shorts, the lot. He was fine and then it must have hit him all at once. He was shouting and swearing at everyone. He tried to pick a fight with Hooper. I've never seen him like that before."

"Brown," Keen shook him. "Oy, Brown. You're going home now." Brown grunted something, looked up, his eyes a guinea-pig pink and then bumped his head back down on the table.

"Where's everyone else?"

"They've all pissed off up Joker's. I'm meant to be meeting them there. What d'you reckon? Should we call him a taxi?"

"I'll take him home. That's if we can get him out to the car."

"You know he's in love with you, don't you?"

Linton laughed, but felt a squeezing sensation around her abdomen.

"After he'd finished calling everyone an arsehole he calmed down a bit. He told me about the baby. I asked him if he loved the mum, and he said the only person he's ever loved is you."

"That must be why he's so nice to me." She tried to sound casual, but she could feel the blood rushing to her cheeks.

"You know why he's never made a move, don't you?"

"Because he doesn't like me?"

"He thinks you're better than him."

"No one is better than Brown, according to Brown, that is. He's an arrogant twat."

"Not with everyone, he's not. He's just trying to impress you."

***

It was after ten o'clock when Sheila's doorbell finally rang. She stormed out into her hallway, her retort of 'where the hell have you been?' ready on her lips. She'd been cross with Heather before she'd even gone out. Her daughter had been full of '*I told you sos*' when she'd rushed round after Brandon's murder charge had been announced. And then she'd had the cheek to ask Sheila to watch Toby, while she 'nipped out' for a few things.

Sheila had been expecting her back at least an hour and a half ago; had been trying her phone since nine o'clock, but to no avail. To begin with she was furious, convinced Heather was taking advantage of her, imagining her popping in to have a natter with a friend on her way home from the supermarket. But then she'd begun to worry.

Now her daughter was safely home, she felt her anger taking over again. At least she did until she flung open the front door. On the doorstep stood two solemn-looking officers and one of them was a woman. She knew instinctively it could only be bad news.

***

Brown was snoring. Linton looked across at the slumped bulk on her passenger seat and realised she hadn't thought this through. How the hell was she going to get him out of the car once they reached his house? She knew his lodger wouldn't be in. According to Brown, he went to the pub every evening.

She pulled up on his deserted street and cut the engine, expecting him to wake with a jolt, but he didn't.

"Brown." She shook him. "Brown!" she said, more loudly. She pinched him. Nothing. She pinched him harder. Still nothing.

She rummaged around under his feet and found a half-drunk bottle of water. She opened it, put her finger partially across the top and shook it at him creating a cold shower over his head and face. It did the trick. He stirred and woke. She had a window of opportunity, if she could only get him to get out of the car.

"Brown!"

He sat up. "Uh?"

"Get out of the car and walk."

He started fiddling with the door, but couldn't open it. *For fuck's sake.* She got out, ran round the front of the car and pulled it open.

"Get out and walk."

He did, automaton-like, swaying, pulling out his newly cut keys from his trouser pocket.

"What the fuck got into you? Keen said you completely lost it."

"What?"

"At the pub. What the fuck was all that about?"

"Kelly had an abortion today," he slurred. "Sorry, a *termination*." He stumbled forward trying to insert the key into the lock. He missed. She prised the set from his hands and slotted the correct key into the door. "She didn't tell me until afterwards," he said as he pushed it open with his shoulder and staggered in. She followed him into the hallway.

"But I thought she wanted to keep it," she said, astonished at how they'd managed to squeeze two bikes, a stack of cardboard boxes, a broken lamp, an empty animal cage and what looked like a motorbike engine into the small space.

"She thought it would be better off dead than have a dad like me."

"I'm sure she didn't think that," she replied, glancing to her left at the stairs. Every step was piled high with magazines and junk mail, still in their envelopes and cellophane wrappers. She followed him into the equally chaotic living room and pushed him onto the beige corduroy sofa.

"Are you going to be all right? You're not going to be sick, are you?"

He shook his head.

"I don't understand. I didn't think you wanted her to keep it," she said, looking around the room with a morbid fascination.

"I'd sort of got used to the idea. Of having someone to love. Linton," he said, shutting his left eye in an attempt to focus, "you know how I feel about you, don't you?"

"Do I?"

"I love you."

"I love you too."

"I mean I *really* love you." He collapsed onto his knees on the floor in front of her, his right knee missing a plate coated in the remains of what looked like rice and curry. "Will you marry me?"

"Of course I'll marry you. Now, do you want some coffee?"

"I'm being serious. And I don't want coffee. I wanna go to bed with you. I always have done." He grabbed at her hands and tried to pull her onto him. She yanked away from him and looked at him properly. His forehead was sweaty, his mouth foamy. He smelt of alcohol and sweat. She thought of how suave Mark had looked the night before.

"I'll make some coffee," she said, turning and running out of the room. He didn't follow her.

She physically recoiled when she walked into the small room at the back of the house that an estate agent might've described as a galley kitchen but she would've described as an unhygienic hovel. Her eyes followed the stack of precariously balanced plates, mugs and bowls along the worktop to the draining board where it ended in the cluttered sink. In amongst the food-encrusted crockery were empty tins and cans and there were probably enough ingredients to make a couple a meals if someone ever got round to scraping the mess from the hob's splashback.

She gingerly opened and shut cupboards, their knobs sticky with God knows what until she found a jar of instant coffee and a cup without a handle that looked suspiciously like a sugar bowl.

The fridge was covered with paper, photos, and a couple of takeaway menus. His sister's scan was there, next to some pictures of a pretty blonde girl with a huge smile. She assumed it must be Brown's niece. His sponsorship form was next to one of the photos, attached with a magnet in the shape of a pint of Guinness. She hadn't realised he was doing it for a children's cancer charity. Glancing down the long list of names he'd collected she could see he'd already raised hundreds of pounds. She opened the fridge and looked for milk but there wasn't any. He'd have to drink it black.

She walked through to the front room, a dirty tea towel wrapped around the cup to stop it burning her hands, and said, "I'm going to go home now. Do you think you'll be all right?"

Brown looked up at her from the sofa through slitted eyes. "That night at the wedding. You would've, wouldn't you?"

"Look, Brown…"

"I wanted to tell you how I felt about you before," he slurred. "That night I rang you from the club. The night after we caught the Ley Line Strangler. Do you remember?"

It was weird, thought Linton, as she looked down at his mottled face. She'd imagined this moment for such a long time but now it felt wrong. He was drunk and his flat was a mess. A woman he'd had a one-night stand with had just had a termination. She felt suddenly dark, dragged down; completely at odds with the lightness she'd felt during the evening she'd spent with Mark.

"It's that fucker Hampton, isn't it?" She started. It was if he'd read her mind. "It doesn't surprise me," he sneered. "You're just his type."

"What's that supposed to mean?"

"He likes his women to be in control."

"Are you comparing me to Elizabeth Hampton?" she said angrily. "I'm nothing like her. She was a bitch and she abused him. I've seen his chest. It's covered in scars where she chucked boiling water at him."

"You've seen his chest, have you?" he scoffed, sounding suddenly sober. "What is it, Linton? Are you so desperate you're shagging the suspects?"

She couldn't think of anything to say so she turned around and walked out.

***

She came in early, hoping to finish reading through the rape cases before her day off and was astonished to find Brown already at his desk. She'd assumed he'd still be in bed recovering from the excesses of the night before.

He was sitting straight-backed, to all intents and purposes looking recovered from the previous night's events, but as she reached her desk and took a closer look, she could see he was suffering. His eyes were red and puffy and he was clutching an empty bottle of Lucozade.

He glanced up as she sat down. She expected him to look apologetic, after his parting words the night before but instead he looked murderous.

"What the fuck was that all that about?" he snarled in a low voice.

She pulled back, feeling like he'd physically slapped her. "What?"

"Turning up like that and taking me home. I don't need babysitting. It was embarrassing."

"Keen asked me to come. He reckoned you were out of control."

"I was fine."

"He said you were shouting and swearing at everyone. He was worried you might get into a fight."

"Next time, why don't you stay at home and clean your house or whatever it is that you do with your sad little life?"

"At least I'm not a slob," she said gesturing at his desk with her hands.

"You know what they say. A tidy house is for someone who's got no life."

"And living in scum means you've got one? What kind of narrow-minded crap is that?"

"Narrow-minded? That's rich coming from you."

"What the hell is wrong with you?" she exploded. "I'm not the one you should be angry with. I'm not the one who had the abortion."

"Fuck you, Linton. It's got nothing to do with that."

"Then what it is? Can't your ego take it because I turned you down last night?"

"Don't flatter yourself, Linton. If I came on to you, I don't remember it. I was so pissed, I'd have tried it on with anyone. I don't appreciate being patronised, that's all."

"You know you're the one with the sad little life. You can't cruise on your looks forever. One day you're going to wake up and find you're past it and on your own."

"Like you, you mean."

"That's out of choice."

He made a noise halfway between a grunt and a laugh then said, "Another woman was attacked yesterday evening, in case you're interested."

"You know I am."

"So do you want to know who it was?"

Oh God, she thought. Not someone else she knew.

"It was Sheila Martock's daughter."

"What?" she said, stunned. "But that's bizarre. What happened?"

"Keen's in charge of the case. Go and ask him."

"Can't you just tell me?"

Brown shrugged. "She was raped on that derelict site by Moorlands," he said speaking in a monotone, as though he was reading from a report. "The attack was even more violent. He punched and kicked her and it looked like he'd tried to strangle her. He probably thought he'd killed her. She's on life support with some sort of traumatic brain injury."

"Who found her?"

"A couple of teenagers. They were doing a recce for the Skate Park they're trying to get the council to build."

"Bloody hell," she said. "Sheila Martock's had a bit of a week of it. Her employer's murdered, her son's arrested. And now this. Do want me to cancel my day off tomorrow?"

"I'd take it if were you," he said, icily. "This could go on for weeks." He didn't need to add that he'd be glad to see the back of her, his tone said it all.

***

Just before Linton left for the day, a card and collection came for Emily Woods, a dispatcher who'd recently left on maternity leave.

"Congratulations on the birth of your daughter!" the caption exclaimed above a drawing of a pink rabbit tucking her baby into a cot.

Linton dropped her obligatory pound into the collection envelope and tried to think of something original to add to the messages of 'Happy Nappies!' and 'I can't wait to meet her!' But all she could come up with was, 'I'm really pleased for you'.

She passed the card to Brown, watching him carefully as he pulled it out of the envelope. She saw him wince and felt a sudden rush of unexpected tenderness.

He looked across and she smiled, but his expression remained stony.

TWENTY-ONE

"Are you sure it's not too cold to do the jump today?" Linton asked, as she clambered into Mark Hampton's car the following morning. She was wearing a hat, scarf and gloves and she'd zipped her Puffa jacket up to her neck. She'd still felt cold as she waited outside her house for him, half-hoping he wasn't going to turn up, her arms wrapped around her body in a pathetic attempt to keep herself warm.

"You're not trying to wriggle out of it, are you?" Hampton said, turning to her. She couldn't help returning his lop-sided smile.

"I'm really nervous," she admitted, pulling her seat belt on, enjoying the warmth of the car.

"What's worrying you?"

"That I could end up dead. Or paralysed."

He laughed as he signalled and pulled away, "I promise to bring you home in one piece."

They were quiet for a few moments as he negotiated his way along the narrow road, pulling in to let two cars and a Royal Mail van past. As he pulled up at the junction and then out onto the main road, she said, "I'm so sorry about what happened to Heather Martock."

"What do you mean?" he asked, turning to look at her with an expression of confusion.

"Didn't you hear the news this morning?"

He shook his head. "I had the radio on, but I wasn't paying much attention to be honest. What's happened?"

"She was attacked last night. Out on that bit of scrubland by the old Moorlands' site."

"Jesus," he said glancing at her again quickly, before turning back to study the road. "Is she OK?"

"It was a pretty brutal. She's on life support."

"Christ. That's awful." Linton could hear the distress in his voice. "Poor Heather. And Sheila. No wonder I didn't see her this morning. I just assumed she was running late. Jesus. I ought to ring her. See if there's anything I can do."

"There's a lay-by up ahead if you want to stop."

He pulled in after a few seconds later and reached into his pocket for his phone.

"Sorry," he said, moving his fingers deftly over the touch screen. "I hope you don't mind."

"Of course not."

He held his mobile to his ear, chewing anxiously on his bottom lip. After a few seconds, he said, "Sheila. It's me, Mark. I'm so sorry to hear what happened. Please ring me if you need anything. Anything at all." He put the phone back. "I'll try her again later."

"Do you know Heather well?" Linton asked, as he pulled out of the lay-by a moment later and rejoined the road.

"I haven't seen her for years, but she was always around when I was growing up." She caught the ghost of a smile as he said, "I think she had a bit a crush on me to be honest. She used to follow me around like a little puppy dog. It was very sweet actually."

"She's got a kid, hasn't she?"

He nodded. "A boy. The product of a one-night stand apparently. I've never met him though. Heather hasn't been near the house for years."

"Why not?"

"She hated Lauren. She thought she was a freak who had to control everyone around her. To be honest, I think she resented her because she took up so much of her mother's time."

"Sheila's very loyal to your family, isn't she? Despite everything that happened."

He nodded. "I think she was grateful for all my help after her husband died."

"What sort of help?"

"I used to mow her lawn, and do odd jobs for her around the house."

"But you were only fifteen."

He sighed. "I was old enough to know that her layabout son wasn't going to pull his finger out. I felt sorry for her. And in a way she'd been more of a mother to me than Lauren. It was the least I could do." Once again Linton marvelled at how differently Mark could've turned out. He'd had no father, a mother who appeared to be a complete narcissist. And yet he'd grown into a sensitive and thoughtful man.

A mile down the road from the skydiving centre, Mark pulled over at a roadside café.

"We're early. Shall we grab a quick drink?"

"A double vodka sounds good."

He laughed. "Stop worrying. You'll be fine."

The café was a time warp of faded brown floral tablecloths and matching curtains. They ordered tea and a bacon roll from the hard-faced woman standing behind the counter. She was wearing a dark green tabard and a streak of unflattering red lipstick that was already seeping into the harsh lines around her mouth. Her put-upon expression reminded Linton of Sheila.

They found a table near the window and a few minutes later

the woman brought their order over. She dumped their drinks unceremoniously on the table, causing tea to slop over the sides of the mugs. Mark still thanked her profusely, telling her the bacon rolls smelt delicious and Linton caught a faint smile tugging at the corner of the woman's lips. Hampton had the same gift as Brown, a strange, innate ability to charm. Linton tried to strike up a conversation about the skydiving centre but Mark seemed distracted, sipping half-heartedly at his drink. He left his food untouched.

"Look," she said eventually, "you're obviously upset about what's happened to Heather. If you want to call today off I'll understand."

He smiled. "You're not getting out of it that easily. And to be honest it'll help me to take my mind off everything." He pulled his phone out. "I'm going to try Sheila again."

"Whilst you call her I'll nip to the loo."

As she got up from the table, Hampton's mobile started ringing. She couldn't help glancing down at the caller display.

"Jonathan Baines," said Mark, reading the name aloud. "I wonder what he wants."

"You take it. I'll be back in a sec."

When she got back to the table a few minutes later, Mark was no longer on the phone. He was staring out of the window, looking deep in thought.

"Is everything OK?"

He frowned. "I think so."

"You look concerned."

"It's just something Jonathan said."

"Go on."

He shook his head unhappily. "He's asked me do to him a favour."

"What sort of favour?"

"He asked me to…" He stopped.

"Asked you to what?"

"Lie, basically."

"About what?"

Hampton picked up one of his gloves and began fiddling with the Velcro strap. "He said if anyone asks, I was with him on Saturday night."

"But you weren't."

"No."

"So why would he ask you to do that?"

"I think I can guess," he stopped then let out a deep sigh. "I'm assuming he was with Sally Hughes and he wants to cover his tracks."

"I'm sorry," she said shaking her head. "I still don't understand."

"They're having an affair."

"No!" she said, genuinely shocked. "Your solicitor and my ex-headmistress. How do you know?"

"Lauren told me," he said. "She spotted them together outside Sally's cottage. It was obvious they were more than just friends. I've never mentioned it to Jonathan. I was too embarrassed to bring it up to be honest."

"That's ironic," she said. "After his campaigning against the dating agency that encourages people not to have affairs."

"That's often the way though, don't you think? People getting angry because they're really angry at themselves."

"Why didn't you tell us that Lauren knew about their affair?"

He frowned. "Why would I? It's not important." After a few seconds he laughed. "Surely you're not thinking he killed Lauren to stop people finding out? That's actually quite funny. Anyway, you've got your man now."

As the waitress ambled over to clear their table, he glanced down at his watch. "Let's forget about Jonathan Baines and his sordid going ons. We'd better get going."

***

Earlier that morning, the consultant had presented Sheila with all the facts and figures; the percentage of how many patients came out of a coma, how many went on to die and how many remained in a vegetative state for the rest of their lives. She heard the statistics, but she couldn't take them in. When it came to numbers, it was like her brain was covered in cling film, a protective layer that they simply bounced off.

She'd always been better with words, so it was the phrase beginning with, "I'm afraid…" that left her with the impression that things weren't looking promising.

But then, not long after the consultant left, Heather had opened her eyes. Sheila had raced into the corridor, calling for help and within minutes there was a flurry of doctors and nurses around her daughter's bed. Sheila could sense a cautious excitement but their optimism didn't last for long.

"She's not reacting to environmental stimuli," said the doctor whose blonde pigtails made her look more like an orphan in a rendition of *Annie*, than someone in the medical profession.

"What does that mean?" Sheila asked, stalling for time, giving herself a few more seconds before she had to face up to the truth.

"At the moment she looks as though she's awake, but she's not actually conscious," said the doctor gently, reaching out to touch Sheila's arm. "I've seen coma patients grind their teeth, swallow, smile and even call out, but I'm afraid it's an involuntary action."

"Will she ever wake up?"

"The possibility of recovery from a vegetative state depends on how long it lasts and at the moment, I'm afraid we've got no idea."

"Do you think she can hear me?"

"There's a faint possibility, but it's widely accepted that patients in VS have no awareness of their surroundings," replied the doctor.

"But she *might* hear me."

The doctor smiled sadly. "She might."

***

It was PC Wilshaw who picked up the dispatch. He was closest to Nutmeg Lane, having taken a drive round the bottom of the Tor to check the disabled parking bay wasn't being abused again.

"Nothing urgent," the dispatcher assured him. "We've had an anonymous caller. He says he's worried about Miss Sally Hughes as he hasn't heard from her for a couple of days. She's a pensioner, so possibly vulnerable. The address is Lavender Cottage. He says, if she doesn't answer, there's a key in the rusted watering can."

The two pints of milk on the doorstep – one cool, one warm – worried him. But it was easy to forget to cancel an order, especially if she'd been called away unexpectedly. The fact that an upstairs window was slightly open bothered him more.

He rang the doorbell twice and knocked a few times. Either she wasn't in, or she was unable to get to the door. He was definitely leaning towards the latter possibility.

He looked inside the rusted watering can. The key was at the bottom, as promised. He fished it out and unlocked the door, tentatively pushing it open.

"Miss Hughes," he called out. Once inside he recognised the pungent smell immediately and moved reluctantly down the bright hallway, certain of what would greet him when he reached its source.

Sally Hughes was sitting in her armchair, her head lolled over to one side and her bloodshot eyes staring straight ahead. She had a colourful, Mexican-looking embroidered cushion resting in her lap.

A couple of hours later, this innocuous-looking item of soft furnishing was being bagged up and sent to the FSS lab with the assumption that this was the murder weapon.

Sally Hughes, former headmistress, talented gardener, member of a book club and lover of Jonathan Baines, had almost certainly been smothered to death with it.

**

"A twenty-minute brief!" Linton whispered urgently to Hampton as the course instructor reached the end of his talk. "That's not long enough." She could hear the panic in her own voice.

He squeezed her shoulder reassuringly. "If you were jumping on your own, you'd do a day's course, but you don't need to when you're in tandem. I'll be doing all the work. You look great by the way," he winked. "I love a woman in a pair of overalls."

She couldn't help laughing. "Just wait 'til I get the helmet and goggles on. You won't be able to resist."

As they walked across the concourse to where the plane was parked, words and phrases swept through her mind. *Fifteen thousand feet. An adrenaline-fuelled minute of freefall. Reaching terminal velocity at one hundred and twenty miles per hour. Once in a lifetime opportunity. The most amazing experience of your life.*

Her mobile rang. "You're supposed to have left that with your other stuff," said Hampton. She glanced down at the caller display. It was Brown. "Leave it. We've got to get going. The aircraft's waiting for us."

"It's work."

"Kate. It's your day off."

"Brown wouldn't ring me unless it was urgent."

She pulled off her glove with her teeth and answered. As usual, Brown didn't hang about.

"It's Sally Hughes," he said. "She's dead. Suffocated. Wilshaw found her at home this morning after an anonymous phone call. Police surgeon's initial estimate is Saturday evening, early hours of Sunday morning."

"Carrier bag?" she said quietly, walking away from Hampton so he was out of earshot.

"A cushion over the face. It's got to be linked to Lauren's death. Two women who knew each other suffocated within the same week."

"Have you spoken to Brandon?"

"About half an hour ago. He couldn't have done it. He was fishing on Saturday night. Remember?"

"So he says."

"I've rung the fishing lodge in Andover. Three witnesses say he was there all night. All weekend in fact."

Linton looked across at Hampton. He was pacing up and down, looking at his watch. "I think you need to speak to Jonathan Baines," she said quietly.

"What's he got to do with it?"

"He's been having an affair with Sally Hughes."

Brown sounded sceptical. "Says who?"

"Hampton told me," she said looking across at Mark again to check he couldn't read her lips.

"How does he know?"

"Lauren Hampton told him," she paused. "Apparently Baines was terrified she was going to tell people. Shit! What if he killed Lauren to stop her telling anyone?"

"That's a bit drastic, isn't it?"

"Remember what you said when we thought it could be the man who slept with Sophia? About reputations being destroyed? Well, Baines' reputation would be destroyed if it got out. Not only is he a solicitor, he's got his campaign about infidelity. Imagine the humiliation if his affair became public. He'd never live it down."

"But why kill Sally Hughes?"

"Maybe she was going to come out in the open. About their affair. Or maybe she knew about the murder? Perhaps she told him she was going to the police." She paused then said, "I think he was with Sally Hughes on Saturday night."

"How do you know?"

"I spoke to Hampton this morning."

"Hampton's nothing to do with the case anymore," he said suspiciously. "Why would you need to speak to him?"

"He said Baines rang asking him to cover as an alibi," she said, deliberately avoiding Brown's question. "He said if anyone asked, could he say he was with him? If Jonathan killed Sally Hughes on Saturday night, he'll need an alibi."

"You still haven't said why you were talking to Hampton."

"For God's sake. Will you stop worrying about why I spoke to Hampton? Mark said Baines wanted an alibi for Saturday night."

"Hang on," said Brown. "If Baines killed Lauren, then why was the carrier bag he used covered in Brandon Martock's fingerprints."

"Maybe the bag was already in the house," she said thinking it through as she spoke. "He worked there, didn't he? Maybe Baines just happened to pick it up."

"Baines just happened to pick up a carrier bag with Brandon's prints on," he said dubiously. "That's pretty unlikely, isn't it? And I think you're forgetting something."

"What?"

"Baines couldn't have killed Lauren. He was backstage with Hampton."

"Not the whole time. He went to the loo."

"Hang on. All along you're the one saying there wasn't enough time, because you didn't want Hampton implicated!"

"I think you should bring Baines in for questioning. I'll come back now."

"Where are you?"

"Taunton."

"Doing what?"

She looked across at Mark. Why not just come clean? But then she'd have to listen to Brown's mocking taunts. *So you're a skydiver.*

"Shopping," she said.

"Well, finish up and come back in."

She hung up, put her mobile back in the pocket of her overalls and made her way over to Mark.

"Ready?" he smiled.

She shook her head. "I'm really sorry. I'm going to have to go back. Something's come up."

"Really?" He looked so disappointed that Linton felt an immediate pang of guilt. "Come on, Kate. Please. It'll take us fifteen minutes to fly up over the area of the jump. Ten minutes to land safely. Ten minutes to get the kit off. That's not even forty-five minutes."

"I can't."

"Why? What's happened?"

"I can't say. But I need to get back."

"What if I take you straight back to work afterwards?"

She couldn't help laughing and, as she did, she realised she was starting to really like this man. A lot. Her mobile rang again. It was Brown.

"Sorry," she mouthed at Hampton, as she picked up and walked away again.

"Baines isn't at his office," said Brown. "He's called in sick. I rang his home and his wife answered. She thought he was at work. It's going to take a while to track him down. I've got Hooper ringing friends, relatives. I'll let you know."

She looked over at Hampton. He raised his eyebrows at her beseechingly.

"I've got something to finish here. It's going to take an hour. An hour and a half tops and I'll be back. Is that OK?"

"All right," said Brown reluctantly. "But if we find Baines in the meantime you'll need to come straight back."

***

"I'm really not sure about this," Linton shouted again, in an attempt to be heard over the roar of the plane's engine. "What if the parachute doesn't open?"

"You'll be fine," said Mark laughing. "They make a big deal out of any accidents because they so rarely happen. And I'll be with you the whole time. I'll look after you. I promise."

"It's all right for you. You've done it hundreds of times."

"That's the whole point. You don't have to do anything. You're going to be harnessed to me and I'll control the whole jump, the freefall and parachute."

"But what if I become unattached? I won't have a parachute and I'll end up plunging to my death."

He placed his hand gently on her shoulder. "Stop worrying. That's not going to happen. Just trust me."

***

At 2.15 p.m. in the Avon and Somerset Police Contact Centre, a call was logged.

Caller: I, um, I'm ringing with some information regarding the Lauren Hampton murder.

Operator: May I have your name please?

Caller: It's, um, Liz. Elizabeth Hampton. I was married to Lauren Hampton's son, Mark.

Operator: And you say you have some information?

Caller: Um, yes. It's important. Really important. I'd like to speak to someone working on the case, please.

Operator: Let me take your number and I'll ask one of the investigating officers to ring you back as soon as they can.

Five minutes later, Elizabeth Hampton answered her phone on the first ring. She'd sat next to it waiting, knowing that if she didn't say something now she never would.

"My name's Detective Sergeant Rob Brown," said the voice on the other end. "I'm working on the investigation into Lauren Hampton's murder."

She liked the way he sounded although she knew that didn't mean a thing. In her former life, when she used to rely on instinct, she'd have said he had the voice of someone who could be trusted, but since Mark, she'd lost her faith in it.

"You say you were married to Mark Hampton?" he said.

"For almost six years," she replied, aware of how unsteady her voice sounded. She paused, took a shaky breath, trying to steady herself. "I know you've arrested someone for the murder of Lauren Hampton, but you've got the wrong man. Mark killed her."

There a short pause. "Do you have any evidence of this?"

"Well, no."

There was a long drawn-out sigh. "So what makes you say that?"

"Because I know how much he hated her."

"That doesn't mean he killed her. Now Mrs Hampton…"

"Osborne," she interrupted quickly. "I've gone back to my maiden name."

"I'm afraid without any evidence…"

"He talked about killing her," she interrupted again. "All the time. He even said how he'd like to do it. That he'd suffocate her; because he'd enjoy watching her struggle as she died."

There was brief pause, then the man on the other end said, "I understand from Mr Hampton that when you split up, there was a lot of bitterness."

She knew straight away what he was driving at. She wasn't stupid, despite what Mark had spent most of their marriage telling her. "Do you think I'm phoning up to get him into trouble because we split up?" she snapped. "Leaving him was the sanest thing I've ever done."

"When I interviewed Mark Hampton, he said he left you because, amongst other things, *you* hated his mother."

"That's not true!"

"You mean you didn't hate her."

"He didn't leave me," she said, choosing to ignore his question. "It was the other way round. I ran away from *him*. I've been in hiding ever since. I was afraid he'd come after me."

"Because of what you did to him?"

"I'm sorry?"

"The burns on his chest." *What?* "The boiling water you threw at him. He told my colleague about it."

Oh my God! She'd forgotten how insane the man was.

"Is that what he said? He's unbelievable. He got those burns on his chest when he was a child. He pulled a pan of water onto himself from the stove. I had nothing to do with that." She swallowed. She wouldn't cry because, once she started, she wouldn't be able to stop and then she wouldn't be able to finish what she had to say. She felt a twisted knot in her chest.

"This is what he does," she said. "He turns things around. He lies. Until you don't even know what's true anymore. I used to watch him in public. I didn't know who the man was, but it wasn't Mark. Everyone told me how lucky I was. What a wonderful man he was. After a while, I thought I was going mad. I don't know how he's charmed you, but he is an evil, violent man who'll do anything to get what he wants." She paused, afraid to ask the question. "What else did he say about me?"

"That you had a problem with drugs."

"That's complete crap."

"That you were jealous. That you didn't like him doing charity work."

"Charity work? He said he did charity work? He's never done anything for anyone in his life unless he was going to get something out of it."

"You described him as violent."

"That's why I left him in the end. He…" she stopped.

"Look, would you feel more comfortable talking to a female officer? I can ask for one if you like."

"It's OK." She took a deep breath. "We were married so

some people might see it as their wedded duty, but no wife should endure the things he did to me." She stopped again. The officer didn't need to know the finer details. He didn't need to know how Mark had pinned her down, tied her up and etched out the word WHORE with a pen knife, so that it sat above her appendix scar, looking like it was neatly underlined.

"The last time he raped me," she continued, trying to push the images from her mind, "I thought he was going to kill me. That's when I ran away."

"Why didn't you report him?"

"Because he said if he ever found out I'd gone to the police, he'd kill me. And believe me, he would."

"So why are you telling us about this now?"

"Because I know you've charged another man with Lauren's murder and I don't think it's fair he should be punished for something Mark Hampton did. It's time he stopped getting away with it."

***

With his pathetic lunch of a Ryvita and three tomatoes at an end, Hargreaves plonked his considerable weight onto the nearest available chair and pretended to study his notes in an effort to try to get his equilibrium back. Ever since he'd started on this stupid diet, he'd felt woozy and lightheaded and it still hadn't made any bloody difference to his sodding weight. He looked across at Brown who was pacing up and down the incident room, his mobile pressed to his ear, and felt something akin to hatred. It wasn't fair that the gobshite with his easy manner and film-star looks could pour pint after pint of lager down his neck and still look like a sodding athlete.

As he took another couple of deep breaths to try and steady himself, he heard Brown shout across the office to Keen. "That's odd. Linton's still got her phone turned off. She never does that. I've been ringing her for ten minutes."

It was Hooper that replied, in his usual excitable manner. There was another one who seemed to eat what he wanted without ever putting on any weight.

"She might have turned it off for the jump," he said.

"What jump?" Brown's tone turned instantly from irritated to concerned.

"Um, er, she's gone skydiving."

"What?"

"I overheard her on the phone. Arranging it with someone. I'm guessing it's with Hampton. I saw them out together the other night."

Suddenly Brown was out of his chair yelling at Hooper, demanding he get the number for the skydiving centre in Taunton. It all seemed very surreal to Hargreaves, as though it wasn't happening. He stood up, overcome by a wave of nausea and managed to say, "Can someone tell me what the hell is going on?" before he felt his legs collapsing from beneath him.

***

So this was what the instructor had meant by staring down into infinity. Linton felt sick and dizzy. Her heart was thumping so hard in her chest that it actually hurt. She glanced back at Hampton, who grinned back in acknowledgment of what was about to happen, then back down at the wispy threads of cloud below.

She took a couple of deep breaths – tried to steady herself. *What the hell was she thinking? She couldn't do this.*

"Shuffle forward towards the door," shouted Hampton. "I'm right behind you."

"Oh, Christ," she mumbled, as she slowly approached the door feeling the temperature drop as she moved closer, inch by terrified inch. The parachute and the jumpsuit were uncomfortably heavy, but she knew that wasn't the reason for the persistent shaking in her legs, which matched the rhythmic chattering of her teeth.

"I don't want to do this," she shouted, but Hampton continued to edge her forward, his body weight propelling her, until she was standing, hunched over in fear, at the edge of the open door.

The next few seconds passed in a terrifying blur and suddenly she was out, dangling from the plane, her legs up behind her, and the rest of her body on the underbelly of the aircraft, secured only by the straps holding her to Mark.

"What if they come undone?" she screamed, but he didn't hear. She tried again, louder this time, "Mark. I've changed my mind, I don't want to do it," but she knew it was pointless, he wouldn't hear her over the roar of the wind and the plane engine.

She had to hang for several more seconds, suspended in open space and then suddenly Mark was rolling out and they were falling away from the aircraft. She felt a slap on her shoulder and she released her hands, splaying them out in front of her.

She was rushing downwards now; the green earth thrusting its way towards her as cold air blasted past and she had a sense of an endless plummeting, without any control of descent.

Down, down, down she went. Wind, fear, wind; cold, cold wind, wondering why she hadn't yet felt the jerk, jerk, jerk she was promised she'd experience when Mark's parachute went up. Hundreds of images and thoughts swept through her mind, a jumble of faces, patterns and flashes of colour, but the overriding one was that she was about to die.

***

For a few seconds there was chaos in the Incident Room, all thoughts of Linton momentarily forgotten. There was a flurry of movement as everyone reached for their phone, but Brown stuck his hand in the air, signalling he had it under control.

"Ambulance," he yelled into his mobile. "Glastonbury Police Station. Possible heart attack." He threw his phone down and ran across to where The Toad was lying, slumped on the floor next to Hooper's desk. He leant over and loosened his tie, then picked up his wrist and pressed down on it with his index and middle finger.

"I can't find his pulse," he said, moving his fingers up to Hargreaves' neck. He held them there for a few seconds, then stood up, looking anxiously round the room until his eyes came to rest on the trainee detective.

"Hooper," he ordered. "Go outside and wait for the ambulance. Tell them to come straight up."

"But, Sir..."

"Now!"

"But, Sir..."

"WHAT?"

"It's Hargreaves, Sir. He's stirring. Look, he's opening his eyes."

"What the bloody hell just happened?" The Toad murmured, rolling onto his side, as Brown dropped back onto the carpet beside him.

"Sir," said Brown. "Wait. Don't move. Have you got any chest pains or shortness of breath?"

The Toad pushed Brown's hands roughly away, then pulled himself up into a sitting position. His face looked flushed and he was breathing heavily, but whether it was with pain or anger, it was difficult to tell.

"For God's sake, Brown," he barked, removing any uncertainty about the way he was feeling, "what are you, a bloody doctor now? Let me get up. I haven't had a heart attack or whatever else you might wish on me. It's that bloody diet I'm on. Not enough bloody sugar. Now what the hell is all this about Linton and Mark Hampton?"

***

"Oh my God," said Linton, dancing about on the tarmac, while Mark grinned at her. "That was amazing!"

"Exhilarating, isn't it?" said Mark, as they made their way back across the field towards the hanger.

"I don't think I've ever felt so invigorated in my life," she said. "It's crazy. I was absolutely terrified but I'd do it again in a heartbeat."

"We could go up again this afternoon if you like."

"I'd love to. But I promised Brown I'd get back. Is it all right if we dump this stuff off and go?"

"It's fine. I'll take you home and come back later and sort it out."

"Are you sure?"

"You kept your end of the bargain. The least I can do is keep mine."

***

Hargreaves was doing his best to concentrate but he still felt lightheaded.

"You're saying that, based on a phone call from Hampton's hysterical ex-wife, you want me to get Taunton police out and bring him in? That's completely ridiculous. Listen to yourself."

"She told me he raped her when they were married. That he was violent. What if she's telling the truth? What if he attacks Linton?"

"For God's sake, Brown! She's gone on a date with him. They've gone skydiving. Why the hell would he attack her? And the reason why her sodding phone is turned off is that she's probably jumping out of a plane…"

"Brown?"

It was Hooper. "I got through to the centre," he said. "They've just finished the jump. It went really well. Everything's fine. They're on their way home now."

"Right," said Hargreaves. "There we go, Brown. She's fine. So now get on with what you're supposed to be doing and find Jonathan Baines. Someone who might have actually done something to someone."

***

It took a while for Linton's adrenaline to ebb. It was only when her equilibrium had fully returned that she began to think about the conversation she'd had with Brown before the jump.

She hadn't had time to process what he'd said about Baines, but now, as Hampton drove back towards Glastonbury, she went back over it in her mind.

She thought back to her initial meeting with Baines. She'd put his unease down to a general anxiety around the police that was often displayed by people who were entirely innocent.

She remembered the dark circles beneath his eyes, his cup that shook and juddered in his head as he'd passed her the tea.

Could he have killed Lauren Hampton to keep her quiet? It seemed over the top, murdering someone just to maintain a reputation, but for some it was more important to them than anything.

"What's up?" asked Hampton, jerking her from her thoughts.

"I'm fine. Still recovering from the excitement, I think."

"Are you cold?" he asked glancing at her. "You've still got your coat on."

She laughed. "I think my body's gone into some sort of shock. She pulled her Puffa jacket closer to her, feeling the heavy lump in the inside pocket. The deodorant can she'd put in the other night and forgotten to take out. She should try running again; if she could do a parachute jump, she could do anything.

She went back to thinking about Baines. Could he really be a murderer?

"Mark?" she said, attempting to sound casual. "You know you said Jonathan asked you to cover for him on Saturday night? Has he ever asked you do that before?"

Hampton glanced at her again, "I know where you're going with this and I can tell you you're heading in the wrong direction. Jonathan Baines isn't a killer. You've only got to look at him to know that."

"I'm not saying that he is. I just need to get a few things straight in my head. On Monday night," she persisted, "was he definitely only out of the room for only ten minutes?"

For a moment he didn't say anything. "Mark?" she pressed.

"You're going to think I'm a liar if I tell you."

"I'm going to think you're one if you don't."

He sighed. "It just seemed easier to go along with it."

"What did?" She could feel her heart accelerating, the adrenalin returning.

"It was Jonathan's idea. To lie about how long he was out of the dressing room for. Obviously I was innocent, but I was worried you wouldn't believe me so I went along with it. He told me to say he was only gone for ten minutes at the most."

"How long was he out of the room for?" she urged, as they slowed down at a set of traffic lights.

As they pulled to a halt, Hampton said in small voice, "Twenty five minutes."

"Where did you think he'd gone?" she said exasperated.

"To the loo! Look. I'm sorry. I didn't think he was using me as his alibi. I thought it was the other way round." He'd taken his hands off the steering wheel and was fiddling nervously with the ring on his little finger. Twisting it round and round between the thumb and finger of his right hand. It wasn't the ring he'd usually worn, Linton thought absentmindedly.

As he twisted it back the other way, the tiny emerald in its centre caught her eye. She looked more closely. It looked familiar. How odd. She'd seen it so many times before, watched someone else turning it round and round on their own finger. It was such a distinctive design.

Hampton must've noticed she was staring at the ring.

"What?" he said, turning to look at her, a puzzled expression on his face.

"Your ring," she said, as a myriad of reasons raced through her brain for why Mark Hampton would be wearing Gemma's wedding band.

"My friend…" she began, then stopped as she watched Hampton's eyes turn from a warm dazzling gold to something dark and hard, feeling a cold snake of fear slither across her gut.

TWENTY-TWO

L auren Hampton pushed her front door shut causing the heavy brass knocker to strike against it forcefully. It was a noise that carried a considerable distance. If anyone was waiting at the bottom of the gravel driveway or concealed within the copse of trees at the bottom of the garden or even hiding in the arboretum, they would've heard it. From inside though, it had a muffled quality, something of a thud as if the metal was covered with velvet.

She left her handbag on the side and picked up a packet of white manila envelopes then walked slowly along the wooden expanse of the entrance hall, her heels tapping out a rhythm like the curt tick of a metronome, and entered the drawing room.

Her desk was on the other side of the room, near one of the large, sash windows. She walked over to it and ran her hand underneath the desk top, feeling for the tiny key that she'd stuck to the underside of the wood with Blu Tak. She couldn't be too careful, not with Sheila snooping around.

She unlocked the desk drawer, lifted out two pieces of folded paper and slipped them into one of the envelopes before sitting down and picking up her fountain pen. She wrote a name carefully across the envelope, realising as she did that the address she needed was out in the hall, written at the back of her appointments book.

Except that when she went to look for it, the book wasn't there, which was odd as she was certain she'd put it in her handbag. She'd spoken to Fenn just before she left for her book club and he'd given her his home address. She must've left her appointments book at Sally's after she'd taken it out to make a note of next month's book.

She'd ring Fenn in a minute and ask him for the address again but first she needed a drink.

Back in the drawing room she poured herself a small sherry and settled down onto the leather chair with its back to the doors that led out onto the terrace. With no one to watch her, she finished her drink in two greedy gulps, sighing as the phone in the hallway began to ring.

She started to pull herself up when she heard a sound behind her. The creak of the French windows opening wider. A moment later the person she least expected to see stepped into the room and in front of her chair.

"What the hell are you doing here?" she said.

***

Linton didn't think that any other sound could've filled her with such dread. The clunk of the automatic car lock. A sound that in less than a second had turned her from passenger to prisoner.

"Just in case you get any stupid ideas," he said coldly, pulling away as the traffic light turned green.

She swallowed, her mouth suddenly dry. Her mind was racing in every direction, frantically trying to find another explanation for what was happening. But there was only one reason why he'd have Gemma's ring; why he'd looked at her with those dead eyes. Mark Hampton was a violent rapist.

"Where are we going?" she said, trying to keep her voice steady.

"Back to mine." He turned to look at her, a sickeningly, cold smile on his face then said, "I'm meeting someone there. Someone else I need to get rid of."

"Get rid of?" she faltered. "What do you mean?"

"Well, I can hardly have you going round telling everyone, can I?"

"What if I promise not to say anything?"

"Don't patronise me Kate."

"But if anything happens to me they'll know it was you."

"Why? No one suspects me. And no one ever will. I'll deny it. Like I did everything else."

Everything else? She tried to sound calm and controlled but as she spoke she could hear the quiver in her voice, "What are you planning to do?"

"To deal with you. Like I dealt with Lauren."

"What are you talking about?"

"Your DI," he said with a sneer. "He thinks he's so bloody clever. I hated him the moment I set eyes on him. Calling me a fairy. Thinking he had one up on me. I've got the last laugh though. I've got you."

"Brown doesn't give a shit about me," she said, "so why don't you let me go? It'll work in your favour if you do."

"You know I've had you two running around like a couple of dogs pointlessly chasing their tails," he said, as though she hadn't spoken. "Every time I suggested something, off you'd run again. I can't tell you how much fun it's been."

He stopped talking as they reached the junction that met the road leading to Glastonbury. It was always difficult to pull out; cars whizzed past at a frightening speed, with rarely a gap in between. It required concentration. If she could just move her arm quickly enough, she could unlock the door, push it open and jump out before the car started off again.

"Don't," he hissed, as she shifted her hand slightly. "I know what you're thinking. There's no way you're getting out of this car until I say so."

A few more cars shot past until eventually there was a break in the traffic. She needed to keep him talking, she thought, as they pulled out – to distract him. Then she could try reaching for the lock again. Even if she had to jump out while the car was moving, it would be better to try and escape now. Once he got her back to Elmtree with no one around, there was no knowing what he would do.

"What did you mean when you said you'd dealt with Lauren?" She tried to keep her voice light, as though they were having an everyday conversation. "Are you saying you killed her?"

"Of course I did," he said looking at her with surprise. "Who else do you think could've done it?"

"But how?" she said, sliding her left hand a couple of centimetres along her thigh.

"It was foolproof. All I had to do was frame Brandon Martock. I sacked him, so he'd have a motive; told him Lauren was firing him because she thought he was a thief. Before he cleared his stuff out of the shed I made sure I took the carrier bag he carried his sandwiches in." He laughed suddenly. "The B in the diary. That was a stroke of luck."

"What do you mean?" Her hand was almost at her the top of her thigh now. Just a couple more centimetres.

"It wasn't anyone's initial. It was Lauren's appointment for Botox."

"Aphrodite's," said Linton, remembering the sign she'd seen outside the beauticians'. "She was one of their clients."

"It had nothing to with Brandon but it pointed you in his direction, along with the silver pot of course that I took the night I said my goodbyes to Lauren."

Linton's hand had reached her thigh now. She glanced at the door. She'd need to free her seatbelt first and then she'd have to release the lock before pulling back the handle on the door.

"All I had to do was feed your suspicions," he continued, gazing at the road ahead. "Make you think it might be someone from the past. Leave the letter I found to Fenn on the side." *Letter? What letter?* thought Linton. "Tell you how much Elizabeth hated Lauren, how she'd blackmailed her and abused me. And of course I made sure I looked like Mr. Generosity himself." He laughed. "I thought the note I left for you to find in my briefcase was a touch of genius."

"You were outside my window that night, weren't you? Watching me to see if I'd read it."

"I knew you would."

They were silent for a moment. Linton glanced at the door again then back at Hampton. He was studying the road ahead, occasionally looking in the rear view mirror. The speedometer said they were doing fifty-five miles an hour. Even if she managed to escape from the car they were travelling too fast. She'd end up killing herself.

"Do you know what my favourite bit was?" he said suddenly.

"No. Tell me."

"The purple earrings. I knew that would confuse everyone. And I loved the idea that Lauren would've hated them." He held his little finger, the one wearing Gemma's ring and gave it a wriggle. "Especially if she'd known where they'd come from."

"They belonged to one of your rape victims, didn't they?"

said Linton, feeling bile rise in her throat as she thought of what he'd done to Gemma.

"Don't worry," he smirked. "I made sure I cleaned them before I put them in her ears."

They'd turned onto the Glastonbury road now. In a couple of minutes they'd be approaching a roundabout. He would have to slow down, thought Linton and concentrate on the traffic coming from his right. If she could keep him talking, maybe he'd be distracted enough for her to make her move.

"But I still don't understand," she said. "How did you do it? Lauren wasn't killed until after half past eight but you were back in your dressing room fully dressed at twenty to nine."

"No I wasn't."

"But one of the cast saw you."

"It was Baines, not me. He was dressed in my costume. I wasn't due on stage until five to nine. I killed her just after eight forty, got back at eight fifty and still had five minutes to swap clothes."

They were almost at the roundabout. Only another few seconds to go. "So Baines was a part of this as well?" she said, as she felt the car begin to slow down. "He knew you were going to kill Lauren?"

"He didn't have a clue."

Linton moved her hand slowly towards the seatbelt holder. She could feel the tip of the plastic with her little finger.

"Don't!" The change in Hampton's tone was so sudden, Linton recoiled. "Move your hand away from your seat belt. Now! I want both hands in your lap where I can see them."

For a second Linton almost refused, thought *fuck it*, I've got to try something but she knew it was pointless. Even if she made it out of the car he'd just come after her. He was bigger and stronger and he had nothing to lose.

She moved her hands into her lap. Until she saw them she hadn't realised how much she was shaking.

"Now where was I?" he said in a friendly tone that was far more frightening than his angry one.

"You were talking about Baines."

"Ah yes! I arranged for him to come to the dressing room that evening. I told him I needed him to cover for me because I was popping out to see someone on a bit of business. He refused at first, thought I was up to no good, so I simply threatened him. Told him if he didn't, I'd tell everyone about him and Sally Hughes."

"But he's not going to cover for you this time. Not now he's under suspicion."

"Or course he won't because I'm going to shoot him. After I've shot you of course."

She felt the spike in her blood as she remembered that Wells had found a gun cabinet in Hampton's cottage.

"He's waiting for me, you see," he continued. "At the pigeon tower. I've told him the police are after him. That they've found evidence he was at Sally's. I've said if he doesn't meet me, I'll tell the police he killed her."

"Except *you* did."

"I had to. I heard her telling Sheila she'd been up at Elmtree that night. I couldn't take the chance she might've seen me."

"It isn't going to work, Mark."

"Don't tell me what will or won't work," he said, his voice suddenly icy. "I know exactly what I'm doing. I'll just act the hero; say you spotted Baines out in the arboretum and went after him. That I grabbed a gun and followed but Baines wrestled me to the floor before shooting you and then shooting himself in the head."

It was a ridiculous plan, thought Linton. So many things

could go wrong and even if it worked, ballistics would eventually find the truth.

"I know what you're thinking," he said. "They'll never fall for it. But look what happened with Henry. Your lot completely messed it up that time."

"Henry?" So Lauren was telling the truth after all. It wasn't an accident. "Did you kill him as well?"

He laughed, "For God's sake. Can't you lot work anything out for yourselves?"

"There's still one thing you haven't told me," she said. "Why did you kill Lauren?"

He turned to her and smiled. "We're almost home now. Why don't I save it until then?"

***

Sheila pulled the notebook out of her handbag, leant across the hospital bed and gently touched her daughter's arm. There was no response.

"I've finished writing it, Heather," she said. "I think it's only fair that you finally know the truth. About everything."

She turned to the first page of the book, cleared her throat and began to read:

"Did you know that Henry means 'ruler of the home'? That's exactly what your father was. The name Sheila comes from the Latin for 'blind', which I must have been to have walked into my marriage.

"The early days of our dating were incredibly romantic. He could be charming when he put his mind to it, when there was something he wanted. He proposed to me within a few weeks. I said yes of course, but told him I wanted to wait until I'd finished university.

"Getting pregnant was never part of the plan, but he was persuasive and I decided that getting a degree wasn't everything. The most important thing was I'd found my soul mate and we were going to raise a family together.

"So there we were living happily ever after, until gradually the real Henry began to surface. The change was slow and insidious.

"Nobody could've guessed what went on behind our firmly closed door. In public he acted like the perfect husband but in private everything I did was wrong. The way I spoke, the things I read, the way I tried to bring up you and Brandon.

"So why didn't I leave? For a start I had you two. And I was so drained, so emotionally exhausted I didn't have the energy to think about it. I felt ill all the time. I couldn't eat or sleep and I walked around with an impending sense of doom. I lost count of how many times I went to the doctors, but they could never find anything wrong. One of them suggested counselling, but I knew Henry would kill me if he ever found out.

"It was Henry himself who told me he'd slept with Sophia. One night when he was drunk. It wasn't a confession, a way of getting his guilt off his chest; it was simply a way to taunt me; to tell me how much better she was than me.

"But there was worse to come. He told me about Lauren, how he'd got her pregnant too. That Mark was his son, your half brother.

"I knew why Lauren had slept with him. It was obvious. She wanted to prove to herself that she was as desirable as her daughter. And I'll bet you she flaunted her pregnancy in front of Sophia, telling her she was carrying Henry's baby; that she was going to keep it. It's no wonder she was driven to suicide.

"Your father made me stay on at Elmtree Manor after

Lauren sacked him. I think he liked having a spy in the camp. He became obsessed, wanting to know everything that was going on at the house. He'd ask me question after question about Mark. When he was home from boarding school he took to hiding in the arboretum, so he could watch him around the house and gardens. I don't believe he ever loved his son, it was more about possession. It frustrated him that he couldn't control what was rightly his.

"Of course nobody else knew Henry had another son. He was too anxious to preserve the reputation he'd made as the friendly, family man. He was 'good old Henry', not the sort of bloke to sleep with his employer, behind his wife's back.

"Then the summer that Mark was expelled from University, the stack of secrets and lies finally collapsed.

"I was in the kitchen of Elmtree house when I heard Lauren and Mark arguing. She was screaming at him, accusing him of being like his father. She told him it wasn't Joseph but Henry; that he'd raped her one night – which wasn't true. She'd never have allowed him to get away with it if it was.

"I knew there'd be an argument. That Mark would confront Henry who'd simply come back and take it out on me. And when the phone rang that night at home and Henry said he was going out, I decided I couldn't stand it anymore.

"It would be a lie to say I didn't know what I was going to do, that it all happened in the spur of the moment because if that was the case then why did I pick up Henry's gun and check it was loaded before following him up there?

"By the time I'd caught him up, he'd reached the middle of the orchard, not far from the ruins of the dove tower and was deep in conversation with Mark. Even from a distance I could see from their stances and the space between them, that a confrontation was taking place. I trod slowly through the long damp grass, careful not to stand on any stray twigs, hiding behind the dense cover of branches and leaves as I went. I moved closer and closer until Henry was only a few feet away.

"I could hear Mark ordering Henry to leave Glastonbury. 'I don't want you anywhere near me. You raped my mother. She'd never have willingly slept with a lowlife scum like you.'

"I charged forward from the shelter of the apple tree. Henry turned to me, apparently unsurprised by my appearance and said in his most menacing voice, 'Put that down, you stupid bitch. I'll deal with you later.'

"I'd never fired a gun before and the force of it sent me flying backwards, the shot ringing in my ears, my trigger finger feeling like it was broken. When I looked up, Mark was standing over me, his hand outstretched. 'Good shot, Sheila. I couldn't have done it better myself.'

"He told me he'd sort everything out. I'd shot Henry at close range, so it would be easy to pretend he'd tripped and shot himself by mistake. There was no need to worry about my fingerprints being on the gun, hadn't I moved it yesterday because he'd left it out on the side?

"Of course I was covered in blood, so he went up to the house and came back with a skirt and blouse belonging to Lauren. He took my bloodied clothes and said he'd burn them. Before he sent me home, he made a deal. As long as I didn't tell anyone Henry was his father, then he wouldn't tell anyone about the murder.

"I shouldn't have been surprised; I'd seen what he did to Lauren's dog. He was an evil bastard but it was hard to believe a fifteen-year-old could be so conniving.

"'And don't think about getting a job anywhere else, Sheila,' he said, with that lop-sided smile of his. 'I like the idea of being able to keep my eye on you.'

"So I'd released myself from one incarceration, only to find myself in another. A lifelong prisoner of the Hampton family."

***

As Hampton turned into the driveway of Elmtree Manor, Linton had a nightmarish sense of driving into a horror film; of entering a surreal world of madness and terror.

"So where were we?" he said, conversationally, as his car grinded and crunched along the gravel. "You wanted to know why I killed my mother."

Linton tried to answer but her mouth was too dry. *Why hadn't she told someone she going skydiving with Hampton?* Nobody knew she was here.

"There's lots of plausible motives," he said, as he pulled to an abrupt halt next to Lauren's car. "Perhaps it was because I held her responsible for my sister's death. The sister I never got to meet. Perhaps it was because she was cruel and manipulative and only thought of herself. Or maybe it was because of the punishments she meted out to me on a daily basis when I was young. Giving me the option of which one I wanted, making me recite her horrid little nursery rhyme."

He cut the engine dead then turned to her and said, "You're the expert. Why do *you* think I killed her?"

Linton looked across at his tussled hair and gold speckled eyes, his tanned skin, crinkled laughter lines and lop-sided smile and wondered how someone so innocuous-looking could be so terrifying. He smiled and she felt the snake of fear again, writhing up in her stomach.

She swallowed. "I don't know. Money or revenge? A combination of both."

"Is that really the best you can come up with?"

"You'll have to tell me, Mark."

It was as she pulled her coat closer that she felt it. The can of deodorant in her pocket. All at once she was focused, thinking clearly. This could be her way out.

"Maybe it was because she gave what was rightly mine to charity," he continued. "Don't you think that might've been a good enough reason?"

"Yes," she said, her hand resting on the bulky shape of the canister, "I do."

"Except that it wasn't that either." He wiggled his little finger at her again and said, "Come on I'm sure you can guess. There's one thing we haven't mentioned yet."

"The rapes. It's because she found out, isn't it? It's why she left the money to Rape Crisis. As a warning to you."

"Congratulations! You got there in the end. And as a special reward, let's go and find Jonathan."

"No! Wait!" she said, as he moved towards his door. "Please. I want to know the whole story. At least give me that much. How did Lauren find out?"

"It's not important."

"But surely you didn't tell her? Please. Tell me. How did she know?"

He shrugged. "She simply put two and two together. They didn't start until I'd moved back."

"But that could've been coincidence."

"Lauren wasn't a fool. She knew I was up to something. And she was bound to be suspicious. After what happened before."

"What do mean by before?" *Just keep him talking*, she thought, all she had to do was yank the can out her pocket, aim it at his face and spray.

"When I was fifteen I was expelled for having sex with a girl from a neighbouring school. Apparently my actions constituted rape. The police weren't called of course, it would've brought the school into disrepute, but they had to let me go."

"But what did it matter if Lauren knew you were the rapist? Surely she wouldn't have told the police."

He laughed. "You didn't know my mother. Once the papers were bored of all her other stories she'd have moved onto telling them about what I'd done. I couldn't stand the thought of it. Living on a knife-edge for the rest of my life. Wondering when she'd spill the beans. Anyway," he said abruptly, "I've thoroughly enjoyed our chat but now it's time to find Jonathan. I think he's waited long enough. You stay where you are. I'll walk round the car and help you out. And don't even think about running off because I'll come after you and I'll kill you and I'll make sure that when I do, it hurts."

He moved his hand towards the door handle. *This was her only chance.* She yanked the deodorant can out of her pocket. Alerted by the sudden movement he turned, his hand outstretched to grab her but he wasn't fast enough. She aimed the canister at his eyes, pressed the nozzle and sprayed. As he let out a painful cry she released the lock, grabbed at the door handle, pushed her hip against it, flung herself out on to the gravel and was on her feet within seconds.

She began to run.

***

MONDAY EVENING, TEN DAYS EARLIER

In the end it was easier not to struggle. She felt her body slumping forwards as she listened to her son's jeering voice, giving herself up to the rhythm of the familiar words.

Eeny, meeny, miny, moe,
Catch a tiger by the toe,
If it hollers let him go,
Eeny, meeny, miny, moe you are it
My mother told me to pick the very best one
And that is y-o-u

TWENTY-THREE

She could hear him behind her, the crunching of gravel getting louder and louder in time with the steady pounding of his feet. Closer and closer. She could hear his breathing now, strong and steady, the path darkening beside her as his shadow caught up with her. The game was up.

The shock though, when he reached out and grabbed her still took her breath away. With one deft movement, he yanked her down until she was lying level to the ground, her face in the gravel.

"Got you," he hissed. The sharp stones dug into her face and she heard herself cry out. Within seconds he was on top of her, cradled across her back, her lungs and ribs being crushed beneath his dead weight.

He slammed his hand over her mouth and she smelt soap. Imperial Leather. She could feel the spiky stones through her jeans now as his legs squeezed her waist.

She couldn't breathe. Struggling she tried to twist her head but he simply held her more firmly.

"I'm going to enjoy this, you bitch."

A mosaic of images flashed through her mind. Her front door… her sister's smile… a perfume label… her nephew's trainers… the sign outside a swimming pool… the sponsorship form on Brown's fridge… the picture of his grinning niece… his face… his scent… his voice yelling, "Get off her! Get your fucking hands off her!"

A moment later Linton was gasping for air, her throat and

lungs burning. Somewhere to her left she heard a loud grunt followed by Brown's murderous tone. "Don't... you... ever... lay... a... finger... on her... again... you... fucking... ANIMAL!"

His words were punctuated by a series of painful groans followed by a single yelp of agony and another voice she recognised.

"Get off him. Brown. You're going to kill him."

Then everything went black.

***

Sheila stopped reading and slid the notebook into her bag.

"I'm making a fresh start," she said. "I'm going to be a better person, a kinder person, like I was before Henry came along and poisoned me. I'll look after Toby until you're better and I'll do a good job of it, I promise. He'll be a credit to you. I'll make sure of it. You'll see."

She looked down at her daughter and, for a moment, she could hardly believe what she was seeing. Hands shaking and heart fluttering, she pressed the buzzer next to the bed. A few seconds later a nurse bustled in, her homely face expectant.

"Look! She's crying!" Sheila said, pointing at the tears running down her daughter's face. "She must have heard me. I think she's coming round."

As the nurse moved closer to Heather, Sheila expected her to call out with excitement, but instead she simply sighed. As she turned away from the bed, she was slowly shaking her head, her lips pulled into a perfect hybrid of grimace and a smile.

"I'm sorry, Mrs Martock," she said gently. "I know it's hard not to be hopeful, but I'm afraid we see this a lot with VS. It's a spontaneous movement. It doesn't mean she's responding to anything."

She paused, as though deciding how to word her next sentence, but Sheila knew exactly what was coming. She seemed to have a sixth sense about her these days.

"I don't believe in keeping people in the dark," said the nurse gravely. "It's only crueller in the long run. The consultant phoned to say he's coming down to see you later. He wants to speak to you. About turning off your daughter's life support machine."

***

The paramedic was insistent.

"We're taking you in. You need checking over. There's a good chance you've got concussion."

Linton could feel the tears coursing down her face, stinging the small open wounds left by the gravel. "I just want to go home," she whispered.

"Sorry, love. It's got to be the hospital."

"What if I come with you?" It was Brown. Linton looked up at him from the trolley they'd forced her to lie on. He was still clutching a blooded tissue to his nose, his expression serious.

"What about Hampton? Shouldn't you go straight back to the station?"

"He can wait. Now just shut up and lie down, will you?"

As the paramedics lifted her into the ambulance she realised that tears were still streaming down her cheeks, soaking the red fluffy blanket she was lying on.

"I can't stop crying," she said, as Brown clambered in behind and sat down next to her.

"I'm bloody not surprised."

"How did you find out? About Hampton."

"His ex-wife rang the station. She told me what he was *really* like. And then when Hooper said you'd gone skydiving…" he paused. "The Toad said I was overreacting but I had a bad feeling. I persuaded Keen to come as well."

"But how did you know I'd be here?"

"I guessed," he said, grinning. "I thought, if I'd been on a date with you, I'd want to take you home as well."

"Brown," she said, flushing in spite of everything, "I've seen your house. You might want to rethink that tactic."

The road leading away from Elmtree felt bumpier than she remembered it. Every bounce and jolt made her flinch. Brown moved closer.

"Are you OK?" he asked. "Does anything hurt?"

"I'm fine."

"Look at your hands. They're shaking."

He leant across and laid his left hand over hers. Linton shut her eyes and listened to his breathing, deep and steady, inhaling his scent of fresh sweat and aftershave. She shifted her hand slightly and as she did, she felt his little finger gently stroking her own. A second later he'd hooked his finger through hers, pulling on it tightly.

A memory sprang to mind, listening to Brown in the hallway at the wedding reception as she pulled her coat on.

Once they've found their lifelong partners, they link their tails together and stay like that forever.

"All right?" he whispered.

She nodded, then opened her eyes. "Brown?"

"What?" He looked down at her, his eyes heavy with concern.

"Don't let me forget to sponsor you, will you?"

She closed her eyes again and drifted off, thinking of seahorses.

***

They warned Sheila that Toby might be difficult for a time. It was only to be expected, after what he'd gone through. The nursery had already raised some concerns, taking her to one side to tell her that his aggression was beginning to become a problem.

"I expect it's his way of masking his grief," said the counsellor they now saw once a week. "I'm sure it's only a temporary thing."

Sheila nodded and glanced across at her grandson who was playing with a plastic kitchen in the corner of the room.

"Five more minutes," she said. "And if you come without a fuss, we'll get some sweeties on the way home."

He rewarded her with a lop-sided smile that sent a shiver down her spine.

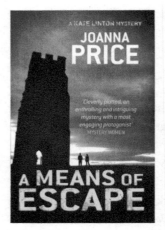

A grizzly and cold November morning. Detective Sergeant Kate Linton is called on Glastonbury Tor, where a young woman has been strangled. Twelve holes are found at the scene, surrounded by wax, evidence of garden flares – the only connection to two other unsolved cases. When another young woman and a TV celebrity go missing, Linton is in a race against time to find the serial killer before he strikes again. But, when her journalist ex-boyfriend is singled out as a chief suspect, Linton feels that events are heading a bit too close to home. *A Means of Escape* presents an intricate, gripping mystery plot, combined with a focus on the heroine's personal life as she juggles an unwelcome attraction for her good-looking and charismatic superior with her efforts to become closer to her estranged family.

'An absolute commitment to believability, which has few equals within crime fiction. Overall a thoroughly accomplished debut and a match for the very best of the genre.'
www.bookgeeks.co.uk

'It will keep you on your tenterhooks throughout.'
www.louisereviews.com

Hardback: 9780956983008
Paperback: 9780956983015